BENEATH THE YELLOW LIGHTS

ISBN 978-1-7333938-4-3 (paperback)

Edited by Jacob Jones-Goldstein, J. Patrick Conlon, and Shasta Schatz
Cover art and Interior Layout by Jennifer Marang
OPP logo by Steve Myers

Published by
Oddity Prodigy Productions, LLC
302 Arbour Drive
Newark, DE 19713

www.oddityprodigy.com

BENEATH THE YELLOW LIGHTS

AN URBAN FANTASY ANTHOLOGY

Edited by
Jacob Jones-Goldstein
J. Patrick Conlon
and Shasta Schatz

DEDICATION

During the making of this anthology, we lost founding member of Oddity Prodigy Productions, Steve Myers.

He was an artist extraordinaire, creator of Superchum, cartoonist, friend, and our guiding light.

This book is dedicated to him.

For Steve, The O.G. O.P.

TABLE OF TALES

INTRODUCTION
by Shasta Schatz

Can you recall the first time you were touched by magic? I can't. Fantasy has always just existed in my life, not necessarily as an enchanted spinning wheel or a cursed royal, but certainly as the result of imagination getting me through the day. I don't have a particular formative moment for what is arguably my favorite genre, but I do know that my first set of magic stories became the ley lines upon which I've traveled. I still have the books in our home library—cautionary tales more specific than fables and no less traumatic than an 80s science fiction thriller. I staunchly remember putting myself into those narratives as an observer only, lest the crone come for me next. Living in a bustling city where I was more likely to see a rat at the bus stop than a helpful bird giving directions to the new bookstore, those stories were best left as a passing interest rather than a lifelong hobby. Ever the nostalgic, decades later, I read selections to my kids until they were old enough to flip through the tomes on their own, hoping they'd embrace a sense of longing for the familiar changelings, enchanted animals, and spell-wielding outsiders that I had. My attempts were not in vain, but I will give credit to modern media for the "Hey, I know that story" that comes as a result of the latest pointy-hatted, demon-possessed, trickster god drama developed for a new audience on a streaming platform. It is with that contemporary whimsy that we, Oddity Prodigy Productions, present to you *Beneath The Yellow Lights*—An Anthology of Urban Fantasy Short Stories.

Since the time of perceived witches of old, humanity's dichotomy of distaste for and fascination with the unexplainable has evolved into a lush and verdant tree of popular culture twists on all things fantasy. The human condition is one of relative struggle, but what about the fae condition? Real or imagined, are they not subject to the same efforts to live fulfilling or at least entertaining lives? The fae can't be trusted, and humans are easily influenced, so there exists a perfect gray area of culpability that we are not afforded in real life. Historically, we condemn the widowed village healer and praise the court astronomer, acclaimed as a scholar. Our colicky infants have clearly been replaced, but maybe we can teach this little horned fae understudy how to love. Literarily, that townie becomes our heroine, the high-ranking occultist is our clear and present villain, and the baby is a long-lost prince of Queen Mab. Magic has and will always have a place in society. We need it to stay hopeful. The sense of possibility pushes us forward. And, on the darker side, putting the onus of a bad situation on the unseeable as a culprit or a benefactor is quite truly a tale as old as time.

In long-told magic stories, the arcane is held high, but by who's decree? Is it to keep the assumed unsavory at bay? To keep the dispossessed at a disadvantage? If you genuinely believe that blood magic is practiced by licensed warlocks alone, then I have a bag of beans to sell you at a steal of a deal. Who is magic for? The simple, the children, the artists, the dreamers? Do we not all pass through those "eras" (as the kids say these days) on our path to whatever is next? Are our lives not enriched by the way time seems to stand still to hold the yellow light for just an extra second on the way home from work? That's true magic. To talk of power struggles between the Seelie and the Unseelie is to only touch the surface of how our minds fight daily to separate the good and the bad--whether it be an inferred slight from a co-worker or the sudden appearance of the refilled coffee cup that you know for certain was left in the kitchen. Or do you?

Urban fantasy--the mythical creatures, the daily grind--this is Bronze Age folklore for a modern world. Names change, environments develop and expand, but the lessons are the same. In the tradition of faerie queens, elves, and sorcerers, the mundane in our world is only so because the sparkle has been lost. Allow our authors to sync your senses to the fully possible. Whether your flavor is romantic comedy or murder mystery, the assortment of magical delights that have been curated for you in this volume will certainly inspire you to see the exceptional in the everyday. For your consideration, we have tales of revolution, nostalgia, monotony, love, law, loss, deals with all sorts, age-old pantheons--literally and figuratively "same story, different day", and a sprinkle of customer service. Let us be your intermediary. We'll walk the line between worlds while you hover just out-of-body to the left of what is.

And with that power of belief, you have a book before you that seeks to possess your mind, if only for a span of hours. When you emerge into your world on the other side, take what you can recall of these tales along your life path, like the cobbled-together stories of another age, transformed across cultures and time. Perhaps remember to leave a patch of local flora in the corner of your fenced yard so that the pixies stay motivated to keep the bogies at bay this fall.

We could all use a little magic, and OPP is here to give it to you.

THE EYES OF THE CITY
by David T. Shoemaker

As he left the New York Public Library's Schwarzman Building, passing between the stone lions Patience and Fortitude—though he preferred to think of them as Leo Lenox and Leo Astor, their original nicknames—art historian Dr. Caradoc Crydd thought he heard a low growl. His hair stood on end as goose pimples covered his flesh. He shuddered.

Caradoc headed north along 5th Avenue towards Grand Central Terminal. He was excited because he thought he had finally found proof that Richard Morris Hunt had used alchemy and other arcane arts in the planning and construction of his buildings. WHY Hunt had used alchemy was still unclear, but Caradoc was convinced it was part of Hunt's progressive era campaign to create safer streets and neighborhoods.

As he approached the 42nd Street corner, the crossing signal suddenly switched from "Walk" to "Don't Walk". The speaker on the sign announced: "Don't Walk...Don't Walk...Caradoc...Don't Caradoc...Don't Talk...Don't Walk...Don't Walk." Caradoc was shaken out of his reverie by the sound of his name and quickly looked around. Normally crowded with tourists, there were only a few people on the other corner—none of whom he recognized. The light changed to green, and he crossed the street, still puzzled by what he had heard.

As he entered the station, the departures board went black, then flashed the message: "STOP LOOKING FOR US, CARADOC!!!" Caradoc shuddered again and quickly went down to the subway level. He boarded a northbound 6 train heading for his offices at Hunter College. Caradoc was grateful to find an empty car. He dropped into a seat by the door, trembling.

Between the 51st Street and 59th Street stations, the subway stopped. The lights went out, and the driver announced, "Ladies and Gentlemen, we apologize for the delay. We are waiting for the train ahead of us to clear the station, and then we will proceed." Seconds later, a different voice came across the speaker. "CARADOC CRYDD, WE SEE WHAT YOU ARE TRYING TO DO. OUR EYES SEE ALL. STOP NOW, OR WE WILL BE FORCED TO PUT AN END TO THIS." With the last word spoken, the train lurched forward and picked up speed. Caradoc didn't wait until 68th Street to exit the subway. He got off at 59th street, ran up to the street, to the fresh air and comparatively open space, and walked the rest of the way.

"You needn't think I'm crazy, Nicholas. Plenty of others have queerer prejudices than this. You might as well laugh at Jakob for wearing two T-shirts in August. And it's only an umbrella. Plenty of people have them." It had been two weeks since the subway incident, but Caradoc's sense of being watched had only increased.

"Yes, but they use them when it's raining! It's 96 degrees and sunny. People are staring and starting to cross the street to avoid us, Doc! Why don't you put it away?" replied Nicholas van Sarnath testily.

"Yes, I know it's not raining. I don't care if people are staring. There's plenty of reason, God knows. Why the third degree? You never used to be this inquisitive..." he answered. "Well, if you must know, I don't see why you shouldn't. Maybe you ought to—the arcane arts are kind of your specialty."

"Ha!"

"As you know, I've been working on a new biography of Richard Morris Hunt, the architect and founder of the Municipal Art Society of New York. Well, I was in Boston trying to track down his early influences following his father's death in 1832.

"One of his classmates at Boston Latin was Samuel Pierpont Langley, 3rd Secretary of the Smithsonian Institution and inventor of the Bolometer. In one of Langley's diaries, I found a curious reference to secret study groups held by Epes Sargent Dixwell, the Principal of the Boston Latin School. In addition to the usual Cicero and Virgil, it seems that Dixwell was teaching some of his brighter students the works of Robert of Chester, Peter Abelard, Paracelsus, and Roger Bacon. This, in and of itself, wouldn't have caught my attention, except for the fact that Hunt—after graduating from Boston Latin—studied in Rome, Geneva, and Paris—all cities associated with alchemy."

"Was he trying to change lead into gold? Beats being a starving artist!" Nick joked.

"No, I don't think Hunt was trying to change lead into gold. Jesus! What would that have to do with my umbrella?! Be patient, Nicholas—I'm getting to the point," answered Caradoc.

"As you wish," replied Nick with a bow of his head.

"When Hunt was in Rome, he was studying to be an artist. He was obsessed with the classical sculptures in the Capitoline Museum. But he suddenly abandoned his study of art and transferred to Geneva to study architecture. Richard Saltonstall Greenough hinted in a letter that the reason had more to do with Hunt's failed experiment to recreate Judah Lowe's golem than the urging of his family towards a more profitable career," said Caradoc. Nick's eyes started to glaze over.

"Don't worry about all the names; you can Google them later if you have to. It's Hunt's story that matters anyway…At any rate, after two years in Geneva, Hunt moved to Paris and joined the atelier of Hector Lefuel. At the time, Lefuel was working on his plans to convert the Chateau de Meudon into the headquarters of the Ecole Polytechnique and had access to the private library of Louis-Philippe I. I think Hunt wanted to study with Lefuel because of his access to this library. I think he succeeded in creating a golem in Rome, but he could not control it. His brother William helped him destroy the golem, then urged him to take up architecture to distance Hunt from the association with sculpture that the local constabulary were investigating. I've become convinced that Hunt found the secret to animating inanimate objects during his time in Geneva and Paris, at least to a limited degree…"

"Riiight!" Nick said, rolling his eyes.

"Don't look at me like that, Nick! I'm not insane—I know the Statue of Liberty isn't going to step down off her pedestal and go skinny dipping in the Hudson. That's not what I meant.

"Since ancient times, there have been references to the "All-seeing Eye" of Providence. Egypt had the Eye of Ra; the Norse had "One-Eyed Odin"; the Chinese had Qianliyan. In all of those cultures, public buildings (temples, forums, palaces, etc.) have been decorated with sculptural friezes or other sculptural guardians like the Foo Dogs. I think the ancients knew how to use the eyes of those sculptures to keep watch over the people. I think the Templars found this secret in Jerusalem and brought it back to Paris. I think Jacques de Molay was burned at the stake because he refused to give King Philip IV control over the Eyes of France."

"The fact that he owed De Molay a shit ton of money he didn't want to repay had nothing to do with it..." replied Nicholas.

"I think Richard Morris Hunt found this ancient secret, and he entrusted it to the Municipal Art Society," Caradoc plowed on, ignoring Nick's comment. "I think MAS commissions public art in order to place Eyes where they want. And the Eyes are everywhere—there isn't a square or park in the city without a sculpture or mural! Laugh if you must, Nicholas, but I'm telling you--the only way to move around the city unrecognized is beneath an umbrella," concluded Caradoc with a scowl as he and Nicholas walked up Broadway towards Amsterdam Ave. Nicholas stifled his laughter but was eager to get to Senn Thai. Both for the food and so Caradoc would put his damned umbrella away.

Ten days later, Nicholas was attending the opening of a new exhibit at the New York Historical Society with his wife, Grace, and mother-in-law, Edda. One of the artifacts on display was the sculptural frieze from the south pediment of the (now demolished) Lenox Library. It caught Nicholas's attention because it had been designed by Richard Morris Hunt. As he examined the piece, he noticed the logo of the manufacturer carved into the stone: an All-Seeing Eye contained within a circle surrounded by "The

Metropolitan Grand Ornamental Limestone And Marble Company." As he looked at the logo, he wondered how they managed to stay in business, considering the sloppy job they did with the lettering. The now missing letter "e" from the word "The" appeared to have been separated from the rest of the word by a space. In fact, the entire name seemed full of errors--"Th eMet ropolitan G rand O rnamental L imestone A nd M arble Company". Nicholas supposed it was a good thing it was on the back of the sculpture where no one would have seen it. As this thought crossed his mind, his cell phone started ringing insistently.

Nicholas was sure he had silenced the phone before entering the museum. He glared at the screen, surprised to see that Jakob Skreestraat was calling. He stepped to the lobby to answer it.

"Ahoy! Sarnath speaking," he said. Nicholas always felt Alexander Graham Bell's wishes should be observed.

"Hey Nick, It's Jake. Did you hear about Caradoc?" came the reply.

"No, what's happened?"

"He's in a coma at the hospital. Hit by a truck on 6th Avenue."

"Oh My God! Which Hospital?"

"Mount Sinai. Room 610. It's the strangest thing. Lily was with him, She said they were walking along sixth when a gust of wind from a subway grate blew his umbrella into the street. Caradoc stepped out to pick it up, and suddenly the traffic lights changed, and a U-Haul turned and hit him. The driver said the GPS told him to turn, even though it was the opposite direction to where he was heading. And the subway line was closed for repairs, so where did the wind come from?"

"I'll stop by in the morning to check on him," Nick said. "How's Lily holding up?"

"Shaken up, but she refuses to leave his side. She's a trooper!" replied Jake.

"Yes, she is. Thanks for calling. See you at the Book Thing," said Nick and hung up.

The next morning, Nicholas and Grace went to visit Caradoc in the hospital. Lily was sitting in the chair beside his bed. She looked like she hadn't slept in days. Grace rushed over, gave her a hug, and asked, "How's he doing?"

"He's been fading in and out all night. Muttering strange things before falling back to sleep..." Lily said with tears in her eyes.

"What kind of things?" Nick asked.

"He thinks the accident was deliberate. That the building pushed him into the street, he really sounds paranoid!" Lily replied.

"It's probably just the pain medicine. I wouldn't worry about it." Nick said, despite his own worries. He thought about Caradoc's rant about the umbrella and wondered if the two were related. "Did you have breakfast? Why don't you and Grace go to the cafeteria and get some coffee? I'll sit with him 'til you get back."

When they were alone, Nicholas sat in the chair and held Caradoc's left hand. Caradoc's eyes fluttered a little, then were still. "I wonder what really happened," Nick said softly.

"We were walking along 14th Street...heading towards Union Square... We were passing the Red Brick building...with all the ornaments...at the corner of 7th Ave...when I noticed the Caryatid by the door...looking at me... like it recognized...and despised me. Then I felt a gust of wind... from the subway grate...and the umbrella...flew out of my hand...into the street. That's the last thing...I remember..." Caradoc gasped.

"It doesn't make sense. Why would a building despise you, even if it could? Which it can't—It's just bricks and wood and glass and plaster!"

"Therefore, as a stranger...give it welcome. There are more things... in Heaven and Earth...Horatio," replied Caradoc with a chuckle.

"You think it was a ghost, 'Doc?" Nick asked.

"Not a Ghost...but perhaps...a Spirit....or.....a Golem...."

Caradoc gave Nick's hand a slight squeeze, then went limp as he passed out again. The nurse came in to check on him, followed by Grace and Lily. The nurse noted Caradoc's elevated heart rate and said visiting hours were over. Lily could stay, but the patient needed rest. Nick and Grace meekly said goodbye and left.

Nick and Grace stopped at Soothr for lunch after leaving the hospital. The Thai noodle house occupied the ground floor of a 5-story brick townhouse in the East Village. The layout was similar to any number of hole-in-the-wall restaurants in New York, but the owners lovingly cared for the wood and tile bar, ornately carved wood and glass screen separating the bar from the dining room and the backyard patio that was one of the city's hidden gems. No wonder a prominent food critic declared, "It doesn't get any better than Soothr!"

"I'm worried about 'Doc,'" Nick said after the waiter had taken their order. "He seems obsessed with this golem idea of his."

"Let's say for the moment that he's right," replied Grace. "You've been ghost hunting. How would that work?"

"It wouldn't, as far as I can tell. Ghosts rarely materialize on this plane and almost never have the energy to manipulate objects."

"What about poltergeists?" Grace countered. She loved playing devil's advocate.

"Those are usually manifestations of a hormonal teenager's psychic energy rather than a separate entity," Nick replied. "Besides, why should a ghost target Doc?"

"Caradoc said golem, not ghost. But isn't that just a ghost trapped in an object, like the Annabelle doll?"

"No, not quite. Golems are…different—Man-made, not possessed. If I remember correctly, they are Jewish helpers or protectors created by a Rabbi. But Doc's not antisemitic! Why would a golem attack him?"

"What if it wasn't created by a Rabbi? Who was he researching when he found the golem stuff?" Grace asked.

"An Architect…Hunt. Richard Morris Hunt. He designed the Lenox Library that was featured in the exhibition last night."

"Could he have made a Golem to help him build? Cheap labor?"

"Labor was already cheap in the nineteenth century! I doubt he'd have needed one for that."

"But if he had wanted to, how would he have done it?" Grace asked.

"He would have...I don't know. The stories I've read are vague about it. Probably to prevent every Tom, Dick, and Sally from making one." Nick replied.

"Who would know?" Grace asked.

"Not many people, assuming the legends are true."

"I bet Jesse would know...or at least know whom to ask!"

"You're right! I'll call him later. He owes me a drink, anyway. It'll be good to catch up."

Nicholas met Jesse ben Solomon at the Dead Poet's Bar on Amsterdam. Jesse was wearing his usual uniform: the long black coat, white shirt, and wide-brimmed fedora of a rabbi, the pink socks of a rebel. They had met in a comparative religion class at Columbia and had bonded over a shared love of Star Trek and Zecharia Sitchin's 12th Planet series.

"Why the urgent summons? It's not my birthday. There's still 63 shopping days until then!" said Jesse with a grin.

"I'll make sure to get you an appropriate pair of socks!" countered Nick. "It's about Caradoc. He thinks he was attacked by a Golem."

"I see..." Jesse was suddenly profoundly serious. He glanced around the bar to be sure they weren't overheard. "Perhaps now is not the time... or the place...for such an open discussion."

"Wait, you think it could be true?!" asked Nick in surprise.

"I don't know if it is true or not," Jesse replied, "but I wouldn't want strangers to get the wrong idea. Why don't we finish our drinks and head back to my place? One of my students gave me a bottle of 12 year old Mortlach I think you'll like."

"Okay," Nick replied. He felt goosebumps along his spine, but Nick couldn't tell if they were for the whisky or what Jesse was going to tell him.

Jesse hung up his coat and hat on the hall tree, then ushered Nicholas into his study. He placed two perfectly round ice spheres (can't really call them "cubes") into tumblers and poured three fingers of the Mortlach over them. He handed one to Nicholas, then settled into his wing chair and took a sip.

"Ah, that's better. Now tell me what happened," Jesse prompted.

Nick outlined the events, beginning with his conversation with Caradoc about the umbrella, then describing the accident, and ending with Doc's theory about the Golem.

"Interesting," Jesse said when Nick was finished. "He specifically mentioned Judah Loew?"

"Yes," replied Nick. "Is that important?"

"Maybe. It would at least suggest how this…'golem'…was made." Nick could hear the air quotes around golem in Jesse's inflection.

"Okay, I'll bite. How do you make a golem?"

"Me? I wouldn't—dangerous things. More trouble than they're worth," scoffed Jesse. "Judah Loew, on the other hand…"

Nick leaned forward in anticipation. "Yea?" Nick prompted.

"The legends vary, but they all involve using one of the Holy Names. Sometimes, the name is written on a piece of paper, which is then placed under the golem's tongue. Sometimes, the name is written on a sign the golem wears around his neck. The golem is only active while the name is in place, and the name must be removed before sunset on the Sabbath every week. But Judah Loew…" Jesse let the thought trail off.

Nick decided to take a guess. "Rabbi Loew made the name a part of the golem, didn't he?"

Jesse sighed and looked at his hands for a few moments. There was a worried look in his eyes when he looked up at Nick. "Yes. The good citizens of Prague did not respect the Sabbath, so Rabbi Loew decided to create a golem that could not be easily deactivated. The Jewish Quarter needed a protector on the job 24/7/365. But it was an abomination to the LORD, for G_d commanded us to remember the Sabbath and keep it Holy…"

"How did he do it? What happened?" asked Nick.

"Rabbi Loew shaped the golem out of clay from the banks of the

Vltava river. He carved the shem—the Holy Name—into its forehead. And for a brief time, all was well. Golems are said to be soulless—animated, but not alive. Emotionless, unfeeling, impervious to pain or suffering. But the Maharal's was different. They say the golem fell in love with a beautiful woman. How is that possible without a soul, a spirit? Can a brick love? Impossible...At any rate, the creature was smitten and followed the woman around Prague. Some say she was the daughter of a rich merchant, others a nun from the Convent of Saint Agnes. There's even a version that says she was the daughter of the Holy Roman Emperor himself! At any rate, Rabbi Loew had locked the golem in the basement of the synagogue to prevent it from pursuing the young woman, but it broke out during the Sabbath prayers and destroyed the synagogue. Rabbi Loew was forced to deactivate it. Some say the golem's body is still stored in the attic of the Old New Synagogue in Prague, waiting to be reactivated in times of peril to the Jewish population."

"How did he deactivate it if the...shem?...was carved into his forehead?" Nick asked.

"Rabbi Loew had used the name "אֱמֶת"—which means 'truth'—to activate the golem, so he used his thumb to erase the "א" and change the word to "מֵת" which means 'dead,' or 'corpse.'" Jesse wrote the characters down as he said this.

"Wait!" cried Nicholas. "Say that again slowly."

"Say what again?" asked Jesse.

"The name! How it sounds in English!"

"Emet?"

"Yes, and when you remove the character, you are left with"

"Met." They said in unison.

"Would the name HAVE to be spelled in Hebrew characters to work, or would it work in English?" Nick asked.

"I have no idea. As far as I know, no one has tried it in another language..." answered Jesse.

"I think Richard Morris Hunt may have," Nick replied.

Nicholas left Jesse's apartment in the Apthorp Building and turned east on W. 79th Street. Despite the fact that he only passed a few couples and a dog walker, he had the distinct sensation of being watched. He cut through the Theodore Roosevelt Park and around the Hayden Planetarium to Central Park West. He couldn't shake the feeling that someone—or something—was following him.

He turned north along the west side of the avenue, heading for his apartment in The St. Urban Building. As he passed beneath the yellow lights and Art Nouveau limestone face on the building's porte cochere, he thought he saw her eyes narrow, coolly observing him. "Must be shadows from the lamp globes," he muttered to himself, chuckling. Nick took the elevator to the fourth floor. He nodded to the ghost of Joseph Gellerei—the Jules C. Weiss & Co. delivery boy who fell down the elevator shaft in 1906—as he passed him in the hall on his way to the former home of Mr. and Mrs. J. M. Main, where Joseph had made his last delivery. He had been able to get the apartment at a reduced rate because of its tragic history. It allowed him a level of luxury seldom achieved by horror writers, even wildly successful ones like himself. Since ghosts are part of his stock and trade, he was never bothered by Joseph's presence.

Nicholas looked in on Grace, but she was already asleep. His mind was too active to go to bed, so he went down the hall to his den. He poured himself another drink, settled into his green leather Richmond chair, put his feet on the ottoman, and tossed a blanket across his legs. Aziraphale, his white Maine Coon hopped into his lap and lay down along his legs, purring. Nicholas turned on the television to catch the late-night news.

"In local news, a ten-year-old boy who had fallen through the floor of an abandoned building earlier this morning was discovered when a passing postal worker heard what he thought was a smoke alarm sounding in the building. Firefighters responded and found Ronny Allina unconscious in the basement with a broken foot and ankle. It is unclear what triggered the disconnected alarm, but Ronny's mother credits his guardian angel. After the break, Jeff Smith will give us a preview of this weekend's weather..."

Suddenly, the TV screen went blank, replaced by static. Aziraphale's hackles rose. He hissed at the TV, then ran from the room.

Nicholas took a sip of his whisky, then said, "I know you've been watching me tonight. Can you speak?"

The Echo Dot on his desk glowed blue and said Yes.

"Who, or what, are you?"

What am I? I don't have the words to tell you, even if I wanted to. I am spirit, but I am also substance. I am many things, yet I am one. I am ancient, yet I am modern. I am unchanging, but I continue to evolve. I am one of five, and We are One...

"How very 'New Age' of you."

Maybe an analogy would help. If you think about Muir Woods or Sherwood Forest, what are you thinking about? Is it the trees? The mosses and ferns? The rocks and land? The green polygon on a map? It is all of these and more. Each tree, rock, and stream has a spirit, an individual identity. But the forest also has a spirit, an espiritu loci. A collective identity greater than the individual spirits of the trees and streams.

"Like the Manitou of the Iroquois?" Nick asked.

The entity ignored him and continued: *Inanimate objects—things that are made—can have Spirits, too. These are somewhat rarer, but by no means uncommon. Most people recognize the "Blood, Sweat, and Tears" recipe, but most think that just refers to hard work. Alchemists know they are, in fact, elements—or perhaps catalysts. Without them, the base materials remain inert.*

When a bird is building a nest, or a woodcarver is making a rocking horse, a piece of their spirit—their hope, their love—infuses the object and gives it life. The same is true of buildings, great and small. The conversion from house to home occurs when the owners infuse the structure with their blood, sweat, tears, hopes, dreams...when they fill it with their love. The structure breathes in this love, feeds on it, and, in return, protects and cares for the family that owns it. A symbiotic relationship exists that allows both to thrive.

"Ah, I see..."

Great buildings like The Woolworth Building, The Flatiron Building, The Empire State Building, even the phallic Chrysler Building have their own spirits. These spirits feed off the occupants and, in return, protect the building and nurture the businesses within. When the spirits are well fed, the businesses thrive. When the spirits are weak, businesses go bankrupt; vacancies appear, and the strength of the entire neighborhood wanes. But we are greater than any of these. They are like organs within our body.

I am one of five, and we are one. We are the buildings, the streets, the subways, the parks, the bridges, the sidewalks, and yes, the sculptures, murals, and mosaics. We are the eyes of the city.

"What should I call you?"

The Munsee called us Manaháhteenk. The Mahicanni used Manahah Tank. Your people call me Manhattan. I am the sibling of Bronx, Brooklyn, Queens, and Staten. We are New York.

"Manhattan, did you save that boy today? Did you sound the alarm?"

Yes, just as we tried to save Joseph. Sadly, we had fewer ways to communicate in his time. We nurture and protect the inhabitants that live and work in us.

"Why did you attack Caradoc? He's one of your inhabitants!"

We also defend ourselves against those who would destroy or blind us. He was about to reveal us, which would lead to the removal and destruction of our eyes.

"Caradoc wasn't trying to hurt you. I'm not even sure he fully understands you. His interest is in the architect Richard Morris Hunt."

We were here before Hunt, before the city, even before humans. We were rooted to this ground. We could feel the world around us, the movements of other beings, but we could not see them. Hunt tried to trap us in his constructions, to contain us, but in truth, he opened our eyes and set us free. The interconnectedness of the city allows us to roam beyond our original grove—sewers, telephone lines, electricity flow from one building to the next. Buildings touch sidewalks, which touch streets. Even in the open parkland, sidewalks and streetlamps connect us. We have seen how violent—how destructive—humans are when faced with a power larger than themselves. They would rather isolate than integrate. It is too dangerous to allow ourselves to be revealed.

"Humans don't always respond in fear—sometimes they respond in love. When tornados or hurricanes destroy communities, humans from all over the country or the world pull together to help rebuild. I am sure many would work to restore and preserve you if they knew the truth! Caradoc is an art historian! He lives to preserve and protect art and architecture. I'm sure he would fight to protect you, too."

Though he might fight to protect us, human life is short. His words would last longer than his support. It is too dangerous. Only if he ceases to uncover and expose our origin will he be spared. Otherwise, he must be silenced.

"Caradoc can be stubborn, especially when his professional pride is on the line. I will try to convince him to drop his inquiry, or at least not publish anything that would directly reveal your presence, Manhattan."

We are grateful. We do not enjoy the destruction of others. Farewell.

Instantly, the TV picture and sound were restored. A late-night talk show was on. Nick had missed the weather report.

Nicholas went to see Caradoc in the morning. Nick told him about Manhattan's visit and passed on the warning. At first, Caradoc doubted Nick's sanity. As Nick's story continued to confirm his research, he became more excited, more eager, to publish his results. Nick left the hospital certain Doc was signing his own death warrant.

As Caradoc was eating his dinner that night, he turned on the evening news.

"Our top story tonight: Billionaire Real Estate Developer Ronald Ace was killed when a piece of the iron facade fell on his head while he was announcing plans to demolish the Roosevelt Building in Soho. Ace's plans to build a new high-rise hotel and casino in lower Manhattan had been fiercely opposed by the local population and historic preservation groups, but he had recently received a green light from the city planning commission and the state gaming board. The future of the Roosevelt Building is uncertain at this time..."

Caradoc started hyperventilating, and his blood pressure soared. Alarms sounded at the nurse's station. Caradoc was given a sedative to calm him down, and he quickly drifted off to sleep. In his dreams, buildings swung their fire escapes like boxer's arms, throwing punches at him as he walked through the city.

A week later, Caradoc's doctors informed him that he was ready to be discharged to a rehabilitation center. They recommended several in the city, but were surprised when he requested one in Syracuse, NY.

WE BREAK ANY CURSE

by Jorie Rao

I couldn't wait any longer. I got up, brushing the dirt and dead leaves off of my jeans. I'd been sitting thirty yards off in the woods watching the house for the better part of an hour, waiting for my source to get back with information on the problem or if things had gone pear-shaped to send me our agreed-upon signal: a small yet noticeable fire.

So far, he was a no-show. It didn't mean anything terrible; Yardley was scrappy and, on occasion, easily distracted by a mess. His absence could imply immediate danger, but it could also mean someone left a cast-iron skillet soaking in dish soap. Yardley wasn't the kind of Brownie that could let that stand.

The property, a combination petting zoo and chicken farm, belonged to Gilded Hill Farms. From April until September, the place teemed with children pushing their way to the front of the crowd to feed ponies, donkeys, ducks, and the like. In November, the farm remained quiet except for tourists who rented out the farm's Victorian-style house as an Airbnb from Gilded Hill's proprietor.

The frigid wind ripped through my jean jacket without issue, blowing my short hair into my face and stinging my ears even under the protection of earmuffs. I stuffed my hands into my pockets and said a quiet thanks to my roommate for insisting I bring hand warmers, but I should have grabbed a pair for my boots, too; the snow had melted, but the ground remained frozen, making my poor choice in footwear abundantly clear. Scrunching my toes, trying to warm them inside my Doc Martens, I set off.

The smell of *farm* had shifted from an assault on my senses into a barely noticeable stench. Most of the animals slept, but one mare trotted up to the wooden barrier, knocked its hoof against the bottom rung, and whinnied at me. A beautiful specimen with a freckled white coat stared at me with wondering eyes that asked, "Where's the food?"

"I'm sorry. I don't have anything." I reached a hand to stroke down the bridge of his nose. "I'll bring some after, okay?"

The pony considered my offer, nudged my hand, and then trotted off to a far corner. I took that to mean he was okay with our deal.

As I approached the house, a two-story Victorian with pale blue shutters and a wrap-around porch, I heard the sounds of frantic slamming. Every light on the first floor seemed to be on. Someone had pulled the curtains closed, but I spotted silhouetted figures pacing back and forth in what I guessed to be the living room.

"We have to change him back!" One of the figures shouted, throwing their hands up in frustration.

My eyebrows shot up. *Change back?* That sounded intriguing.

Once on the porch, I realized why Yardley hadn't made it back. The toddler-sized Fae had been distracted by cleaning, after all. His earth-tone rags that passed as a tunic, tied at the waist with twine, ruffled in the wintry winds.

I crouched down next to where he aggressively scrubbed a stain out of the welcome mat. His petite, surprisingly sturdy arm moved with inhuman speed. Next to the mat, he'd laid out the tools of his trade: a Tide-to-Go pen, a Mr. Clean Magic Eraser, and a bottle of OxyClean.

"Hey," I whispered, doing my best not to startle him into disappearing into a cloud of Pine-sol scented mist.

Yardley turned. A line of sweat beaded across his furrowed brow. "It's a tough stain." "I can see that." I looked over my shoulder at the window closest to us. Inside, the pacing and frantic calls to "change him back" continued. When I looked at my companion, he had the Tide pen, gripped with both of his tiny hands, working at the stain. If I had a death wish —which I don't, for the record— I'd film him and post it on TikTok because it was one of the cutest things I'd seen in a long time. Since I didn't want to mess with the Fae lords, I refrained and enjoyed the scene for myself.

"I became distracted, Sidney Spectre," Yardley said—his version of an apology. "But I did notice that someone inside is a goose."

I felt his power flutter around me, skimming across my skin like a feather duster whenever he used my (almost-full) name, which he'd won in an ill-fated game of Boggle. I shook off the feeling and refocused. "Meaning?"

"He was a man. Now, he is a goose."

While I processed that information, he leaned down to inspect the mat but seemed dissatisfied. He sprayed the OxyClean and grabbed the Magic Eraser, then scrubbed.

I couldn't see anything, but I wasn't a Brownie. Creatures like Yardley were supernaturally programmed to be excellent cleaners, or at least they were obsessive about it. Never tell them they did a good job, though; that's a sure-fire way to make certain they never come back.

"Did you see him turn into a goose, or is your fae-sense tingling?"

Yardley chuckled. I amused him. "Tingling. Already a goose. Tall blonde one is dating the goose. He is upset."

I thought I'd be upset, too, if my partner turned into a goose. "Okay, so how many people in total?"

"Four. Two couples. Brother and sister, both with their mates."

I winced at the archaic use of 'mates' and stood up. "And one of them is a goose." He nodded but otherwise ignored me. Having a Brownie as a scout had its perks, but conversation wasn't one of them. After a minute of silent scrubbing, the air around me felt like silly putty, and poof, Yardley disappeared before my eyes, and the lingering scent of Pine-sol tickled my nose.

"Guess it's showtime." I pulled out my wallet, slipped one of my cards from the billfold, and knocked on the door.

The shouting ceased and turned into conspiratorial whispers before someone opened the door. I bit my bottom lip to keep from laughing. The man who answered, the tall blonde that Yardley mentioned, brandished a whisk.

He looked over my shoulder, possibly to assess if he needed to add a spatula to his arsenal, and when it became clear I'd come alone, he narrowed his eyes at me. "Can I help you?"

I extended my hand, the business card pinched between my index and middle finger. "I'm here about your goose problem."

He lowered the whisk and took my card. I waited as he read my details. I'd agonized over the wording. Mercy, my roommate, ended up convincing me that "We break any curse" inspired more confidence than "I can break curses." Sadly, it also inspired a bunch of confused looks whenever I showed up alone.

Faint sounds emanated from the adjacent room: a table being knocked over, followed by an agitated honk, then another honk accompanied by hissing. Someone yelped. The man looked over his shoulder, tensing as the noises died down. When he faced me, he asked, "'We break any curse'?" He sounded skeptical for someone whose partner turned into a goose. "Are you for real?"

I nodded. "Sidney Spectre, curse breaker, at your service." I craned my neck to see further inside and spied two people, a man and a woman, peering out from behind the pocket door. The man had a tear in his flannel shirt, his hair rumpled. The woman had a red mark on her face that would be a decent shiner by morning.

He looked at the card again. "Where's the 'we'? I only see you."

"My associate already left." The 'we' thing confused people, but the cards were already printed. *C'est la vie.* Plus, Yardley counted as part of the 'we' since he did all my scouting. After a beat, he thrust my card back at me. "Look, we don't..." He moved to shut the door, but I wedged my boot in before he could.

"Did something weird happen? Like, say, you found an object that turned your friend into a goose when he touched it?"

"How ..." the blonde said, stepping back.

I pushed the door open and stepped inside. Warmth circled me, and the smell of a lit fireplace drifted in from the living room. Sufficiently warm, I pulled my earmuffs down to rest around my neck. "Where is it?"

The woman spoke, her tone careful. "In the kitchen where Matt left it."

"And Matt is the goose?" I asked.

As if summoned by the mention of his name, Matt the Goose waddled out of the living room and into the entrance hall. He ruffled his feathers and honked at me before sidling up to stand at the woman's feet. The man beside her took a tentative step away, keeping his gaze on the goose as if it were an active landmine.

"Yes." She grimaced. "He's my brother. I-I'm Charlotte."

The man, presumably her partner by process of elimination, said, "Is that going to happen to all of us?"

"Really, Ash?" The tall blonde sounded disgusted.

Matt, the goose, hissed and moved to attack but stopped when the blonde waved the whisk at him.

Ah, so that's what the whisk was for.

"Come on, Nate, like I'm the only one thinking it?" Ash asked. "We all touched that stupid thing."

It was a valid fear and the first question I needed to answer. Cursed objects, depending on their age and the level of power used to create the curse, could grow a mind of their own, occasionally deviating from their original purpose.

Matt honked, whether in approval or annoyance; I had no idea. Goose wasn't one of the languages they offered in school.

"Ash," the woman begged, pulling his arm so he had to face her. "We need to help my brother." She turned to me. "Can you actually help us?"

I nodded. I hadn't met a curse I couldn't undo with the right time and supplies, but it only took one stubborn curse to end my streak. She didn't need to hear that, though. "This is insane," Nate informed the room. "This can't be happening."

I checked my watch. The moon would be at its peak soon. If Plan A didn't work, I'd need the moon for Plans B through Z. "Not to be rude, but can we save the 'this can't be happening' monologues for after I figure out why your boyfriend is a goose?"

Nate, still holding the whisk, scowled but said, "Follow me."

As I walked the hallway, I noted the portraits that lined the wood-paneled walls. Gold-coated frames held images of Victorian-era people. Some showcased young children, others a study in adults or a group of people lounging on a hill eating a picnic; in each appeared a white goose upon someone's lap.

Nate sensed me lingering and turned. "Part of the charm, I guess, but they creep me out. Matt was so excited to stay in a Victorian, so when we found one on AirBnB, he practically forced all of us to go. He loves this— all of the lace and woodwork. *Downton Abbey's* his favorite show."

"My roommate loves that show," I told him, at a loss for anything more significant to contribute. The only other thought that came to mind would undoubtedly upset him. The kitchen, true to the era in which the home was built, remained threadbare with only the basics: a sturdy wooden island in the middle of the room, a cast-iron stove, a deep-set sink, and a hearth. Atop the wooden island sat a substantial golden egg.

"There." Nate pointed as if there were any questions about which item held the curse.

"Okay, I'm sensing a theme here."

"We found it in the safe," he told her, tucking the whisk in his pocket. "The one over near the butler's pantry. Matt said it's where they used to store the silver and other valuables. He wanted to look, so we did, and that thing was just there by itself, so Matt picked it up, and a little while later, he was a goose."

"A removal curse," I said, digging around in the pockets of my coat. I found my white candle and portable candle holder, a small iron circle, and placed it on the wooden table as far from the egg as possible.

"A what?"

"A curse that activates when the item is removed or stolen," I told him as I pulled a compact mirror out along with a few small baggies of herbs and salt as well as my dropper bottle of Anointing Oil—a.k.a olive oil—and a matchbook.

"You know you sound insane, right?"

"You know your boyfriend's a goose, *right?*"

Nate started to protest but instead asked, "What's that?"

"A shortcut. Not breaking the curse, just redirecting the magic."

"Will it work?"

"One way to find out." I opened the dropper, poured oil onto the wooden surface, and sprinkled in oregano, crushed bay leaf, and salt. "Get the others. If this doesn't work, we'll have to try something else."

Nate's eyes went wide, but he dashed out of the kitchen.

"So, you're a cursed egg? Well, I eat eggs for breakfast, so *ha*." I eyed the object, feeling its magic as surely as I felt Yardley's. In contrast to the silly putty feeling whenever Yardley disappeared, this felt like walking on rocks coated in slimy algae. The magic held hints of something old as hell, possibly one of the capital "P" Primordials. An involuntary shudder went down my spine.

The vague feeling of old-ass magic paired with the goose thing suggested a *specific* Primordial—one that hadn't been seen in a century.

Crap.

The thought that a spell reflection might work felt less likely, but I had to try. Any other avenue would alert the caster, giving them time to intervene.

"Here goes," I said, rolling the white candle in the oil and spice mixture. I placed it in the holder and put it all on the mirror. With the candle lit, I began the spell, repeating it thrice. *"Return to your maker. Leave in peace. Should your way be barred, your power shall cease."*

The candle flickered, shot up a white-blue jet of flame, and then snuffed out. The slippery algae feeling didn't dissipate, and the adjoining honk confirmed what I already knew—this curse couldn't be redirected.

"Matt's still a goose," Ash announced.

I chewed the inside of my cheek. This was gonna suck. "Time for Plan B."

"What's that?"

"We're giving Matt a bath. Nate, fill the sink with ice-cold water."

He nodded, thankfully done protesting the insanity of his situation, and dashed to the deep-set sink.

Without warning, Charlotte choked. She brought her hand to her throat and squeaked when she saw feathers growing out of her skin. Her pupils dilated until only black was visible. She hunched over, retched, and collapsed. More feather's sprouted out from under her clothes as her body began the shift.

"Char," Ash shouted, rushing to her side. He tried to touch her, but when he reached for her arm, it shrank back into a wing. "Oh, God."

"Wow," I said, unable to tear away from Charlotte's shift, "we need Plan B.S."

"And what's that?"

"I've gotta bitch-slap that curse."

Nate and Ash looked lost. Eventually, Nate said, "Okay, what do we need to do?" "There's a creek. I passed it on my way here. We need to gather supplies and get there before the rest of you go the way of the goose."

Five minutes and one canvas bag of supplies later, we headed toward the back of the property. The pony from earlier trotted along the fence, whinnying expectantly. I rifled around in the tote and returned with an apple.

I held it out. The pony crunched into it with delight.

"Why'd you do that?" Nate asked.

"I promised."

He looked at me like I was the one holding my goose boyfriend. "Horses don't understand promises."

"Don't they?"

Nate considered that but didn't comment. He carried Matt close to his chest, cradling him tightly. It would have been sweet if it hadn't been out of necessity. Matt kept trying to fly away.

In perfect contrast, Ash carried Charlotte with his arms extended to keep her as far from his face as possible. She didn't try to fly away, but she'd pecked him a few times, finally biting him on the nose. Even at arm's length, she snapped her beak at him.

"If this doesn't work," Ash said, jerking back to avoid another goose attack, "then what? We take them to the ocean?"

I picked up my pace. "Not quite," I called back, expertly avoiding the real question. If brute force didn't work, then we'd have a slightly bigger problem on our hands. The caster would sense my magic, find us, and, depending on their mood, either kill us or very helpfully remove the curse and let us go on our merry way.

Don't laugh. It happens—well, happened. Once. Rumpelstiltskin gets a bad rap. Kinda creepy but otherwise totally chill.

"How much further?" Nate struggled to keep hold of Matt.

"Almost there," I said, sensing the running water.

My skin felt sweaty under my clothes, a side effect from the strain of the magic I'd already performed. Even the tiniest bits of magic need to come from *somewhere*. If no other wellspring is available, I take it from myself.

Out here, in middle-of-nowhere Connecticut, magic existed in abundance—yet I couldn't access it on this farm thanks to the capital "P," pain in my ass, Primordial. When one settles down, the ambient magic around them follows 'finder's keepers' rules and doesn't like to be used by outsiders.

The dark woods engulfed us. If not for the flashlight on my phone, I'd be traipsing around blind with only my Sense guiding me to the water. How did curse breakers do this before flashlights? Honestly.

I stepped over a fallen tree waiting for Nate and Ash to catch up. Nate stepped over easily, but Ash's foot caught on a broken branch, bringing him down. Charlotte skittered away, honking as she disappeared.

"Char!" Ash groaned, holding an arm to his chest.

"You okay?" Nate asked.

"Yes." His voice cracked, and for a moment, I thought he might cry, but he shook it off and said, "We need to get her."

"You go. Leave Matt here. I'll get to the water and set up." I held out my arms for Matt, but Nate hesitated.

"Dude, I promise I won't run off with your significant goose. Scouts honor."

He took a deep breath and handed Matt to me. "You were never a scout, were you?"

"Not in the traditional sense." I tried for levity, but he looked like he wanted to throw up and slap me, not necessarily in that order. "Look, I don't break promises. Just ask that horse." Nate didn't respond, but he quit staring at me and helped Ash. They both lit up their phone flashlights. We exchanged numbers in case they got lost, and then they headed off. Matt tried his wings. I narrowed my gaze. "Do you wanna be a goose forever?" That stopped him dead. "Good, now behave so we can get this curse broken."

The rest of the path to the embankment went off without a hitch. My heart pounded anyway, waiting for the other shoe to drop. I crouched, placing Matt on the ground. I didn't release his wings. "If I let go, will you stay?"

He honked at me, which could be 'goose' for "yup" or "hell no." I decided to interpret it as "yup" and let go. He didn't fly off, so maybe I was fluent in 'goose.'

I looked up at the canopy of bare trees. The waning moon shone brightly in the cloudless sky. New moons were better for curse-breaking, but the waning moon would suffice.

With Matt silently pecking at the ground, I unpacked the supplies, some of which I'd brought with me, others pilfered from the house. The clay, candles, herbs, and sun water all came from my coat pockets. From the house: a slip of paper, a pen, a hammer, and a fire-safe bowl.

I hummed my favorite Queen song as I worked the clay in the light provided by my candle. "Fat-Bottomed Girls" had the beneficial effect of chilling me the heck out while also clearing my mind enough to perform the brute force spell. Magic *knows* when you're distracted. Spells cast like that are hit or miss—sometimes both. Don't ask.

My phone didn't ring, so I hoped that meant they had found Charlotte and were on their way. I texted Mercy to have an Epsom salt bath ready for me when I got home. I'd need to soak the algae feeling off me before I felt right. She sent back a thumbs-up emoji, then a question mark. Stregas weren't big texters.

The sound of a snapping twig pulled my attention away from the phone. "Nate? Ash?" No answer.

There's that other shoe—dropping way before I was ready.

Matt sensed the badness of our situation and hissed, scrunching his neck into an "S"-shape. He flapped his wings and stood behind me.

"You're trespassing," a deep, velvety voice came from the cover of a boulder.

"Am I?" I tried to sound cocky, but it came out too fast.

Matt hissed as the figure stepped into view. They were tall, that much was obvious, and they moved with achingly slow movements to show they had all the time in the world. Primordials were like that because *they did.*

"By rights, these humans belong to me."

"They might disagree."

Each step brought them into the cone of light from my phone, finally illuminating the porcelain features of a Primordial who'd been AWOL since sometime in the 19th century. "Mother Goose."

She smiled at me. "That is my most recent name. I have others, as you well know, Breaker."

I did know. She'd gone by many—most notably, the Beast of Gevaudan. Any infamous shape-shifter was an aspect of Mother Goose or one of her children. If I didn't break this curse, I could count Nate, Ash, Charlotte, and Matt among them.

"You *really* leaned into the goose thing."

"This has been my land for a century. Those who remove my egg become one of my flock. You are interfering in something you do not understand."

"I understand that cursing people who see a golden egg and get curious enough to touch it is a bit melodramatic, even for a Primordial."

"You call it a curse. I call it new life."

"You say tomato. I say you're a supernatural rapist. No means no, Mother Goose." She laughed at me. A hearty, silken sound that cut off so abruptly I balked. Emptiness surrounded me. She called the ambient magic to her, leaving me in a magical dead zone. Because the universe has a sense of humor, the others joined the party in time to see Mother Goose shift from her human aspect into a goose large enough to lay truly humongous golden eggs. She was the size of a velociraptor from *Jurassic Park*.

"What the literal hell?" Nate shouted, stopping short and tripping over the supplies I'd laid out. He tumbled into the water, bringing Charlotte, whom he'd been carrying, with him. Ash stood stock still. "D-did that woman just turn into a massive goose?

"Water. *Now*," I said, shoving both him and Matt toward the freezing water, where Nate shivered, holding Charlotte close.

I'd need to do a speed run. Super Mario, give me strength. Writing the spell on the paper and doing the burning ritual were scrapped. Luckily, I'd carved the runes into the clay and anointed it with the sun water before the goose-shit hit the fan. I dripped wax onto the clay and started shouting. "No *more befouled, again unbound, again unbidden."*

Mother Goose lunged at me, her white wings spread. I rolled away before her colossal beak slammed into the ground where I'd been. In the roll, I'd squished the clay, so I tried reshaping it, dodged a hit, and fell on my ass.

"H-hurry," Ash chattered at me.

"Trying to avoid a veloci-goose over here." I narrowly missed getting whacked by one of her wings. I pooled my own wellspring of magic and repeated the spell.

"Ha," I said as she launched another attack, missing me as I sidestepped. She let out a honk that vibrated the earth beneath me. I faltered as she tried to seal me in a dead zone again.

Clearing my mind. I hummed *Fat-Bottomed Girls,* pulling the final remnants of my own wellspring. Sweat dripped down my spine.

Mother Goose leaned back, wings flapping, beak to the sky, and roared as I said the spell one final time, sealing my intention. She clocked me with her wing. I hit the edge of the water and tossed the clay poppet to Nate, who caught it without any hesitation.

"Go under. Count to thirty."

They did as I said, but I'd taken my eyes off the goose for too long. She closed her beak on my shoulder. Agonizing pain washed over me, dissolving my pool of magic. I shook violently.

Another blow, this time a head butt, landed between my eyebrows. I blinked away the pain. "Jump over *this* candlestick!"

I tossed the candle at Mother Goose. It hit her neck, singeing her feathers. She honked, hissed, and tried to put out the fire.

I spared a look at the water. Four humans popped up, shivering and ghastly pale but sans feathers. Yay me!

My glory was short-lived because Mother Goose extinguished herself and lunged full force. I scrambled back, crab-walking along the water's edge. Nate called my name, and when I turned, he tossed me his whisk.

I caught it, dumbfounded. What did he expect me to do with this?

I got my answer when Mother Goose stopped dead. She eyed the whisk with the same caution that had kept Matt in line earlier. If I hadn't been so tired, I might have laughed. "Back, foul creature," I shouted, both loving and hating my pun. She backed away, scrunching her large neck in derision.

The gaggle of shivering humans swam to the embankment. Ash hugged Charlotte, kissing the top of her head. Nate and Matt held hands. All in all, I felt pretty good about this one. "You'll want to leave a bad review."

"Se-seriously?" Nate said, teeth chattering.

I shrugged. God, did it hurt to move. I pulled my phone out, steadying the whisk, and called for my ride. Mercy laughed into the receiver when I told her how I was keeping Mother Goose at bay.

"Why isn't she changing back?" Matt asked. His voice hoarse, likely from all the honking.

"Great question." *Would it be unprofessional to say I had no flipping clue?*

"Will we need to worry about her coming after us?" Ash asked.

"I don't think so, but Primordials can hold a grudge. Maybe avoid geese for a while."

Charlotte laughed, but when she saw my face, she stopped. "You're serious?"

"Creatures like Mother Goose have a long memory, but her magic is rooted to this farm. She can't leave the property, which is likely why she turned it into an Airbnb, but she has children. She also seems stuck shifting into a goose — a massive goose, but it doesn't inspire the same fear as a werewolf. Maybe a side effect of rooting herself to the land."

"What?"

"Primordial beings can do two things for power: connect to a place abundant in ambient magic or cast the same way us measly mortals."

"There's more power connecting to a place?" Nate asked.

"Yes and no. The other way takes longer and is messier but allows more freedom—literally and magically. Connecting to a place is a Hail Mary, albeit one with an endless wellspring of ambient magic. A Primordial will do it when they are weak and have no choice. Getting stuck isn't ideal for their kind."

"So she's stuck here?"

"A century ago, she was persona-non-goose with a few of her fellow Primordials and got a butt-whooping from what I heard."

"None of this makes any sense," Nate said.

I shrugged. "When Mother G connected herself to the magic here to recoup, she got chained here forever."

"Forever-ever?"

"*Forever-ever. They're immortal.*"

"And she chose *Connecticut?*" Ash asked.

I thought Connecticut was an okay-ish spot if you liked idyllic scenery and antiques, but he's right. I might have chosen somewhere warmer.

"You guys go pack while I use the whisk," I stopped mid-sentence to laugh because come on — *a whisk?* "— to hold her back."

I stayed outside, wagging the whisk at Mother Goose while they packed. I had maybe five minutes before my body would give out under the strain of all the expended magic and energy.

Nate, Matt, Ash, and Charlotte carried their luggage down the front porch and met me at their car. They'd all changed out of their wet clothes but left their hair soaked. Couldn't blame them for prioritizing getting out of here over a quick blow-dry.

"Thanks, Sidney." Nate smiled, then tugged Matt, who shuddered when Mother Goose hissed, toward the car.

"I hope I never see you again." Ash patted me on the shoulder. "No offense."

"None taken."

"Can I have a card?" Charlotte asked. She winced at Ash's snort but took the card when I handed it to her. "Just in case."

I waved goodbye as they drove off. Around me, the farm was silent except for the frustrated honks coming from Mother Goose.

Finally, the sound of Mercy's all-wheel-drive Chevy crunched on the driveway. Lightning fast, thanks to her Strega-ness, she stood at my side, eyed the Mother of all Geese, and wrapped a hand around my waist before yanking me into the safety of her truck.

I slumped in the passenger seat and slept the whole way home.

CUSTOMER SUPPORT

by Alice Avoy

"Well, well, who decided to show up fifteen minutes *late* with a Starbucks? *As. Always.*"

Maja froze and sighed inwardly. Her hopes that she'd be able to sneak to her desk undetected hurled themselves through the window and hit the sidewalk. Still, not batting an eyelid, she twirled around and met her boss, leaning against the doorframe of his office with the most impeccable, obsequious smile in existence.

"Ah, Principality Dantaniel, you look... radiant today. Absolutely resplendent! Have you groomed your wings?"

The angel furrowed his perfect eyebrows. The boss, who could smell bullshit on default, seemed like a true supervisor from Hell, even though his place of origin was actually in the opposite direction. Always serious, hyper-responsible, and pathologically punctual–the perfect opposite of Maja, who snorted chaos for breakfast and downed it with lightheartedness in true Rusalka fashion. The only thing they had in common was blond hair, and that was it.

"Please, Maja, spare me your placating efforts as they are empty, and you are frankly wasting both of our times. I expect you to stay after work today and make up for all the minutes you have squandered this week. They've accumulated to an hour already."

"But–"

"No buts. I expect full efficiency and commitment."

Maja couldn't stop herself from whining. "It's not like we're saving the world or anything!"

"Helping our customers is extremely important. As is the bi-monthly evaluation of your performance, so don't forget about that."

Maja bit back a reply, knowing better than to offer him a piece of her mind. Working as a customer service representative at the Magical Emporium, the biggest online store for all things supernatural wasn't the most glamorous job in the world, but it paid the bills. Definitely better than working in retail–she had her fair share of that during her first year after emigrating to Chicago. Never again, thanks.

"Yes, I know, I know. I'm sorry. I'm getting to work right away."

"Good." Without sparing her another glance, the angel withdrew to his office.

Maja suppressed a craving to stick out her tongue at him. Angels having hundreds of pairs of eyes was just a stereotype, but she didn't want to risk it. Like a good corporate drone, she walked straight to the end of the corridor and across the room with three desks. Samira, the prettiest sphinx Maja had ever seen, was on holiday. Iraklis was the only one holding down the fort. The satyr's booming voice bounced against the walls as he spoke on the phone. She'd feel bad for leaving him on his own that morning, but he usually left earlier than he was supposed to, so they found a good balance.

"No, as I have already told you, we're not selling dragon eggs. That's people trafficking. Highly illegal." His gaze met Maja's, and he rolled his eyes. She gave him a thumbs-up in solidarity—no escaping idiocy in this job. "Yes, ma'am, you can write a complaint to my manager, but that won't change our stock or the laws of this country. Good day to you." The satyr hung up with a long-suffering sigh. Even Iraklis, the most chill person she knew, had his limits.

"Tough crowd, huh?" Maja flopped on her chair and sipped her coffee–a luxury she could barely afford, but there was no other way to survive Friday morning.

"You have no idea. It's the third Karen today already. Are we going for a record?"

"I sincerely hope not. Not sure if I can handle that today."

"Why?"

"I'm fighting against the stereotype of Rusalki being bloodthirsty. Don't wanna hate on humankind too much. Bad PR, you know?"

"Come on. You're working in customer support; of course you hate humanity. Would be weird if you didn't."

Maja laughed and turned her computer on. She checked her email and noticed only a handful of new messages that required a reply. Perfect. Hopefully, there wouldn't be any phone calls...

Ring ring!

Ugh, of course.

"Your turn now, Maja. Have a smattering of excrements thrown your way." Iraklis indicated the phone with a charming smile and an eyebrow wiggle.

"Right..."

Heaving a sigh, Maja put her coffee away—time to earn her paycheck and take a nosedive in the sewage. Looking straight into the satyr's dark eyes as if to challenge him, she picked up and spoke in a perfectly friendly customer service voice, oozing enthusiasm and eagerness to please. "Hello, good morning! My name is Maja. I am a representative of the Magical Emporium, and it will be my utmost pleasure to assist you in whatever issue you are having. How may I help you?"

"Um..." The young woman's voice coming through the receiver was so tiny and timid that Maja instinctively leaned forward as if that could make her hear better. "Hello... I'm... I'm calling about one of your products."

"Certainly. Which one? Would you like me to make a presentation of the product for you? Give you more details? Or do you have any questions about ingredients? I can assure you that all of our products do *not* contain any genetically modified or unethically grown plants and they have been tested in proper clinical trials on an assortment of willing participants, who have been generously renumerated."

A stretch of baffled silence. "Um... No, I don't want that. Um, it's about your product. The... Cat's... Whispers?"

Maja looked to the side, going through the entire inventory of the company's products in her head. None were called that, but the customers were usually dumb, so she went for the closest approximation.

"The Cat's Whiskers?"

More heavy silence. Maja wanted to repeat what she had said, but then she heard a soft, resigned gasp. "Oh... That's... That explains... things."

Maja rolled her eyes. Iraklis snickered from behind his computer screen. He could pretend all he wanted that he was working, but he couldn't fool her. Who, if not her, was a master of slacking off, after all? "Did you have any problems with that product?"

"Um, yes. It seems that I... I misunderstood what it does."

"Could you elaborate?"

"Um, yeah... I... Well, I thought that when I drank it, I would be able to speak to cats. You know, like cat's whispers?"

"Ah..." Maja found it really, *really* hard not to burst out laughing. Especially since Iraklis wheezed openly now. She rammed her nails into her thigh to add some physical pain to balance the mental anguish of hilarity suppression. "No, unfortunately, that is not what our product does. One dosage of Cat's Whiskers turns you into a tabby cat for a period of twenty-four hours."

"Um, yes. But I, um... I didn't read the instructions first. And I drank the entire bottle. The, um... the large one."

Oh, man. Maja ran quick calculations in her head. The small bottle had about thirty dosages, and the large one... a hundred. A hundred days of being a cat... Then a thought hit her, strong like a brick to the head. "Ma'am, please do not take this the wrong way, but... how are you able to talk to me if you turned yourself into a cat?"

Silence yet again. Huh. Was it just a prank call? Maja traded glances with Iraklis. Time to end the conversation firmly but politely. As Maja was opening her mouth to give the caller wasting her time some much-needed passive-aggressive what for, the woman on the other side decided to reply.

"Um, actually... It's pretty embarrassing. I'm a shifter, you know."

"A shifter?" Not many of those around, not in Maja's experience at least. Shifters, as shapeshifters were colloquially known, were a magical subspecies of humans who could change their bodies into various animals at will. Exactly the kind of people who shouldn't be messing around with magical items that turned you into anything. "So... it didn't work on you? Or were you able to change back?"

"Well... partly. Oh, I told you it's pretty embarrassing... I drank the entire bottle, and the potion changed me into a cat, so I kind of panicked, got horribly entangled in the strap of my bag, panicked even more, and then somehow tumbled out of the window of my apartment together with it. I landed in the branches of a tree, where I tried to change back into a human, but... it didn't exactly work. I managed to shift my head and right arm, but the rest... Eh, let's just say I'm a three-quarter cat hybrid that's stuck in a tree, and I don't know what to do. It's a blessing in disguise that I still have my bag with me. At least I was able to call you."

Iraklis mouthed helpful advice so that only Maja could hear it. "Call the firefighters. I heard they're pretty good at freeing kittens from tall trees!"

Maja told him nonverbally to can it. Her focus moved back to the client. "I'm sorry to hear about your situation. It is certainly difficult. We will send someone with the antidote as soon as we can." The girl was lucky that she'd called in the morning. If she called after 5:00 p.m. or on the weekend, she'd be on her own. "Where are you, ma'am? Please give me your location, and we'll dispatch someone from the field division to deliver the antidote to you."

"Thank you." The relief in the girl's voice was palpable. "I'm in Chicago right now, just like you guys—935 West 83rd Street, near the Lutheran Church. Please hurry. Being in this form is... ugh, it's so weird. I have no idea what my body is doing. I want to scratch parts I don't even have anymore!"

"Please, remain calm, ma'am. Help will reach you soon. Goodbye." Maja hung up. She let out a long breath, staring at Iraklis. "Well, that was a journey I didn't think I would go on today."

"Pfft, right? Shifter turned into a half-cat, that's amazing!" He laughed so hard his whole desk shook. People on the floor below could probably hear him. "Cat's Whispers! I'm gonna print that one out and stick it to the wall for posterity."

Maja cracked a smile, the corner of her lips twitching uncontrollably.

"Every time I think that our customers have reached the peak of stupidity, something like this happens and proves me wrong. But anyway, we can't leave that poor cat idiot *hanging* there. Gotta let the boss know." Maja picked up the phone again and called Dantaniel's office on an internal line. "Hey! You won't believe what happened!"

"You do not need to scream at the top of your lungs. I am perfectly capable of hearing you at lower volumes. What is the matter?"

"I just got a call from a local client. A shifter drank Cat's Whiskers. She needs an intervention and some magical antidote. Are any of the teams available?"

Dantaniel replied immediately, not needing to consult the log book. The guy had everything memorized. Maja was somewhat impressed but mostly horrified. "No, they are all on a mission currently. They will not be available sooner than four to five hours."

"Ah, shit. Not good. She's stuck in a tree right now."

"Where is she exactly?"

"Just round the corner, really."

"In that case, you can go yourself and deliver her the antidote in person."

Maja blinked. "What? You want me to go in the field?"

"Precisely. Iraklis will be perfectly capable of covering for you. He is used to it by now with how poor your work ethic is."

Freaking *ouch*. Maja opened her mouth but closed it immediately. Your boss being right while reprimanding you was the worst feeling in the world. Guess she didn't really have a choice here. Ugh.

"Fine! Fine. I'll go."

"I'm happy that you've decided to treat your work with the seriousness it deserves."

Maja did her best not to cringe. "Sure. I'll be back in an hour."

"Good luck. Don't bring shame to our company."

Dantaniel ended the call. Maja sighed, gulped down the rest of her coffee, and gathered her things. Iraklis shot her a sympathetic glance as she headed out the door.

Maja walked down the street, hands in the pockets of her coat. She was out of the office, yes, which was nice, but the purpose of her outing wasn't all that great. Customer service was hard enough when done over email, nearly impossible on the phone, and apocalyptic face-to-face. At her last retail job, she'd been fired after a conversation with someone who shared IQ levels with an amoeba got slightly out of control. Getting here, to remote support, seemed like a huge step up the social ladder. But now she was back to direct interventions. Damn. Just her luck.

At least the shifter girl on the phone didn't sound bitchy. Maybe she wouldn't be too problematic. Maja fiddled with a small bottle hidden in her left pocket, hoping for a smooth operation. She buttoned her coat properly and put the collar up. The last days of September felt kind of chilly, even for someone whose ancestors soaked in the icy cold lakes of Masuria.

Maja blended in seamlessly with the throng of people running errands. No matter the hour, the streets of Chicago were always bustling with life. Most faces she passed by belonged to humans–at least it seemed so at first glance, although appearances could be deceiving–but the number of out-and-proud magicals was sizeable as well. She sometimes wondered if people hundreds of years ago could have guessed that one day, all the "monsters" spoken about in fairy tales would actually cross the veil between worlds, strike a truce with humanity, and somehow become a part of polite society. Things weren't always easy, sure, but Maja still preferred living in a city to squatting somewhere in ancient forests. At least here they had coffee and junk food. Civilization had spoiled her.

Maja slid her gaze across the buildings, searching for the address indicated by the unlucky customer. It should be here somewhere...

Yes, she'd arrived. The big oak tree must be the spot where the temporarily cat lady took her refuge.

"Um, hello?" Maja came to the trunk and craned her neck. She could feel people's eyes on her, although no one seemed to judge her too harshly. They probably thought she was some homesick nymph. She could live with that. "You there? I'm from the Magical Emporium. We talked on the phone? I'm here to help."

Branches rustled high above Maja's head. She squinted but couldn't really see anything through the canopy of leaves. For everyone's sake, she hoped this wasn't some stupid prank.

"Hey." A quiet voice near the treetop oozed embarrassment. "Could you... come up here?"

"What? Are you seriously asking me to climb a tree?"

"Please. I can't really move."

Maja swore under her breath. Dantaniel owed her a bonus for this insanity. He'd better not say that she never went above and beyond for a customer ever again.

Maja bent her knees and then jumped up, grabbing the sturdiest-looking branch. She rocked her body, caught another branch with her ankles, and all but catapulted herself upwards. The last time she did anything similar, she was still a little girl, but it was good to know she hadn't lost her touch.

"Where are you?" she asked, reaching approximately the middle of the tree.

"Here."

Leaves rustled again. Now, Maja could see the creature in all her glory.

"Oh shit..." The lady on the phone hadn't exaggerated. A human hand was attached to a human shoulder and a human head, but the rest of the body belonged to a ginger tabby, still entangled in a bag's strap. A sight straight from a macabre horror movie. Shame, since the human head was kind of cute, showing features of a young woman of Asian descent with a perky nose, bright blue hair, and beautiful brown eyes.

"I haven't seen myself in a mirror, but I'd probably agree with you." She smiled meekly.

"Sorry. That wasn't very professional of me."

"It's fine. I'm just happy that you've come. Do you have the antidote?"

"Yeah. Here." Maja grabbed the bottle, uncorked it, and gave it to the other woman. "You just need to drink it. It will transform you back into your original shape."

"Thank you."

In her place, Maja would immediately down everything in one gulp, but the girl hesitated.

"Something wrong? Adverse side effects of the antidote can't be ruled out completely, although, personally, I think that acne or hair loss are better than not having most of your body..."

"Ah, it's not that... Could you just... um, turn around while I shift back? I'm actually naked."

"Oh." Maja should have expected that. "Sure. No problem."

Changing your position while sitting astride a tree branch wasn't the easiest feat, but thankfully, years spent in her grandmother's forest hadn't been wasted.

"So, are you done?" Maja asked after a long moment filled with silence.

"Yes..."

"Great, we can go down now and–"

"I'm still naked."

"Oh. Right." Huh. Maja wished she had thought about that sooner. Maybe she could have brought a company T-shirt or something. Time to improvise. Carefully, she shrugged off her coat and put it behind herself without taking a peek.

"Come on, take it. It's gonna be too big for you, but we can't have you going butt naked across the city."

"Thanks." The girl really sounded grateful. "You've done so much for me, and I haven't even introduced myself yet. Sorry. I'm Rika."

"Cool. I'm Maja. With a 'j' not 'y,' the Slavic way."

"Nice to meet you. Anyway, I'm ready now. I'll go down first, okay?"

"Sure."

A minute later, both were standing under the tree. Maja's coat on Rika reached almost to the ground, which was for the best as no one would wonder why she was walking around without pants. Adorable. Especially as she was still kind of embarrassed about the whole ordeal.

"Um... My apartment is right in this building here. Maybe you'd like to come in for tea? It's the least I can do to thank you for saving me. Oh, unless you're still at work? Sorry, I shouldn't have suggested that..."

Maja burst out laughing. "I am indeed at work, and that's precisely why I'd love to have tea with you. Why not use the company's time to do something fun for a change?"

Rika beamed at her and led the way.

"It's a bit messy. I didn't really expect anyone," Rika said, turning the key in the lock as they reached their destination.

"Can't be worse than mine. I clean it every equinox to honor my ancestors."

Maja expected the usual bachelor pad with clothes scattered everywhere and takeout boxes hosting a billion strains of bacteria. The reality turned out to be quite different. Almost every free space on the shelves and on the floor by the walls was filled with potted plants. All sizes and shapes, some sprouting flowers, they turned the place into a tamed jungle.

"Wow."

"Yeah. I got a bit carried away. I grew up near a botanical garden in Tokyo, so every time I feel homesick, I buy a new one."

"Ah, I totally get it. When I miss home, I make pierogi. I always end up with too many and have to eat them for a whole week."

"Make yourself at home." Rika picked up a pile of clothes from an armchair by the window. "I'll put these back on and then make us tea."

"It's fine, I'll do it. Tea-making is actually my superpower. That's why I'm considered a magical. The gills on my neck have nothing to do with it."

Rika's smile mirrored her own. "Everything's in the cupboard. Go wild."

Rika disappeared into the bathroom. Maja used that time to boil the water and prepare mugs. The selection of teas wasn't impressive, but she found a tangerine-flavored green tea that smelled divine. Perfect.

Rika returned just in time. In her proper clothes, she looked like your stereotypical art major, although, as Maja learned in the course of their conversation, in reality, she studied computer science. Over tea, they talked about this and that, sharing a laugh over the shared experience of being a relatively fresh immigrant in the States. Maja had a great time.

"No you didn't!" Rika wiped tears of joy from her face, leaning forward and hanging on to every word.

"Totally did! And the–"

A ringing from her pocket cut the story short. Maja took her phone out. One glance at the screen prompted her to curse like a sailor.

"Maja? What's wrong?"

"Shit. It's my boss. I told him I'd be back in an hour, and we're... pushing on three now. Whoops. It's been really nice to meet you, but I gotta go."

"Ah, sure."

Rika looked as if she wanted to add something else, but Maja gave her a friendly goodbye wave, already busy with appeasing Dantaniel. She shot out of the apartment, too preoccupied to look back.

The following Friday, Dantaniel had a breakfast meeting on the other side of the city, so Maja came in an hour late without a shred of regret. Samira wasn't back yet–lucky girl–but Iraklis was already bravely supporting customers. When Maja entered the room, he was talking on the phone with a client. Their eyes met, and he winked at her.

"Ah, you're in luck. She just came in. Wait a second." Iraklis passed Maja the phone, mouthing *For you*. Maja gave him a puzzled look and then responded to the call in her usual service voice.

"Magical Emporium, Maja is speaking. How can I help you?"

"It's me, Rika."

"Rika!" Her work persona mask fell off. Maja smiled in a genuine way. A week had passed since their meeting, but her thoughts still wandered to the cute shifter from time to time. She regretted having left in such an abrupt way. Hearing from Rika again was a nice surprise. Maybe Maja hadn't messed up completely. "How have you been?"

Iraklis pursed his lips and made a kissing sound. Maja chucked a pen at him.

"Um, I need help, Maja... Again..."

"What happened?"

"You have this product on offer, a Plant Glower, right?"

A what?

"Plant Glower? You mean, Plant Grower?"

"Ah..."

"Oh." Maja realized that she already knew everything that had occurred. "I'll come by with an antidote now."

"Yes, please."

Maja hung up and stood briskly, ready to jump straight into action.

"Wow, Maja, what's gotten into you? You actually want to work? Damn, that girl must be really cute."

Maja punched his shoulder lightly on the way out. He was absolutely right, but she didn't have to tell him that. She was glad that Dantaniel wasn't there–he'd probably require an explanation for why she wanted to go herself instead of sending a team. She doubted he would understand. In her experience, angels were terrible wingmen. Pun intended.

Maja took all the items she needed and left the building.

She remembered the way, as Rika's apartment was really close. In no time, she was knocking on the door. No roots or branches stuck out from under the door, so that was definitely a good sign. Perhaps the damage wasn't too severe.

"Hey, it's me! Are you okay in there?"

"It's open, come in!"

Maja pushed through the door. She expected to find herself in the middle of an overgrown forest. Instead, she saw Rika sitting at the table, the same one they had tea at before. In the middle stood a potted plant. A geranium, by the looks of it. Completely ordinary, aside from one leaf that had grown twice in size.

"You must be kidding me."

Rika had enough decency to look embarrassed.

"Well... I kind of forgot to ask for your number last time we met, and I really wanted to ask you out, so I did that on purpose. Sorry. I hope you won't get in trouble at work."

Maja laughed. "Oh, I'm not mad. I'm delighted! People say that Rusalki are so good at using their womanly wiles, but it seems I was completely beaten by a shifter."

When Dantaniel called three hours later, Maja didn't respond. She couldn't, too busy supporting a customer – in a direct, mouth-to-mouth fashion.

BILLIE AND THE SCARY IT

by Brenda Morris

Billie did not like the Scary It. Each night, the Scary It slithered and swayed up the fire escape to her window. It wheezed up all six stories of the rusty metal as the sirens of the city wailed in the night. The entity left slime in its wake. No one could see it but Billie, so she kept it secret.

Every night since they had moved after the accident, the Scary It would slink its way up, up, up. Then it would scratch, and it would claw at her window, calling her name.

Billie. Billie. Billie.

And Billie would squeeze her eyes shut and clench her fists, internally shrieking–

Away! Away! Away!

Eventually, the Scary It would leave, and the fever it induced in Billie would ease. Sweaty fists unclenched, and eyelids rested. Soon sleep wrapped Billie in its embrace. Then the sun would rise, and light would break through the curtains flooding Billie's small bedroom, and all would be well… or as well as it could be.

"How did you sleep, my love?" asked Billie's mother that sunny morning, marking the one-year anniversary of *the accident*. Billie's mother sat at the small, run-down, wooden table, squashed between the small space between counter and wall. There were only two chairs.

"Fine," lied Billie as she took her seat. Off-brand corn flakes sat before her. Not like before. Not like in the big house with brand-name cereal and more than two chairs at the table. The big house with a garden. The big house where the Scary It did not visit.

Billie's mother nodded and reached out for her daughter's hand. Billie tensed. She may have only been ten, but she was bright, and she knew what was coming. She knew what day it was.

"Baby, do you know what day it is?" Billie's mother asked quietly.

Slithering could be heard creeping up the fire escape.

"Yes!" Billie snapped, pulling her hand away.

Billie's mother sighed. "I was thinking about visiting the—"

"I feel sick, and I want to stay home!"

Wheezing, it was crawling up the side of the building. It wasn't supposed to come during the day.

"Billie, you know I can't afford a sitter right now, and I really think you should—"

"I want to stay home alone!" shrieked Billie, fists clenched.

Billie's mother sighed again, and with her sigh, the slithering was replaced by the sounds of city bustle and the honking of cars.

Billie's mother had not wanted to leave her ten-year-old alone, but she had no choice, so she locked the door on her way out and instructed Billie to lock the chain that was just barely in reach of Billie's small fingers.

Alone, Billie crept towards the closet next to the bathroom. Having sold so many items, one tiny closet stored all the belongings they were able to keep from the big house. Never alone, Billie did not want to upset her mother by going through them, but now she had her chance.

Box after cardboard box, Billie sifted through the items from once upon a time. Photo albums, teddy bears, her father's watch...

Billie opened another box and gasped.

A little miniature cottage made of pebbles sat before her. Back at the big house, it had sat in the garden beneath a large tree. There had been toy flowers and little tables with little chairs, a walkway made of stone, and a tiny picket fence. Her father had even hung twinkle lights around the stump of the tree. Now all that was left was the miniature cottage—her fairy house.

By the time Billie's mother returned home and Billie unchained the door, every box was put back in place as neat and orderly as a bunch of cardboard boxes crammed into a small closet could be. The only exception was the fairy house, which Billie had placed under her bed.

They ate dinner in silence. The wailing of sirens and the obnoxiously loud noise of neighbors' televisions filled the tiny kitchen. Billie's mother did not talk about her visit. Billie did not talk about the closet. They went to bed.

After Billie's mother kissed her goodnight and turned off the light, Billie sat up. Carefully she crawled to the floor and pulled out the miniature cottage.

"It's for the fairies. If you are kind to them, they will return the favor."

Billie remembered her father's words as she cradled the house. Carefully, she tiptoed to the window, pulled back the curtain, and lifted the window open. The city sounds grew loud, and Billie hoped her mother would not notice the change. A minute passed, and her mother did not stir. Gently, Billie set the fairy house down upon the fire escape.

She gazed at it. No toy flowers. No little chairs and little tables. No stone walkway. No twinkle lights. No garden. Just rusty metal.

Billie shut the window and closed the curtains. The fairy house belonged to the Scary It now. The entity would surely devour it, and Billie would never have to see the fairy house again. It did not belong in an apartment six stories high.

Tiptoeing back to bed, Billie crawled under the sheets and waited for the slithering. She closed her eyes.

Tap. Tap. Tap.

Scrunching her face in utter confusion, Billie sat up. That could not be the Scary It. It never tapped on her window. But if not, then who was it?

Billie bravely tiptoed back to the window and pulled back the curtain. At first, she saw nothing else other than her miniature cottage. Billie was about to close the curtains when–

"Yoo-hoo," sang a voice.

Billie's eyes opened wide as she beheld a miniature boy before her. Standing at six inches tall, he had the brown and white wings of a moth, four black dots decorating them. Brown antennas protruded from behind his neck, and a furry brown hat sat on his shaggy hair. He wore no shirt, but tan leather sleeves wrapped his arms. He had on what Billie could only assume was a kilt, with black trousers underneath and long brown boots. The boy's face seemed older than Billie's but was not as mature as that of a full-grown adult.

"Hello? You there," the boy called, tapping the window once more. "Open up! I request an audience at once!"

Billie opened the window, eyes blinking at the sight.

"I say, the condition of this fairy dwelling is quite atrocious," the boy continued, moth wings fluttering. "I am not picky, nor do I ask those to give more than they have, but having visited this dwelling previously in its former location, I can say in good consciousness that there is a severe lack of effort here."

Billie blinked again.

"I have waited almost a year for my home to be accessible to me, and this is the state you have left it in? What do you have to say for yourself?" The boy crossed his arms.

"Are... are you a fairy?"

The boy only fluttered his wings, giving Billie a cold, hard stare. "What gave it away?" he asked sarcastically.

"I just thought fairies were... girls..." mumbled Billie.

"And I thought Billie was a boy's name — look at us and our mistaken preconceived notions."

Billie's mouth fell open. "How do you know my name?"

"You don't remember me? We used to play in the garden together. You were very young."

"We did...?" trailed Billie.

"The name's Aloe F. Vera, but friends call me Loe," Loe said, smiling up at Billie.

"It's a pleasure to meet you again, Loe."

"Now, back to the topic of this dwelling," Loe continued. "Where are my flowers? Where is my walkway? What has happened to the chairs and the tables?"

"They got left behind," Billie spoke somberly.

"Why have they not been replaced?"

"My dad always put them there..." whispered Billie.

"And why has he not done so again?"

Suddenly, the fire escape jolted as something began to slither up towards them, it's wheezing echoing into the night.

Loe looked down, eyes growing wide. "What in all nature is that?"

Sweat formed on Billie's palms as her heartbeat quickened.

"Billie?"

"It's coming," Billie spoke. "Quick, come inside."

Loe fluttered into Billie's room, and Billie went to close the window, only–

"It's stuck!" Billie cried, struggling.

"Let me try — I'm stronger than I look," Loe informed her, flying over to the window and pressing down upon the peeling wood. It did not budge.

Outside, the slithering and wheezing continued to sway up the fire escape. Panic began to seize at Billie. She thought about shouting out for her mother, but the words got choked up in her throat.

"Billie?" called Loe, drawing the young child from her panic.

"If we can't close the window, it will get in," Billie replied. "We need to run."

Billie grabbed her jacket, her backpack, and her old baseball cap. Then she quickly threw on her boots as the entity slimed its way up the metal stairs.

"Come on," Billie whispered. She quietly opened her bedroom door and tiptoed into the small hall, Loe fluttering by her shoulder. Billie paused, gazing at her mother's open door.

"What about her?" Loe asked.

Billie only shook her head. "She'll be fine. It only wants me."

With that, Billie tiptoed her way to the front door. She gingerly unchained the chain lock, twisted the lock on the doorknob, and out they went. Being on the sixth floor, most other residents used the elevator. Though it was late, Billie could hear it rising. She quickly ran for the stairwell. Down they went. At the bottom, Billie looked at the fairy.

"Get in my backpack," she instructed. A girl of her age out and about alone at night would already cause too much unwanted attention. Throw a fairy in the mix, and it would be a nightmare.

Loe did not hesitate. He slipped inside, and Billie zipped the bag up just enough that Loe could peak his little head out. Then they exited the stairwell and, with no door attendant in the front to stop them, exited the building.

Outside, the city sounds were even more overwhelming. Honking, shouting, music reverberating. Somewhere a trash can was knocked over. Somewhere else, a cat shrieked. A baby wailed. A horn blared. And people were walking their way.

Billie quickly slipped into the nearby alley on the opposite side of the fire escape. There she crouched, taking off her backpack. Loe flew out.

"Billie, you have some serious explaining to do," Lou announced. "What is after you?"

Billie quickly explained all the details she knew of the Scary It. Loe listened intently with a nodding head.

"And so, you've never actually seen the creature?" Loe asked after Billie finished.

"Only the slime it leaves behind."

Loe nodded to himself. "Well, what now?"

"I guess we should wait here until the sun comes up," Billie spoke. "It usually goes away in the daylight."

"Usually?" inquired Loe.

Billie thought back to earlier that day when her mother asked her if she wanted to go to the–

Something was dragging itself across the dirty pavement, crawling right towards them. Wheezing.

"Actually, on second thought, maybe we ought to keep moving," Loe spoke, staring in the direction of the approaching noise.

Billie nodded her head in agreement. "I don't know where we could go."

"I have a place," Loe replied. "Follow me."

The fairy fluttered forward down the alley. Billie quickly followed. Coming out on the opposite end, Billie was relieved to find the slithering sounds had been left behind.

"Keep your head down, and I'll direct you where to go," Loe said, inserting himself back into Billie's backpack. Billie pulled her baseball cap down, clutched her backpack straps tight, and was off.

Avoiding main streets, she only walked along back roads and alleyways. Billie would have surely been terrified to roam through the cracks and corners of the city amongst the shadows had it not been for her companion's calming voice telling her which steps to take next.

Eventually, they made it to a dark park. A few cats scattered as they entered. The only living soul Billie could see was a man on a park bench, fast asleep. The sound of a distant truck made the atmosphere ominous.

"It's okay to come out," Billie whispered.

Loe fluttered out, stretching his moth wings. "This way," he spoke, and once more, Billie followed. They made their way to a patch of trees.

"Loe, where are we going?" cried Billie. The silhouettes of the twisted trees frightened her.

Loe did not answer. Instead, he stopped in front of a particularly large and gnarly-looking tree. "Here we are," he spoke proudly.

"Huh," Billie muttered, thinking her fairy friend must have lost some marbles.

Loe swayed his hand over the tree. A doorknob, made of bark and flowers, bloomed before her eyes. Billie gasped. Loe looked back at her. "It's meant for the mythical and magical, so if anyone asks, tell them you're a witch."

Billie nodded, clutching her straps tight, and Loe placed his hand on the knob. A door opened up from the tree with a frame just tall enough for Billie to walk in with ease. Jolly music and laughter greeted Billie's ears. Loe flew forward without a second thought, but Billie hesitated.

"Come on, Billie," Loe beckoned.

Billie bit her lip. She was unsure where Loe had brought her or if she really wanted to enter somewhere she was forced to pretend to be a witch. Still, being alone in the city at night with the Scary It following her sounded worse. Billie stepped inside. The door closed.

Inside was dark, only a few lit candles on the wall providing light down a spiral wooden stairwell.

"Loe?" Billie whispered. The music and laughter sounded like it was coming from below.

"Come on!" Loe snapped from somewhere further down the stairs.

Billie made her way down, and her eyes went wide as she took in her surroundings. She seemed to be in a large room made from a hollowed-out tree. The floor, ceiling, and walls were all bark, and the room was circular. It seemed to be a tavern of sorts. There was a bar with stools and other tables scattered around. There was a small stage for entertainment, a few dartboards on the walls, and even a billiard table. Candles lit the walls, and a small chandelier hung above.

But what was even more eye-popping were the patrons. To the side, two men were playing darts. The board they threw at was low to the ground and with good reason since the two men were unbelievably short. The pair reminded Billie of the clay gnomes they once had in their garden at the big house. At the billiard table was a giant, squinting his one large eye, about to make his move. On the table, a little man dressed in green, whom Billie could only assume was a leprechaun, taunted the one-eyed giant. At a table, a creature that resembled both a lion and an eagle sat conversing with a very, very hairy man. And in the corner, a man with large white fangs stood in the shadow, smiling to himself. The sight gave Billie the chills.

Billie quickly caught up to Loe as he flew past a table full of female fairies, giving the ladies a quick nod before setting his sight on the bar.

"Ban!" Loe called merrily.

"Loe!" the bartender, who appeared like a human man, called back equally as merry. Ban had long, thick black hair and a matching beard. He had just finished placing a drink in front of a large white horse, with one singular horn protruding from its head when they approached. Billie was almost certain Ban was actually human until she reached the bar, where Loe instructed her to take a seat. From her new, higher vantage point, Billie could see the lower half of Ban — he had the body of a horse.

Billie quickly snapped her eyes up. It was rude to stare.

"Briar and Edwin sound lovely tonight, don't they?" Ban asked happily, glancing at the bunny and fox singing upon the stage. "They're going to enter the annual talent display at the theatre under the train station. I'm rooting for them."

Loe nodded and then turned to Billie.

"Billie, this is Ban I. Daide," Loe introduced. "Ban, this is Billie."

Ban eyed Billie sternly. Billie gave him a smile.

"Loe!" Ban snapped. Then he spoke in a hushed voice, "You know you can't bring humans round these parts."

"She's a witch," Loe whispered.

"No, she ain't," Ban spoke softly.

Loe sighed. "She needs help, Ban."

Ban looked back at Billie. Billie gazed back. Ban sighed. "What's the matter?"

Billie began to explain the Scary It. Ban listened intently the whole time, even shooing away others trying to order a drink.

"I can't say I've heard of any entity such as... what do you call it again?" asked Ban.

"The Scary It," Billie replied.

"Eesh," shuddered Ban. "Creepy."

"Ban, can you help us?" Loe asked.

"Should've named it, like, Bob or Joe or something," mumbled Ban.

"Ban!" Loe called.

"All right," Ban replied, holding up his hands. "Personally, I know nothing. But I got a mate. A... water mate. She might know something. She's got a gift."

"Who?" Loe asked.

"The name is Medi X. Cine," Ban explained, grabbing something from behind him. He laid it on the bar for Loe and Billie to see. It was a tourist map of the city, only none of the places or names were familiar to Billie. Billie gazed over at Loe, and then clarity struck. This was a map of Loe's world. The city under her city.

"You'll find her at this pier," Ban said, pointing.

"Got it," Loe replied, looking up. "Thanks, Ban."

"No trouble," Ban spoke. Then he turned his gaze to Billie. "You say the Scary It started coming after you moved. May I ask, why did you move?"

Billie felt sweat form on her palms. "We... lost the house after the accident."

"What accident?" asked Ban.

Billie did not answer. A loud thud echoed through the room as the door above was thrust open. This was followed by a slithering sound, and a loud, spine-tingling wheeze silenced the whole tavern. Even the bunny and fox were still.

"Is that it?" cried Ban nervously.

"Don't worry," Billie said to him. "It won't hurt you — it only wants me."

"Ban, is there a backdoor?" Loe cried.

Ban pointed, though his eyes remained locked upwards.

"Let's go," Loe instructed, flying off.

"Pleasure meeting you, Mr. Daide," Billie called as she chased after the fairy, leaving the silenced tavern behind, the sound of slithering sliming its way down the stairs.

They went behind the bar, through a door, up a dark stairwell, and out another door.

Billie nearly tripped on the sidewalk as the city sounds rushed over her. They had entered the tavern through a park, but they had exited out a door on the side of a building.

"Loe," Billie quickly whispered as a group of people approached, laughing in the night. Loe quickly flew back into Billie's backpack, and Billie turned her head away as the group passed. "Where to?"

Loe instructed her, and the pair were off again, keeping to the alleys and shadows. They walked in silence for a while.

"Loe, can I ask you a question?"

"May," Loe corrected.

"What about May?"

Loe only sighed. "Ask me your question."

"Why did you return to the fairy house?"

"Why would I not? It's my home," Loe replied.

"But," began Billie, "it used to be in a beautiful garden surrounded by trees and flowers. Now it sits on a metal fire escape in a noisy city. That doesn't seem to be very 'fairy-like.'"

"You and your preconceived notions," chastised Loe.

"Seriously," Billie went on. "Why would you want to come to the city, to a dirty, metal fire escape outside a tiny, cramped apartment?"

"I see," Loe spoke with understanding. "You have a contrived idea of what a home is, my dear."

"Huh?"

"A home isn't such because it is big and in the suburbs," Loe replied. "A home is where you and your loved ones are safe and together. That includes tiny, cramped apartments."

"Not all my loved ones are together," Billie sighed.

At that moment, she could hear the slight sound of something slithering behind her. It was so faint. Loe must have missed it.

"Maybe they're not because you won't let them," he said.

Suddenly something wheezed loudly behind them.

"Loe!" Billie cried.

"I heard it," Loe replied. "Run!"

Billie ran. She ran as fast as her legs could carry her, following Loe's directions. Eventually, the air became cooler and misty. They were by the water now.

Billie ran down a long, empty pier and stopped at the edge. She panted, trying to catch her breath, as Loe flew out of her backpack. The sounds of the city were dull, just a distant background to the rippling of the water as it collided with the docked boats. A few bells chimed here and there. There was no slithering. The Scary It was far behind them.

"What do we do?" gasped Billie, catching her breath.

Loe gazed out across the dark water. "Let's try calling her. Medi!"

"Mrs. Cine!" cried Billie.

"It's Miss Cine," came a sharp voice.

At first, Billie looked around, confused. She saw no one around but herself and Loe. But then a splash drew her attention downwards. A woman was floating in the dark water. She was older and had frazzled wet hair, and wore a dark, wet hoodie.

"Who are you?" asked the woman.

"Are you Medi?" asked Loe.

"Yes, and again, who are you?" the woman snapped.

A detailed account of who Billie and Loe were, what they were running from, and how they had come to be there was delivered to Medi.

"I see," Medi said when they finished.

"Can you help?" asked Loe.

Medi squinted her face at him. Then she looked at Billie, and her face eased. "Give me your hands, kid."

Billie got on her knees, and Medi swam to her. Medi's hands were surprisingly warm as they took in Billie's. Medi closed her eyes, nodded her head a few times, and then let go.

"To get rid of it, you need to face it," Medi said, eyes gazing directly into Billie's. "There's a tunnel not too far up ahead. It will meet you there."

"But it will devour me!" cried Billie fearfully.

"Only if you let it," Medi replied.

"Billie, we have to do this," Loe spoke somberly.

"Wrong," Medi interjected. "*Billie* has to do this, and Billie has to do it alone."

"But–" Billie and Loe spoke in unison.

"No!" snapped Medi. "You've asked, I've answered. The rest is up to you."

And with that, she swam off. Before diving under, Medi leaped in the air, and Billie's mouth dropped as she took in the beautiful, sparkling green tail. And then the mermaid was gone.

Billie and Loe looked at each other.

"Billie..." Loe trailed.

She held her hand up to him, deep in thought. She wanted nothing more than the Scary It to be gone. And she had gotten this far with the aid of Loe, Ban, and Medi. It was time she stepped up to the plate. She tugged on the brim of her baseball cap and stood up. Billie gazed at Loe, her face fierce.

The fairy nodded. "I'll be right here if you need me."

"Thank you," Billie replied.

"Good luck."

Billie walked back up the pier alone. She spotted a tunnel not too far ahead, and she moved towards it, hands gripping her backpack tightly.

Billie entered the tunnel alone.

"All right!" she yelled. "Come out, come out, wherever you are!"

There was silence.

Then there was slithering. It was coming, wheezing its way over, leaving slime in its wake. Billie braced herself, clenching her fists tight, eyes open for once. Closer, it slinked, dragging itself across the pavement. It was almost there. Heart beating wildly in her chest, Billie stood ready. It was almost there, slithering and wheezing. It was just around the corner. It–

Billie gasped, her fists unclenching.

A version of herself, two years younger, ran in, laughing. The sound of slithering and wheezing was gone, replaced by the laughter that echoed through the tunnel. The younger Billie ran past the older one. Billie turned and saw two figures standing behind her. The younger Billie leaped into her father's arms, her mother standing close behind. The trio laughed.

Billie watched them. They were so happy. And then Billie realized what the Scary It was — what it had been all along.

"You're just... memories," Billie spoke.

The three of them, her younger self, her father, and her mother, all stopped and smiled at the present-day Billie. Billie gazed at them. They were what she had been running from all along. She took a deep breath.

"I'm not afraid of you anymore," Billie spoke boldly. Then she grinned at them. "I love you."

They vanished. Billie was alone in the tunnel once more. The Scary It was gone. And it would not come back. This Billie knew.

Eventually, Loe flew in. "Billie?"

"I'm here," Billie said, smiling at her friend.

Loe stopped, moth wings fluttering before her. "You okay?"

"I am," Billie replied. "And I'm ready to go home."

Walking back through the cracks and corners of the city, Loe and Billie laughed and conversed the whole way. Loe spoke of more details of his world, the world beneath Billie's, and Billie spoke of the details of her life. Life in the city. The city above Loe's.

In time, they came through an alley and crouched down.

Across the street, Billie could see her building. There were about six cop cars in front, all with their blue and red lights swirling. In the distance, dawn was approaching. The darkness of night was shrinking away from the blue of day.

"Loe, I just want to say thank–"

"No need," Loe whispered, smiling at Billie. "Just please do something about the terrible state of affairs my dwelling is in."

Billie smiled at her friend. "I promise."

"Well, I'm off. I bid you farewell," Loe sang.

"Will I see you again?" Billie asked, concern growing on her tired face.

"Maybe... or maybe you'll forget me again," Loe said softly.

"I won't forget you," Billie stated sternly.

Loe smiled at her sweetly. "Either way... you know where my home is."

Billie smiled, and Loe gave her a wink. Then off he rose into the sky, and like a bird, he soared far away. Billie waited until the sight of her friend was gone, then she walked out of the shadow of the alley and into the light.

"Billie? Is that you?" cried one of the officers, spotting her.

Billie did not have time to answer. Out of nowhere, her mother appeared. She scooped Billie up, crying.

"Billie, where have you been? Are you okay?"

"I'm fine," Billie assured, hugging her mother back.

Eventually, Billie and her mother, as well as a few officers, made it up the six stories to their small, cramped home. There, the adults sat Billie down and politely demanded she explain where she had been and why she had left.

"Okay," Billie had responded.

And so, Billie informed them of everything that had occurred. She spoke of the Scary It and Aloe F. Vera. Of how they had run and gone to the tavern in a tree. She spoke of Ban I. Daide and the other odd patrons. Then she spoke of running to the pier and meeting the mermaid, Medi X. Cine. Billie informed them of the tunnel and how she faced the Scary It, and how it turned out to be nothing more than her memories. She spoke truthfully and did not miss a single detail.

They did not believe a word she said.

"Kid's got an imagination," laughed an officer.

"I do, but that does not mean that I'm lying," Billie snapped, quite offended.

The officer smiled at her sweetly. "I didn't say you were lyin', kid. If you say that is the story, then that's the story — just no more running off in the middle of the night, okay?"

"Trust me," Billie replied firmly. "I'm not running anymore."

After the officers left, Billie and her mother headed towards the small, run-down, wooden table squashed between the small space between counter and wall. Once all the chairs were occupied, Billie turned to her mother.

"Are you mad?"

Billie's mother shook her head. "I was just scared, baby."

"I was pretty scared too," Billie responded. "But I'm not anymore."

Billie's mother smirked. "You must be very tired."

"I could use a nap," Billie spoke honestly. "And then maybe once I'm done, you could go back to the graveyard — only this time I could come."

"If that's what you want," Billie's mother spoke softly.

"Yeah," Billie replied.

"Sounds good to me," her mother agreed.

"And... then after, if it's okay, maybe we could go to the store?"

"What do you want there?" asked Billie's mother.

"Remember the old fairy dwelling we had in the garden, the one Dad made?"

"I do."

Billie smiled. "I'd like to make a new one out on the fire escape."

"Oh really," Billie's mother commented, her own smile mirroring Billie's.

"I'd like to make it together if that's all right," Billie said.

"That sounds wonderful."

THE FAERIE WEDDING DRESS

by Rose Strickman

As sunlight struck the cars parked alongside the street, gleaming on the pavement, a small, dumpy figure climbed the stone steps to the townhouse. Milkweed paused a moment, looking up at the white-painted door in weary resignation. Well, no sense in delaying. Raising a gnarled green hand, she knocked on the door.

"Coming," called a voice from within the tall white house. Milkweed watched as an odd, distorted shadow loomed in the warped glass of the door, and then Lord Niall's mortal opened the door.

The mortal's smile froze and fell off the instant she took in Milkweed. Her face drained of blood. Her mouth opened, but only a scratchy, inarticulate noise emerged.

"Good afternoon, Lady...Erica." Milkweed remembered the mortal's name just in time. She curtsied. "I'm here from Lord Niall, to make the wedding dress. May I come in?"

Erica wrenched her jaw up. "Oh—oh, God—oh, all right, *fine*, come in!"

It was not the most gracious invitation Milkweed had ever received, but it *was* an invitation, and so the faerie was now free to enter the mortal's home. Having shuffled in, she looked around curiously. The front hall seemed narrow and bare but very clean and bright. A tall mirror hung behind an elegant side table: Milkweed looked strange and out of place in it, all tough green skin, pointed ears, yellow eyes, straggly hair, ragged dress, and, of course, her large, unwieldy sewing basket.

Erica hovered, wringing her hands. She fit in here a lot better than

Milkweed: tall and graceful, as mortals went, hair black and shiny. Her clothing was severe but, to Milkweed's professional eye, very well-made, in styles and colors that suited her. Her only discordant aspect was her demeanor. Erica jittered and dithered, eyes dancing onto Milkweed and off, obviously longing for her to go away but unsure how to make her.

Milkweed held back a sigh. "Shall we go take your measurements, then?"

"No!" Erica's cry made Milkweed jump. "Sorry. Listen, uh, can I have your name?"

"Milkweed."

"Okay, listen, Milkweed, I, ah, really don't think this is a good idea."

"But I need your measurements if I'm to make the wedding gown—"

"*I don't want the damn—*" Erica stopped herself, took a deep breath. She let it out, visibly forcing calm. "Look, why don't we go sit down in the living room?"

She was going to be difficult. Well, given the merry dance she'd led Niall over the last year, perhaps Milkweed shouldn't be surprised. Resigning herself to the inevitable, the faerie trudged after the mortal through her house.

It didn't match the wonder of Niall's hall, of course: no mortal building could. But Milkweed found herself admiring the house's spare, pared-down elegance, from the shiny floorboards to the tall ceilings. Various artworks hung from the walls, along with photographs of beautiful humans wearing exquisite gowns. The "living room" turned out to be another high-ceilinged chamber, with cream walls and tall, curtained windows overlooking the terrace. Beyond, the river shone wide and sparkling, and the mortal city spread, ungraceful but vibrant. With a little hop, Milkweed seated herself on one of the stiff brocade sofas.

Erica hovered. "Ah—want anything to eat?"

"That wouldn't be advisable." If Milkweed ate Erica's food, she'd be in Erica's debt, and she didn't think that was a good idea. Erica seemed to understand this. She nodded and sat down across from Milkweed.

"Okay." She took another deep breath. "Look—Milkweed—the thing is, I really don't want to marry Niall."

"What?" Milkweed gaped. True, Erica had been refusing Niall's suit for a year, but Niall and his vassals had all assumed she was merely playing hard to get and driving her dower portion up. It hadn't crossed anyone's mind that Erica might *reject* their lord's attentions.

"Come on, I've read the stories!" Erica said impatiently. "These human-faerie marriages don't end well! And I like my life here. I've got family, friends, a career. I'm not going to give that all up to go to another world with some elf lord!"

"So...you weren't just driving up the dower," said Milkweed, trying not to imagine Niall's probable reaction to being described as "some elf lord." "When you were putting off Lord Niall. You were actually...*putting him off?*"

"Yes!" Erica cried. "I kept hoping he'd get the message without me actually having to say no." She grimaced. "Somehow, I don't think he'd take rejection too well."

"No, probably not," Milkweed admitted. "So when you said you wanted the wedding gown..."

"I *didn't* want the damn gown!" Erica said impatiently. "I told Niall I couldn't possibly marry him because I didn't have a proper wedding dress and couldn't get one here in the mortal world. It was my last-ditch attempt. I thought he'd give up finally. But instead, he sends you." She gave Milkweed a dirty look.

There passed a glum silence, broken only by the noise of traffic outside.

Milkweed straightened, hopping off the sofa. "Well," she said, "do you have a stool?"

"What?" Erica blinked, pulled out of some hopeless reverie.

"So I can take your measurements," Milkweed said patiently. "It's better if you stand on a stool."

"Did you hear a word I just said? I don't *want* the wedding dress! I don't want to marry him!"

"And what am I supposed to do about it?" Milkweed put her hands on her hips. "I'm just the seamstress, remember?"

Erica's tone turned wheedling. "Couldn't you go back and tell Niall that you don't think I'd be a good wife? That I don't want to marry him?"

Milkweed stared. "Do I look like I'm suicidal?"

"Come on! Why does he even want to marry some ignorant, stupid human, anyway? I'd be an embarrassment to him."

"No, you wouldn't. Faeries marry mortals all the time."

"Really?" Erica blinked. "I thought it always ended in blood and tears and tragedy. That's what all the stories say, anyway."

Milkweed rolled her eyes. "Well, it wouldn't make much of a story if it went like, *And after a sedate but pleasant courtship, the faerie married the human, and they were reasonably happy together, barring the odd argument over who was hogging the blanket,* now would it?"

"Okay, there's that," Erica conceded. "But I still don't think Niall and I would live happily ever after."

Milkweed shrugged. "Well, anyway, where's a stool?"

Erica glared another moment but seemed to decide against further outright resistance. She stomped off and returned with a plastic stool, which she placed in the center of the room. She climbed aboard, face like thunder.

Milkweed, with some pleasure, got out the tools of her trade: the kit with the scissors, pins, thread, the tape measure, and, of course, the yards and yards of faerie silk, all magically packed into her basket. Erica caught her breath at the lengths of shining red fabric.

"What silk!"

"Yes," Milkweed said proudly. "Essence of fire spun onto the silk of my own spiders. I thought it would look well with your skin tone, though, of course, we can use other fabrics if you prefer..."

"Right." Erica stared at the fabric as Milkweed bustled around her, taking her measurements. "You know, I could really use that stuff in my fashion house."

"Oh, you run a fashion house?" said Milkweed, snapping her fingers so the tape began to measure Erica on its own, zipping through the air.

"Yeah, those are pictures of my creations on the walls." Erica stiffened but didn't pull back as the tape flew around her. Milkweed entered the results in her notebook. "What, Niall didn't tell you?"

"He hasn't told us much about you. Just that you met at a fashion exhibition party, and he got your consent to marry him a few days later."

"*Got my consent?*" Erica spat. "He used a nasty, dirty trick! I didn't know what I was agreeing to!"

"Don't feel too bad," Milkweed said. "Mortals quite often don't."

Erica glowered but said nothing.

Milkweed noted down the last number and snapped her fingers again, retrieving the tape. She raised her hands and the silk rose on its own, wrapping around Erica. The mortal gasped at the touch of faerie silk. "You know, once you marry Niall, you'll have all the faerie fabric you want," Milkweed couldn't resist saying.

"Yeah, but I won't have my business anymore, will I?" Still, there was a speculative gleam in Erica's eye as she ran her hands over the cloth. "There's nothing like this on Earth, is there?"

"Certainly not," Milkweed boasted. "No mortal fabric can match this."

"Oh...really?" Erica's smile widened. "Say, Milkweed, once we're done here, I'd like you to go back to your master with a little proposal..."

"She wants *what?*" Lord Niall blinked slanting emerald eyes at Milkweed, incredulous.

"That's what she said, my lord," Milkweed said helplessly.

Niall paced around his lesser parlor. Around them, the palace was in a minor uproar as his servants prepared for the upcoming wedding: the kitchens were loud with preparations of delicacies for the feast, and outside, faeries were whispering magic to vines and bushes and trees, encouraging them to grow and flower, putting on the very best display. All the rooms were being cleaned for the arrival of the guests. Of all Lord Niall's household, only two people were aware of any further obstacles to the match: Milkweed and Niall himself.

Niall struck out at a chair, making Milkweed flinch. "So," he growled, "Erica Seward sets yet another condition, does she? And with...what is this ridiculous bet?"

"She says that if she can make a wedding gown more miraculous than a faerie gown, unique in both worlds, then you have to grant her three requests. If she can't, then she'll marry you; no further protests, obstacles, or delays."

"A miraculous wedding gown." Despite his annoyance and frustration, a gleam appeared in Niall's eyes at this, a faerie's joy at an unexpected game or challenge. "And...how long does she demand?"

"One week, my lord. She says that if she can make a gown more unique than mine in one week, then you must accede to three demands."

"What demands would those be?"

To leave her alone. "She didn't really say, my lord," Milkweed said. "But she did promise they wouldn't be too ruinous to yourself."

"A mortal's word." Niall sniffed disdainfully. "Worthless. Still...this does have some merit. She'll marry me, will she?"

"If she loses the bet, my lord."

"She'll lose," Niall said dismissively. "No mortal's gown could possibly match a faerie's. This could be good...And I'd like to see what she comes up with." Niall straightened. "Very well. I accept her challenge. In one week's time, we'll see who has the more unique and miraculous gown." He glowered at Milkweed, who shrank. "I hope," he said softly, "that it's you, Milkweed. For all our sakes."

"Yes, my lord," she said, voice trembling, already feeling the lash.

"Very well." Niall waved a green-tinged hand, dismissing her. "Go get the finest silks from the storeroom. Go get the star thread, the flower-gauze, and the diamond lace. I want to see your very best creation, Milkweed, in one week's time."

"What are *you* doing here?" Erica demanded, opening the door on Milkweed the next day.

"We still need to do the final fittings," Milkweed said. "And Niall says I have to stay here to make sure you don't cheat."

Erica folded her arms, leaning in the doorframe. "How do I know *you* won't cheat?"

"I promise I won't." Milkweed knew she should try to keep the weariness out of her voice, but Great Trees, she was so sick of this whole affair. "Nor will I try to sabotage your own gown, I promise."

Erica eyed her sidelong. "You people always keep your promises, don't you?" She sighed. "And I guess...Niall's going to punish you if you disobey, isn't he?"

"Yes, lady," Milkweed said. "He'll probably have me whipped."

Erica flinched. "Marriage to this guy sounds less and less attractive all the time," she murmured. "All right, come in."

Once inside, Milkweed was conscious of a strange humming noise coming from somewhere deep within the house. Erica ushered Milkweed into the living room and closed the door behind them with a glower. "No peeking," she growled. "No taking information back to your master or anyone else. No sending in *other* faeries—or humans—to spy or sabotage either. In fact, don't even *ask* about that noise."

Milkweed stared at her. "You really don't trust us at all, do you?"

"Certainly not," Erica said crisply. "So you see, I would make a very bad mistress for you, really."

"Oh, I don't know." Milkweed began fetching out her tools. "It might be nice to have a lady who's honest, for once. And Niall would probably like your quick skill with the whip."

Erica flinched again. "I'd never whip anybody!"

Milkweed found herself warming to the mortal. "Well, fetch your stool, anyway...or do you have time for a fitting right now?"

Erica cast an odd look at the closed door and the humming beyond. "Yeah...I got time."

She went to fetch the stool. Milkweed nobly refrained from going to spy on the humming noise. She hadn't actually *promised* she wouldn't look, but still, she found herself oddly reluctant to break Erica's trust.

Erica returned with the stool and clambered on top. "Honestly, why do you even work for Niall?" she asked, as if she just couldn't help herself. "He's a complete psycho!"

Milkweed was *really* liking this mortal. "Not a lot of choice," she said, snapping her fingers to summon the silk. "He's my liege lord, after all."

"And Faerie is permanently stuck in the Dark Ages," Erica muttered. "Oh boy, what an attractive prospect moving there is!"

"Really?" Milkweed brightened. If Erica was finally coming around and thought Faerie was attractive, maybe they could be done with all this.

"It's called sarcasm, Milkweed." Erica's voice was flat and tired. "And, I think, yet another reason why I wouldn't fit in terribly well with you people."

Milkweed shrugged. Mortals were strange, with some very strange customs. It was no use trying to understand them. "Well, let's get on with the fitting, anyway..."

Milkweed spent the night outside in Erica's manicured garden. She needed contact with the earth after spending all day inside a mortal building. Erica was endearingly anxious about this.

"Are you sure you don't want to sleep in a guestroom?" She hovered over Milkweed as she settled in a nice patch of grass.

"Quite certain. I will be very comfortable here." Milkweed hefted her magic basket. "And I brought food with me."

"This is insane." Erica shook her head. "Shouldn't you at least go home to spend the night? You can come back tomorrow morning."

"Lord Niall said I had to stay for the entire week."

Erica looked like she was refraining, with great effort, from rolling her eyes. "Okay, then, if that's what *Lord Niall* says...Good night."

"Good night, Erica." Milkweed watched her go indoors. A light appeared in a basement window, but the opening was blocked by a white lacy curtain: Milkweed couldn't see in. Erica was definitely in there, though. She could hear the mortal moving around in the space where the mysterious humming emanated.

Midway through the week, Niall dropped in.

Erica and Milkweed had just adjourned from a very enjoyable lunch. Milkweed no longer needed Erica for fittings, so they each worked separately for most of the day. Milkweed had taken over a spare bedroom for her sewing, and Erica spent long hours in the basement, doing whatever it was she was doing.

Nevertheless, they'd fallen into the habit of lunching together, Erica from her own food and Milkweed from her stores. Erica was surprisingly good company when she wasn't snappish and sullen about the impending nuptials. Milkweed found herself laughing uproariously at some of her anecdotes of the mortal fashion industry, even when she didn't entirely understand the context. Erica herself seemed very interested in Milkweed's descriptions of life as a faerie seamstress.

"I wish we *could* use some of your fabrics here on Earth," she said wistfully as they exited the kitchen. "But mortals can't work with them, can we?"

"Faerie fabrics tend to revert to their original form when worked by a mortal," Milkweed confirmed. "Starlight thread turning back to starlight, that sort of thing. But if a faerie works them, they retain their magical nature."

"How weird!" Erica exclaimed and then stopped dead, face freezing, as the door opened, admitting their most unwelcome guest.

Elegant and handsome as a summer's day, Lord Niall smiled at Erica as Milkweed curtsied. "Hello, Erica." He shut the door behind him; he'd already tricked an invitation from Erica months ago and could enter her home whenever he wished. "I give you my warmest greetings, my lady and my future wife." He knelt gracefully at Erica's feet and kissed her hand.

She snatched it back. "What are *you* doing here?"

"Checking on Milkweed's progress, of course." For the first time, he acknowledged Milkweed's presence. "Well, Milkweed?"

"You know, Niall," said Erica, leaning against the wall and examining her fingernails, "you might get better results from your employees if you didn't treat them like dirt. Just sayin'."

"Oh, do you?" Niall barely glanced at her. "You'll learn better once we're married. Milkweed?"

Reluctantly, Milkweed led him to the spare room where her project was laid out. Erica trailed unhappily behind the faeries but stopped short of actually entering the room. Even now, she wouldn't cheat.

Niall was pleased with Milkweed's progress. "Very good," he said, standing over the half-finished gown with his hands clasped behind his back. "Very nice effort, Milkweed. She won't be able to beat this!"

"No, my lord," Milkweed murmured. She hoped none of her uneasiness—or her increasing guilt—showed in her voice.

But Niall, as ever, heard only what he wanted to hear. "In three days' time," he said, with great satisfaction, "we will win the bet and Erica will return with us as my wife. Fear not, Milkweed, you will be rewarded."

"Yes, my lord," she said, more quietly still, and curtsied as he swept out of the room. She heard him bid Erica farewell and then the front door closing behind him.

When she was sure he was gone, Milkweed emerged, heading down the staircase. Erica sat, head propped in her hands, at the long, polished oak table in the dining room.

She lifted her head at Milkweed's entrance to give her a weak smile. "Are you sure you wouldn't like to come work for me instead, Milkweed?"

Milkweed sighed. "Sometimes," she said, "I wish I could."

The night before the judging, the humming from the basement finally stopped.

"What *was* that?" Milkweed asked.

Erica glanced up from setting up the two dressmaker's dummies in the living room. "You'll find out. Tomorrow." She gave a quick, flashing grin.

"You seem very confident," Milkweed observed.

"Oh, don't worry." Erica's laugh rang out. "Half of it's just nerves. I get like this before an exhibition, too. But I do think you'll find my end results...interesting, at the very least."

"I hope not," Milkweed said. "If I lose this contest for Lord Niall, he'll have me flayed alive."

"Oh, God." Erica's smile faded. "You really mean that, don't you?" She looked at Milkweed with new urgency. "Seriously, Milkweed, is there any way you can get away from that bastard?"

"No." Milkweed shook her head. "Not unless I can trick him into releasing me, or some other lord or lady wins me away from him."

"Well." Erica slumped on the sofa beside Milkweed. All her energy seemed suddenly sucked away. "This *is* a pickle, isn't it? Because I don't want you hurt, Milkweed, really. But I also really don't want to marry him."

Milkweed laughed. Erica looked at her. "What's so funny?"

"It's odd." Milkweed shook her head. "I feel the same way. I don't want you to have to marry him. But I don't want to lose the contest for him either."

Erica gave a small, unhappy laugh. "Like I said. What a pickle."

They sat together in the gathering gloom.

By prearranged agreement, Milkweed brought her dress into the living room before Erica did, while Erica was out of the house. She hung it on one of the dummies, straightening the sleeves and arranging the train. She stood back and looked at it with an odd mixture of pride and despair. For this was unquestionably the finest article of clothing she'd ever created—and it spelled Erica's doom. There was nothing a human, even *this* human, could make that would equal it.

Perhaps Erica would get used to being Niall's wife. There were worse things, after all, than being the consort of a powerful faerie lord. Maybe she and Milkweed could even work together to create new and amazing clothing...But she knew Niall would never allow that.

Sighing, she threw a sheet over her dress, covering it completely, and turned away to head back out into the garden. The curtains were drawn over the living room windows, so she couldn't see in when Erica brought in her own creation. But she saw the golden lamplight shining around the edges and knew that the stage was set.

The next day, Erica appeared in a black suit with gold piping, severe and beautiful, her hair caught up in a neat bun. "One of yours?" Milkweed asked, admiring the suit's straight, simple lines.

Erica smoothed the skirt. "Of course. Got to look my best for such an important day." She eyed Milkweed's dress, her finest, woven from the green of tender young grass. "Though, really, that style's not bad either. We could really do something with it." She waved her hands, excitement lighting her eyes. "I can see the show now: human fashion meets Faerie!"

Milkweed had to laugh. "That would be something! But how do you know there's even going to be another show?"

"Come on, Milkweed, let me have a little optimism."

There came a tread outside the door, and both women tensed, all laughter ceasing. The door opened with a wave of pine scent, and Lord Niall strode in.

At least he'd dressed for the occasion, Milkweed thought as she curtsied, taking in his human-inspired suit of jacket, tie, and long dress pants, all sewn from the finest faerie materials. His shoes shone with polish. The jacket and trousers were midnight silk, the tie woven from the last sheen of a sunset on still waters. Above the tie, Niall's face beamed.

"Good morrow, my wife-to-be," he said, kneeling and kissing Erica's hand with aplomb. "Where are the dresses?"

"This way, my lord," she said, surprisingly cheerful, and led the way to the living room.

There, the two dressmaker's dummies stood like shrouded ghosts. Erica led the faeries in and then turned back to Niall.

"Just to reiterate," she said. "This is a contest to judge which dress is the more unique and wondrous. Do you, Lord Niall, promise to judge fairly, without thought to your own interest?"

Niall stood straighter. "I swear, by the wood and the stone, that I shall judge these dresses impartially and honor the terms of our agreement."

"And the terms?" Erica pressed.

"That if Milkweed's dress is the more unique and wondrous, then you shall return to Faerie with me as my wife." A swift smile gleamed.

"And if mine is judged so," Erica said, "then you will grant me three requests before leaving me alone forever."

"Yes. I swear by the wood and the stone."

Erica nodded, knowing enough of faeries to be appeased by this most binding of oaths. "Okay then. Milkweed, you go first."

Milkweed stepped forward and pulled the sheet off her dummy.

She couldn't help but be gratified by Erica and Niall's twin gasps as they beheld her creation. It was, without doubt, the finest dress she'd ever made. A skirt and bodice of fire, with a train of dusky rose petals, so that the heat released the scent of roses and the silk shimmered and flickered. The skirt darkened in waves, from the palest of flames around the waist to the darkest of smokes at the hem. The bodice was laced with threads of the purest golden sunlight, and Milkweed had woven a choker of sun-diamonds and gold. Any woman wearing this ensemble would resemble a conflagration, a sun in splendor, an exploding star: she stood in danger of outshining the Faerie Queen herself.

Niall drew in a breath and let it out in profound satisfaction. "Well done, Milkweed." He turned to Erica with a smug smile. "And yours, my lady?"

Erica smiled. She went over to her own dummy. With a flourish, she pulled the sheet off.

Niall and Milkweed stared. They blinked. They stared some more.

"What," Milkweed demanded before she could stop herself, "is *that?*"

"Yes." Niall continued staring. "What *is* that?"

"It's a wedding dress." Erica twitched the long, sweeping train, making it clatter and clank. "One I made myself."

"Out of what?" Niall asked.

"Glass."

"*Glass?*"

"Yes." Erica's smile was sharp as a manticore's tooth. "My friend Ivan lent me this marvelous new 3D printer, not out on the market yet, that will print out glass fibers. That's the humming you heard in the basement," she added as an aside to Milkweed. "This dress is absolutely unique, in both Earth and Faerie, made with the most advanced of human technology. Not a bit of magic to it!"

"But it's...it's hideous." Milkweed had never heard Niall sound so dazed and confused.

"Ah." Erica's eyes gleamed. "But the contest wasn't about the dresses' beauty, was it? It was about their *uniqueness*. Their originality. And this..." She swept a hand down the length of the sharp-edged, asymmetrical, sweeping shape on the dummy. "...Is absolutely unique and original, in both worlds."

Milkweed watched in growing horror as her lord's face turned white. He had lost the bet; even he had to see that. Milkweed trembled. She'd lost the contest for him. The punishment would be beyond imagining.

"I cede this contest to you, Erica Seward," Niall said at last, in a tight, white whisper, and so it was concluded.

"Excellent!" Erica brought her hands together in a brisk clap. "So then, here are my requests. First, that you, Lord Niall, give up all plans of marrying me or taking me to Faerie, and, furthermore, that you will do so in a spirit of honesty and honor. No looking for loopholes, no sending other faeries to take me, no persecuting me or my friends, family, or associates in any way. Also, no trying to seduce away my friends, family, or associates. True honor, Niall."

Teeth gritted, Niall swore to it all. At his sides, his fists trembled. Milkweed shook.

"Secondly," Erica continued, "you will provide me with a lifelong supply of faerie fabrics and other materials of the finest quality, without any curses or similar magical or non-magical impediments, in the quantity and type I require, whenever I require."

Niall swore to this as well. "Though it won't do you any good," he added with a sneer. "No mortal can work with faerie fabrics."

"Ah! That brings me to my third request." Erica smiled at Milkweed. "I want you to release Milkweed from your service. You let her go without any punishments or impediments and let her choose whatever life she wishes."

For a moment, Milkweed couldn't believe her ears. Then, with a rushing, soaring sensation, she realized what Erica had just said. She looked at Niall, waiting in agony for his response.

"Very well," he spat out at last, and Milkweed thought she'd leave the floor and fly. "I swear that Milkweed may leave my service if she chooses, free of punishments, curses, or other impediments."

"Wonderful!" Erica gave another brisk clap. "Now, I do believe our business is concluded, Lord Niall. You'll see yourself out, won't you?"

Niall remained a moment longer, trembling with rage. But he was beaten: the knowledge seeped into his eyes, and he turned away at last to stride out of the living room, stiff with shame. The front door slammed shut, and he was gone forever.

Erica let out a long, long breath. She folded down onto the sofa as though her legs just wouldn't hold her any longer. "He's gone," she whispered. "He's actually gone!"

"Yes. He is." Milkweed was still stunned. "So...I suppose I work for you now?"

"Well, I'd like it if you did." Erica looked at her. "But you're free to choose, Milkweed. Would you like to come work for the Seward Fashion House?"

Milkweed thought of her own creation, hanging on the dummy. She thought of the pictures of Erica's works hung up around the house. She thought of glass and 3D printing, and she thought of what a human-faerie fashion show might be like.

"Do you know?" she said, a smile growing. "I think I would."

BRINGING THE HOCUS

by M.C. St. John

"Come on, Hector, you gotta hurry."

"I'm almost done with the eyes."

Hector shakes the spray can, the bat skull rattling inside the cylinder, keeping the creative spirits happy. The charmed paints are his creations. He takes pride in his conjure work.

Shhhh-shh-sh-shhhhh.

On the yellow orb, an iris appears, flecked with white and yellow, a glistening drop of light high in the right corner for perspective. Hector leans back, examines. *Shh-sh.* Under Hector's hand, the eye is real enough to blink, the pupil to contract and grow, to focus and see the world around it. To live.

"There," he says. "You have to get the details right for it to work."

From the lower part of the scaffold, Jayla crosses her arms and cocks her head. Green and purple paint stipple her face and the front of her hoodie. "Tell me something I don't know. But I'm here to tell you time is of the essence here. You know this neighborhood. The tunics can't be too far away."

"Okay, okay. You finish the scales on the hide?"

"Yep. Your stencils made the work go quick."

"And the wings?"

"What do you think I've been doing down here with Sammy D? Reading his Tarot? Drinking tea? Yes, we got the wings finished. Now would you come *on?*"

Hector takes one last look at the eye, mutters a few words—a prayer, an incantation, and some good, old-fashioned words of encouragement—and throws the spray can in his satchel, where it clinks against its brethren of magical colors. From his perch, he shimmies down the scaffold, descending the abandoned building.

Once upon a time, before gentrification, the city likely sold the place to a developer, who promised to make high-rise condominiums, and then skipped out when another neighborhood turned brighter and shinier for the coffers. Now the construction scaffolding itself has rusted, a relic from another time, leaned up against the forgotten building. A faded sign above the dumpsters claims it to be *Augie's Attic—Furniture & Occult Curios*, but it's more like *Augie's Rubble Pile & Debris*.

Until Hector and his friends came in, that is.

"Dang, I was wondering when you were gonna finish."

Appearing from behind the dumpsters, Sammy D trots over. He peeks over his shoulder, then stares past Hector and Jayla to the other alley, even nervously glances up at the night sky, speckled with city lights and gray clouds. He's ground control, the lookout, the heavy, always peeping for security's sake.

Satisfied, he pulls down his balaclava, revealing a sweat-shiny face streaked with blue paint. "Coast is clear for now. Didn't see any tunics cruising down Eldritch Ave."

Jayla wrinkles her nose. "I don't know what's worse, seeing them in plain view or dreading the fact we *don't* see them."

"Watch it, Jay. You're paranoia's flaring up." Sammy D looks toward the building. He sighs softly, a mixture of awe and wonder, and pounds one fist into his open palm. "Oh man, after I finished painting the tail, I bowed out and didn't see the whole thing. Hector, this is so *so* dope, man. How do you come up with this stuff?"

Hector stuffs his hands in his pockets. "It just calls to me. My imagination, it runs loose, and I have to let it out."

"Well, thank the gods you do."

"I couldn't do it without you two," Hector says.

"We know. Who else is going to keep you in line?" Jayla hip-checks him, grinning. "In all seriousness, though. You brought us in for your crew.

Me and Sammy D are forever grateful you did."

Sammy D nods. "Man, I don't know *where* I'd be if it wasn't for you, Hector."

Hector regards each of them, studying their faces, the contours of their mouths and eyes. How can a series of lines and shapes make up the faces of friends whom he loves? Hector can't say. He's just glad that it's true. "Thanks, guys. I appreciate it more than you know."

"Okay, before we go full Hallmark Channel..."

Hector clears his throat. "You're right. Let's see if the charms worked. I haven't used my paints on something this big."

"Go on then," Sammy D says, "get your conjure on. We'll hold down the fort."

In the sodium arc glow of the night, where even the shadows hum with energy, Hector walks right up to his graffiti on the side of Augie's Attic. He cranes his head up to take in the totality of his creation.

The dragon peers back at him.

Three stories tall from snout to tail, the creature clings to the moldering brickwork with iridescent claws. Green and purple scales, as intricately patterned as chain mail, course the twisting length of its ridged back. A majestic set of wings jut from the shoulders, folded in on themselves, ready for flight.

The dragon's long snout ends in a set of nostrils the size of city manholes, which emit plumes of rather realistic smoke. Below is a grinning set of teeth, with the faintest of steam lines coursing out between them.

But it's the eyes that have it: the spark, the *life*.

The great yellow orbs, lovingly rendered with light and shadow and color, contain a sense of power that threatens to break through to the third dimension. The effect is more than an artist's tools of perspective, shading, and proportion. Hector knows this truth not only in his hands but in his heart. It's not just skill or charms or incantations. It's creation—pure, primordial magic.

He loves the feeling so much it frightens him.

Still, he pulls from his satchel a special spray can. Among a mixture of charmed pigments and oils, this spray can also contains the powder from a blessed birch, the sacred tree of life.

He aims the nozzle at the dragon's spiked tail. The paint shoots out as fine and black as a calligrapher's quill. Hector moves his hand in long, elegant strokes, whispering the final words of his spell.

Emblazoned across the tail is his tag, his moniker, his conjure name. *The Hocus.*

Hocus as in *hocus pocus,* as in magic words like *abracadabra* and *alakazam,* but then deeper, older, reaching down to the roots, as in the archaic definition to deceive, to hoax, to trick, as in the power of ancient witches and magicians and sorcerers, of cauldrons and seances and spirituals, of haunted forests and deep caverns below the earth, bursting forth with the powers of mother nature, the elders, the gods themselves—

The dragon blinks, its pupils focusing on the lone boy.

"Hello, beautiful," Hector says. "Welcome to the neighborhood."

The dragon nods its serpentine head in agreement, then stretches out to its full length. The building wall trembles with the dragon's movements. From the facade, a brick falls, *bomp,* then several more, *ba-bomp-bomp,* followed by a shower of old mortar dust.

Hector backs up, taking in the sight. The dragon is still a drawing— glorified graffiti if you get right down to it—and confined to the flat plane of the building. But when it stretches out its wings, giving them a solid flap like an enormous bird, the wind it creates is very real. It blows Hector's hair back from his forehead. The rusty scaffolding trembles like a stand of reeds in a high autumn wind.

Sammy D promptly loses his mind.

"Oh my gods, oh my gods, *oh my gods.* You did it, man. Forget training a dragon. You *made* a dragon." He clutches the back of his head, chuckling. "Can you believe this, Jay?"

"Seeing is believing, and I'm seeing plenty." Jayla watches the dragon thwap the blue underside of its tail against the brickwork, shaking away more dust. Smiling, she turns to Hector. "Congratulations. You brought the hocus tonight."

"I did, didn't I?" Hector grins right back. "I brought the hocus."

Suddenly, the dragon rears back like a man about to sneeze,

scrunching its gold-yellow eyes. Then from its enormous nostrils, it lets loose streams of fire.

Like the wind from its wings, the fire is *very* real and *very* hot. This desolate lot in the rough part of the city glows with the radiance of a bonfire. The artificial lights recede, along with the shadows of the past. The distant drone of highway traffic quiets, the random radio playing hip-hop dies away. The fire is frightening and amazing in equal measure.

All members of Hector's crew wear the same expression of wonder. It's the face of children who knew those fairytales they heard at bedtime were true, and now here, *here,* was the proof, three stories tall and cooking with gas.

Sammy D is the one to break the silence. "Whoo-eee, what a rush." He wipes away the sweat from his face. The blue streaking his cheeks looks like ceremonial war paint. "We have ourselves a pro-level conjurer, Jay. Hector, the *artiste,* the tagger extraordinaire, the man with the plan and the magic spray can. All right, Hector, you should get some video of your Smaug here in action, so—"

"What in the *names* of the gods is going on here?"

From the far alleyway, a broad-shouldered man with a crew cut appears. He gawps at the dragon, then turns belligerent at its presence. After giving the creature a wide berth, he locks eyes with Hector and marches toward him. Four more men snap to attention behind Crew Cut, each one a variation on the theme of clean-shaven, muscular, and stern. They all wear the same dark gray uniform.

"Tunics," Jayla says. "The suspense is over. They're here."

Sammy D's voice squeaks. "Is that supposed to make us feel better?"

"Hey, you. Yeah, you." Crew Cut points a finger at Hector, closing the distance. "You responsible for this Class-D infraction? You know conjuring is a crime in the city. And something *this* big?" He tut-tuts, shaking his head. "You're going to have to come with us."

Jayla leans over to Hector. "When you get the chance, run."

"I'm not leaving you, *either* of you."

But Jayla persists. "We know who they really want, Hector. They'd love to put away a conjurer like you. Like they have with all the others.

Can't have magic on the streets, can we? No, only the *tunics* can have the charms."

"Uh, guys," Sammy D says. "They're getting closer."

Three of the tunics break away and position themselves around the base of the scaffold. The dragon eyes them, a growl rumbling deep in its throat. Its claws punch new holes into the masonry as it changes position. Its movements waver between the second and third dimensions. Flat or solid? Dragon or drawing? The illusion would make M.C. Escher's eyes water. The entry-level tunics, young guys who don't need to shave all that much to be clean-shaven, rub their eyes and squint as they try to keep watch over the magicked, depth-defying dragon.

Meanwhile, Crew Cut and the remaining tunic—Deputy Tunic—do not break their stride heading toward Hector and the gang.

"I'm not going to split," Hector says. "We're in this together. I drew you two into this."

"And what about that imagination of yours? *These* guys will lock it up nice and tight. Your creativity can't run wild in a cell block."

"She's right," Sammy D says. "As much as I don't want her to be. You gotta make a break for it."

Hector stares at each of his friends. Jayla's eyes are hazel and flecked with gold, and her left eyebrow arches when she doesn't take no for an answer, which is right now. Sammy D's eyes are light green, like sea glass, and his lips are set in a tight line of concentration, his major tell for when he's ready to scrap.

Hector knows these details already about his friends, but he wants to experience them as he has in his dreams or the joyful fugue states when he gets to painting and conjuring. To remember those sparks of life. He'll need them after this...if he makes it.

He draws a deep breath. "I love you guys."

"Remember, no Hallmark," Jayla says. She turns and raises her voice to address Crew Cut. "*I'm* the one who conjured the dragon, sir. Isn't it cute?"

Crew Cut changes direction, his curiosity piqued. "The word I'd use would be *illegal*. Let's talk about it downtown, shall we?" He signals his second-in-command. "Cuff the girl."

"Got it, Captain." From his belt, Deputy Tunic produces a pair of enchanted manacles and moves toward Jayla.

"You boys come with me," Captain Crew Cut says.

Hector starts to take the lead, but Sammy D stops him. "Me before you, man. *You* were the third wheel in this crew. The least I can do is get arrested first." The wink Sammy D drops is fast, but Hector catches it.

The Captain is intrigued, even as he removes his manacles from his belt. "So, you and the girl conjured the dragon together?"

"Oh yeah, me and her are tight. We even got these matching tattoos. Check mine out."

And since Sammy D is keeping his talk light and his hands above his shoulders, he has won some leeway with the Captain. Only a little, though. Any wrong twitch of the finger or a quick reach down to his belt for a wallet or a wand could be misinterpreted. This is the city's mage force we're talking about. Discretion has never been their strong suit.

Sweaty and slack-jawed, Hector watches the scene with terror mixed with some envy. Sammy D is a smooth operator, a vibe Hector always aspired to but could never manage himself. Ultimately, he's in awe of his friend's natural charm. Hector also sees what's coming next.

Still smiling and chatting, Sammy D slowly tugs the collar of his sweatshirt down and off to the side. There, underneath his clavicle, are two words written in fine black ink that shimmer as if they are still fresh.

Captain Crew Cut tilts his head to read it, brow furrowing. He briefly lowers the manacles as if puzzling out the words is taking away too much of the limited brainpower needed for apprehending perps. *"The Hocus?* What is that, some gang name?"

"More like a family. And don't you forget it."

The words come so light and easy from Sammy D's mouth that the meaning behind them doesn't register for a beat. Crew Cut is pondering them while still looking at the moniker on Sammy D's skin. He sees Sammy D's left hand holding down the collar of his sweatshirt.

He doesn't see the right hand.

That one has gone behind Sammy D's back and now comes back

around, front and center. A rattle from a bat's skull announces that Sammy D has the charmed spray can, his pointer finger poised on the nozzle.

Captain Crew Cut's eyes widen when he sees he's been bamboozled. A sound halfway between a burp and gasp—*errup*—escapes his lips. Then he is hit in the face with a spray of bright blue paint.

"Gah. *Gah.* Ye *gods*—"

Crew Cut drops the manacles to rake at his face. The blue paint bubbles and grows viscous. It's charmed but not lethal. If anything, Crew Cut's face will look like the underside of a dragon's tail for a few days. He doubles over, swiping at his face.

Deputy Tunic stops in his tracks, manacles dangling from his outstretched hand, his mouth a perfect O of surprise. "Captain, what happened?"

"The paint. Gah, the paint *burns*—"

"He'll be okay," Jayla says. "Just a little blue in the face."

Deputy Tunic jolts at the sound of Jayla's laughter. Before he can remember what he was doing—mainly cuffing this punk girl—and help the Captain, Jayla has already seized her opportunity. She slaps the manacles out of Deputy Tunic's hands and shoves him. Taken off guard, the stroppy dude trips over his own feet and topples to the ground.

Hector watches this handful of seconds unfold. They did it, they *actually* did it. Then Sammy D's voice is in his ear. "Go, man. You gotta go now."

"What about you guys?"

"We'll be fine. I mean, we do have a *dragon*, right? Good thing to have in our corner." Grinning, Sammy D cocks back the empty spray can and lobs it across the lot.

The spray can nails the conjured dragon in the head, who shakes itself, roaring with anger. It narrows its gold-yellow eyes at the surrounding tunics, seeing which one will get the brunt of its fury. It decides all of the above.

With a mighty whap of its wings, the dragon rises with enough power to bow the building front. It's as close to the third dimension it will ever get, and it makes the most of it. The rusty scaffold trembles, squalls, and tumbles forward. The tunics scream and scatter as iron bars, and old wood comes down in torrents.

"You see? Smaug for the win. Now get goin—"

Sammy D pitches forward, his eyes wide. He looks down at the scorch mark on the side of his sweatshirt, which spreads with a curling green fire. He is starting to smoke, too, burning from where the spell has hit him. The smell is a mix of charred paper, aerosol paint, and fried yew powder.

Sammy D opens his mouth to say one more thing, but no sound comes out. He falls to his knees. Not twenty feet away, Deputy Tunic lies on the ground. He is still pointing his wand, the city-issued weapon for tunics, at Sammy D, his intended target.

Hector doesn't give him a chance for another shot.

He runs.

A cloud hovers over the fallen debris from the scaffolding, so he heads there, banking on some cover. The dragon roars again, its massive head rising above the dust, its eyes locking with Hector's. Then a green bolt from a tunic's wand hits it, then another. Distempered, the dragon swivels its head and breathes fire in return.

Waves of heat bake across Hector's skin. He involuntarily touches his forehead, praying he still has his eyebrows. So good so far, for him at least. The tunics? He doesn't stick around to find out. He's already seen one friend burn.

He slips around the dumpsters, avoiding any scaffolding that has tumbled like fallen jackstraws in front of him. Coughing from all the dust, he makes his way farther down the alley, building distance from the tunics and the dragon, Sammy D, and Jayla...

On Eldritch Avenue, he jogs down the street, past an all-night bodega, a string of abandoned storefronts, and empty lots. Eventually, he turns onto Coven Street, which is the start of the hip neighborhood those land developers chose instead of the Land of Augie's Attic.

Hector picks the noisiest, brightest street, of which there are many to choose. Like any other, this street has a line of generic bars and late-night chain restaurants, where the customers enjoy the magic of cocktails, flat screen T.V.s, or their phones. Ordinary, boring people with ordinary, boring things to consume. It's the ideal place to blend into and vanish from attention until he reaches the nearest subway station.

To act normal—and to calm himself down—Hector looks up every now and then to take in his surroundings. But when he sees several restaurants with commissioned street art adorning their walls, he commits to staring at the sidewalk. It's better that he does.

None of the graffiti is conjured. All of it is dead on the wall.

"Where is he?"

Captain Crew Cut's jaw is set, his eyes blood-red and staring. His posture would be more intimidating if his face weren't covered with a certain shade of blueberry goo from the charmed spray can. To compensate, he unholsters his wand and points it at Jayla's chest. "Don't make me ask again."

Jayla doesn't give him the pleasure of showing her fear. She instead decides to watch the lackey tunics, dusty and slightly charred around the edges, surround the dragon. It was a majestic creature, with those massive wings and eyes like pools of gold.

She chides herself for thinking of Hector's conjure in the past tense. She can't help it. She knows what is about to happen, as sure as when she saw Sammy D throw the spray can, leaving himself open as an easy target.

Deputy Tunic gives the command, and the lackeys follow. They raise their wands and fire bolt after sizzling bolt at the dragon. It can't escape the confines of the wall, its home, which sends a particular stinging ache to Jayla's heart. But the dragon doesn't go without a fight, returning fire with fire. She turns away before the scorch marks from the tunics' wands overtake those beautiful green and purple scales.

The wand presses into her chest.

Jayla shakes her head and gives Crew Cut a rueful smile. "Do you ever wonder where magic comes from?"

"You're not answering my question. I don't like it."

"We both know what's going to happen after I do. Humor me first.

Do you wonder?"

Crew Cut takes a sharp inhale and slowly lets out the air—a vein shaped like a fork of lightning throbs at his right temple. "Magic is a tool to maintain order, to enforce laws. You might as well ask me where screwdrivers come from or why we need high-speed internet. *We* made these things to *use*. Magic serves to keep society in order."

"So long as you tunics have the wands."

"I've seen what people like your friend do with magic. Testing boundaries, breaking rules, *personal expression*." Crew Cut purses his lips. "All of it leads to disorder and chaos. Vigilantes threaten to destroy our way of life."

"If only everyone saw it your way. It would be so simple."

"Simple as answering a question?"

"You're assuming a question has only one answer. Most don't."

Jayla wants to do what Sammy D had done. She wants to pull down the collar of her hoodie, to see Hector's tag one more time. But her hands are manacled behind her back. She'll have to settle for imagining those fine, strong letters on her skin. Imagining is better.

"Well?" Crew Cut asks. "How about *an* answer?"

"Okay," Jayla says. She arches her eyebrow, which means she means business. "Wherever he is, he's dreaming up something new. He's making magic. Wait until you see what my man is coming up with next."

Crew Cut tut-tuts. "I'll be here when he does," he says, "but you won't."

When Jayla feels the tip of the wand burn against her chest, she closes her eyes. Yes, she'd rather watch in her mind that beautiful dragon unfolding its wings, sending dust devils across the lot, shaking away the the ordinary world. Better to feel the heat from the plumes of fire from the dragon's snout when she and Sammy D and Hector were watching what they helped create together. When it was just them and the bonfire against the city night.

Shhhh-sh-shhh.

Hector stands back, shaking the spray can. "Almost," he says.

No one replies. The warehouse has been abandoned for years—only tracks from mice and stray cats dot the dust on the production room floor—and so has the loft office where Hector set up his pallet and hot plate.

Sh-sh-shhhhhh.

He grabs another color spray can, whispering an incantation, then a prayer. When he's conjuring at this intimate scale, he doesn't need to recite his spells as many times as he does. The dragon was big, *enormous.* At that size, it would never escape the wall it was made on. He needed all the help he could get to bring it to life at all.

But here, in the comfort of this dusty loft, among his charms and herbs and pigments and books, Hector prays to make sure everything goes all right, that things will turn out, that his imagination can run wild, that the friends he's made will be safe.

Shhh-shh-sh. The right shade of green appears, the color of sea glass. "Yes, *yes.*"

Hector wipes his eyes, clears his throat, and reaches into his satchel. Is it worth it? Is this magic worth the risk? The trouble? He approaches his latest creations and aims the nozzle of the spray can. The black paint shoots out, fine as lace. The rich smell of birch, that tree of lovely life, fills the loft.

"Yes," Hector says. "It's worth it to me. To them."

Having tagged his conjures, he sets down the spray can and observes—lines and shapes and color. Hazel flecked with gold. A jutting chin. An arched brow.

Soon enough, they both blink their eyes and step from the wall, whole and intact, and Sammy D, as usual, is the first to speak.

"Man, do I have to tell you how good you are, Hector? *Every* time?"

"You do," Jayla says, touching her shoulder and *The Hocus* freshly written there. "He drew us into this crew, after all."

"And I'm so glad I did," Hector says. "I've got big plans for us."

LOVE GETS AN UPGRADE
by Tori Miller

My date was waiting at Weston's, which sat at the corner of Grey Street and Alice Avenue. Exhausted from my long walk, I made my way inside the restaurant. A hostess, who was once smiling, became crestfallen when I approached her.

"Can I help you?" She said.

"Yes, actually," I said, defeated. "I'm looking for—"

The hostess stopped me by raising her hand. She picked up a pair of menus and gestured towards the tables with her head.

The well-worn booth of yesteryear provided minimal comfort as I sat across from my date. She was a Kitsune, a fox-person hybrid, with piercing eyes and soft reddish-orange fur. She looked taller than most as she leaned back to roll her shoulders. She was wearing jeans and a plaid button-up top while I was wearing my best dress. I smiled, trying to hide the shame of being late.

"You must be Shelby." The Kitsune said in a warm tone.

A slender hand held up her head as amber-colored eyes made notes about me. I nodded while she took a small sip of her coffee before continuing. "You look nice, by the way."

"Thanks," I said, starting to relax. "And... You must be Zaria? Janet told me a bit about you."

Her eyebrows and ears perked in a smirking fashion. She extended her hand for a handshake. "Yep, I'm Zaria. A pleasure meeting you. Hopefully, Janet told you all of the... good stuff about me."

I reached in for a handshake and played along with her implied sarcasm. "Well, it really depends on what you define as *good*."

She smiled and nodded her head. I didn't realize until I started to pull away, but my hand was beginning to separate from my wrist. I covered the opening with my other hand and pulled it underneath the table almost instinctively. Zaria shot me a quizzical look. Great.

"You ok?" Zaria asked. "Did you— almost lose your hand?"

I looked nervous as I stitched my hand back together with items I had from my purse. Zaria was still waiting on an answer.

"It's... a... condition," I said nervously. "A condition that is a bit embarrassing to talk about. Sorry, I don't like bringing it up. A lot of people look at me weird and—"

"Hey, I get it," Zaria said, casually holding her hands up. "We all got histories that we don't want known to the world. You're good. You don't have to spill everything out on the first date. Just... the good stuff."

I smiled. I wasn't sure about where this was going, but her sense of humor comforted me. Before I could conjure any small talk, a waitress waltzed up to our table.

"Hello there," She said. "Are we ready to order?"

Zaria immediately ordered a Garbage Scrambler while I pondered on what to have. I ordered the Weston's Choice with a coffee to match Zaria's.

"Good choice," Zaria stated, holding the coffee cup close to her. "If you haven't been here before, you have to try a waffle. They're amazing! It's like biting into a buttered piece of frosted cake if that were a thing."

"What's a Garbage Scrambler?" I asked.

"Oh, that?" She said. "It's like four eggs and whatever the chef wants to add in there, all on top of two buttermilk biscuits. It's been my go-to for many years."

I nodded and took a sip of my coffee. "How do you know Janet exactly?"

Zaria shook her head and grinned. "Oh, *her*? That orc and I go back a ways. We've been working at this Steamworks shop called Ticky's. While she fiddles around with clocks and other small things, I specialize in Automatons and fix them should they need repair. The work pays well, and I get to make my customers and patients happy, which is always a plus. How did you meet Janet?"

My face grew slack as I remembered the sheer embarrassment I had brought upon myself when meeting Janet. "Well..." I said."I met Janet by spilling coffee all over her paperwork. You know all that crappy paperwork one has to sign when getting a new wand. You see, my boss was watching my every move and I got very nervous. At least Janet stood up for me while my boss chewed me out."

"Dude, those wand dealerships are the *worst!*" Zaria said. "They take forever with their paperwork, half of them stare at you because you aren't picking a wand that is *in vogue,* plus some of them gouge you with the price that they slap on to those bad boys. That and their coffee *sucks!*"

This came across as a bit strong to me. I didn't know she was super passionate about this sort of subject. I wondered if maybe I should educate her a bit when it comes to selling wands. "Well," I started to offer. "There are some laws that pertain to wand manufacturing and selling. My boss made a point that I knew this process both inside and out. One such law is that you have to buy them from a dealership."

Bringing this point up was a big mistake, as her fur began to bristle. "Oh, don't even get me started on those wand laws." She said. "Half of those crap laws were designed by Humans and Elves in the eighties that were trying to clamp down on crime. Worse yet, if I wanted a wand dirt cheap, I'd buy it from like a street corner or something. They make no sense."

I nodded in agreement. Some of those laws that surrounded wands, or other magical items for that matter, made no sense. This was one of the many political divides that Zaria and I had to face. While I could pass for a Human and remain unbothered by the general public, Zaria didn't have that same luxury. I couldn't imagine the kind of harassment she got because she was not at the right place at the right time. People just suck.

I went for my lukewarm coffee cup and drank a bit. "Kind of like the law stating you can't buy wands on Sundays?" I offered as a weak gesture.

Zaria snorted and shook her head. "Yeah. That used to be the law everywhere in the United States, but we happened to live in the one state that not only kept that restriction to Sundays but Saturdays too." She scoffed at the thought and then continued. "Pft, thanks, Indiana."

I smirked, knowing it was sad but true. She had strong opinions when it came to regulations surrounding wands and other magical issues. Given her profession, I couldn't blame her. She would not only have to buy the right kind of wand for a procedure, but one that's medical grade as well. With wands only coming with a certain number of charges, it can get real expensive real quick.

The waitress came over and brought us our meals. My eyes widened at the amount of food on my plate while Zaria looked for a fork.

"Hope you came hungry, hun." The waitress said as she placed our check on the table. "If y'all need anything, let me know, ok?"

I thanked her as she disappeared to help out another table. We began to eat our food, and I instantly fell in love with it. One large waffle with two eggs, hash-browns, and two strips of bacon that melted in my mouth—a meal fit for royalty served on an extra-large platter.

We mainly sat in silence as we ate. After a while, Zaria's ears perked up, and she asked me a question.

"Have you ever been to Smiling Oaks before?"

I shook my head no as I chewed on part of a waffle. I quickly gulped it down. "Nope. I'm new here, looking for work and a town that isn't just a few traffic lights with some deer."

Zaria nodded and took a large pull of coffee from her cup. "I remember those good ole days. I moved from a small rink-a-dink city to Smiling Oaks once I got my witch's license and never looked back. You'll like it here."

"Well, it's definitely a lot better now that I've met ya," I said flirtatiously.

Zaria blushed beneath her fur, and a happy smirk appeared on her face as she reached for her coffee. After a brief pause, she refocused her attention back to me.

"I'm glad I met you, too. You honestly remind me of when I was starting in this big city," she replied.

Her saying that felt so validating and put me at ease. Even being as passionate about something as mundane as buying wands, she was easy to talk to. I'm glad I met her, but the real thanks belonged to Janet, who pointed me Zaria's way. We eventually paid our separate checks and made the trek back to my apartment. Thankfully, Zaria offered me a lift and her condolences after telling her I took the subway. Once we got back to my apartment, we started to plan for another date. While it would have been better to plan such a thing at the restaurant after our meal, we were both talking too much to plan it out then. I began to offer suggestions, but Zaria was looking about my apartment with a quizzical look.

"You don't seem to have a lot of stuff." She said, looking into the small hallway leading to my bedroom.

"Yeah—" I said, not sure how to address her. "I'm starting fresh, but... aren't we supposed to plan for our next date, or are you going to keep snooping around?"

Her ears perked up, and she turned around. She offered a quick apology as she sat down on my couch in the living room.

After some back and forth, we both landed on going to the local art museum. When I was reading about the place on my phone, they were advertising their newest traveling exhibit. It was called 'Bodies: Art in Motion.' It was an exhibit about the Undead and their plight, all through the lens of art. I'm not sure how Zaria would like this subject matter, but seeing her as more of a medical professional, I don't think it would bother her at all. When we both finalized plans for our next date, we parted ways as I looked fondly toward seeing her soon.

I thoroughly enjoyed the exhibit and didn't notice my date growing more uncomfortable by the minute. Zaria looked ill as we made our way from her car to my apartment. I offered her a glass of water, but she waved it off. I started to notice how pale she was underneath her fur. I was about to say something when Zaria decided to break the silence.

"I don't get it," Zaria said, shaking her head. "Why would anyone think it would be a good idea to make an exhibit out of that? How could anyone call that art?"

"Well," I started to say. "It was interesting. Or at least I thought it was."

I retrieved a bottle of ale for myself and sat on some wooden crates in the living room. It looked tacky, but having minimal furniture and not wanting to be right next to my date made this a viable option. If she were going to get sick, I would rather clean it off the floor than get it on me. Hopefully, it wouldn't have to come to that. Her ears perked in my direction upon hearing a distinct ticking sound coming from me.

"Are you... ticking?" She asked.

I nervously opened the bottle and took a small sip. We ran into this topic before, but outfoxing her was a trivial task. I would typically point to a clockwork object or some other device to create an alibi. Zaria stopped me in my tracks as I started to give my canned answer.

"Look, I get you have a condition of some sort, but you can't hide that from me forever. How can I trust you when you're trying to hide something?" She said, eyes narrowing.

I sighed, knowing that she was right. The problem now is that Zaria wants an answer, and I didn't feel like talking about it. I shouldn't have to hide a huge part of myself, but telling her that I'm Undead would be awkward at best. If she didn't like the Undead that she met as part of the art exhibit, she certainly wouldn't like an Undead for a girlfriend. I didn't want to lose her. She was the one thing that made me feel normal.

"Alright," I said, knowing I had to choose my words carefully. "I was in an accident many years ago. Some doctors got some clockwork parts to work in tandem with the rest of my body. This, of course, did not come without some sacrifices. Instead of a heart, I need to be cleaned out and wound up every year. That and parts of me have to be replaced due to me falling apart. Since then, I've had to make sure that my ticking doesn't give the wrong impression on people."

Zaria still looked ill but wasn't as green as she was before. She nodded her head and sighed, taking in the new information.

"I get it," She began. "You want to appear as normal as possible so that you can make it on your own. Believe me, I know what it's like to give the wrong impression on people. Not many like to associate themselves with a Kitsune. Many think that we steal and trick people into making them do what we want them to do. Sometimes, people think all we do is breed and multiply or have other harmful stereotypes. The problem is, I will never be able to pass for a Human."

Zaria repositioned herself on the couch, looking less stiff than before. "I know we agreed to go to the art museum, but I'm... *shocked.* Shocked that someone thought that it was a good idea to have these Zombies reenact parts of their lives or having some of them talking about their newly found hobbies. It makes me super uncomfortable."

I grew quiet. She used a word that provided a poignant reminder of my current set of circumstances. I knew I had to say something.

"You know those weren't Zombies, right? Zombies and Undead are two different things. A Zombie is a mindless drone that got summoned by a magic-user to do a task. On the other hand, an Undead could be summoned by a magic user, but they are given free will. Those guys weren't hurting you because they found a new lease on life. The least you could've done was be respectful." I said, knitting my eyebrows at her while going for another pull of my ale.

Zaria looked stunned from my vantage point. Her face became red, and she adjusted her position on the couch. Before she could retort, I decided that I needed to speak up for a change.

"Look, I get that you don't like mysteries and want to know every last fucking detail. But if someone is happily living their life, let them live their life. Hell, I'm happy for those people that we saw today! Living in this Human-Elf society, people like them would be living in tent cities. And hun, people like you or Janet wouldn't be too far behind."

Zaria positioned her arm as if she wanted to say something but folded her arms into her lap instead. This allowed me to hop off the wooden crates and dispose of my empty ale bottle.

"All you did today during our date was complain over a few dead bodies, pushing you to question mortality. Sure, it's entirely valid to say it wasn't art, but you were rude. The least you could've done was keep it to yourself."

"Shelby. I–"

"Get out," I said firmly.

"B-But Shelby. I–" Zaria stammered.

In an instant, my temper flared, my blood ran hot, and I didn't recognize the voice that came out of me. *"Get out!"*

Stunned, Zaria got up from the couch and offered her goodbyes. I offered mine with a softer tone but firm because I didn't want to be a complete ass. Quick, like my temper, she was gone. I decided to spend the rest of my evening sitting in the exact spot Zaria sat. All I wanted to do was educate her on the differences between Zombies and Undead, but I let my temper get the better of me. My eyes welled up when I realized the damage that I had caused. I probably lost her for good, and it was all my fault.

I woke up the next morning feeling groggy but comfortable in bed. It was common most days to feel pain upon waking up. As I was getting the covers off of me, my legs didn't want to move. They looked exceptionally pale and devoid of color when I looked at them closer. I touched them, and to my surprise, they felt ice cold. This was not good. I sat on my bed, pondering what I should be doing next. I thought about reaching for my phone, but I left it in the kitchen after Zaria tried to call last night. I swear she kept calling for at least an hour straight. I was too busy finishing another ale and ruminating over our time together and the night's events. At first, I was mad at myself for doing such a silly thing, but then I focused on the problem at hand. I had to get from my bed and into the kitchen. I used my arms, gripped the side of the bed, and pulled hard. My body landed on the hardwood floors with a thud. I realized that I no longer had control of my arms and couldn't move or push away from the nightstand.

This was how I was going to die, I thought, not by old age or some hate crime, but by my stupidity and angering the only person who cared about me in the process. Tears streamed from my face and onto my arm, which was now a pillow of pins and needles. Before I could dive deeper into my sorrows, there was a knock at the door. After some silence, there was another knock. I realized that I couldn't call out for help even as I tried to. All that came out was incoherent gibberish due to my slack jaw.

"Shelby?" Zaria said from behind the door. "Look, I'm sorry about last night and was hoping that we could talk about things." The moments that passed felt like an eternity as I tried and failed again to form something coherent. She knocked again. "Shelby? Are you ok?"

I tried to answer again, but I couldn't make out any words, and my voice was giving out.

Zaria tried the door again. "Shelby? I don't know what's going on, but I'm coming in."

I heard a bag plop onto the floor outside the door. She rummaged through some tools and unlocked the door to enter the apartment. On an average day, I would find this creepy, but I was glad to see her again. She closed the door behind her and started to look for me. She found me wedged between my bed and nightstand after a brief look. I winced as she pulled me from my spot and placed me back on the bed. My left arm fell off, and I felt warm blood from the lost appendage while in transit. Zaria picked up my fallen arm with a gloved hand and placed it next to me. She stared at me with a blank, sunken look in her eyes. I'm not sure if she wanted to say something or if she had come to the realization that I was an Undead who had passed for an average Human woman. I saw pools welling in her eyes before she wiped them off. Zaria paused again as if she wanted to say something but shook her head. She began fumbling through her bag, pulling out an old burlap sack. Zaria dug around the bag as if to test something. Based on her expression, she seemed pretty pleased with the result.

"It's not much, but it'll do for now." She said. "Normally, I would say hold still, but... you're doing just fine." From her bag, she revealed a vial of clear fluid along with a needle. Before I could muffle a scream due to my fear of needles, she pricked me and injected the clear liquid. Shortly after, I then drifted off to sleep as I looked into Zaria's worried expression.

A machine slowed to a dull roar as I lurched myself awake. My eyesight was hazy, and I felt the weight of the world pinned me down. Some muffled voices surrounded me, but I couldn't make out what they were trying to say. As I tried to get up, someone's hands pressed firmly on me to keep me in place. When I gave up trying to move, my vision started to clear up.

"Good, she's breathing." I heard someone say.

"Good," Zaria said. "Thanks for the help. I think I got things from here."

"Sure thing, boss." The stranger said.

The unfamiliar person walked away while Zaria collected several tools from my bedside table. She looked exhausted as she placed metallic tools into a white plastic bin. After she managed all of the tools she needed, she disappeared into the hallway. When she returned, she gave me a quick once over and started to raise my body into an upright position.

"How are you feeling?" She asked.

"Good," I said. The word felt forced out of my mouth. My voice seemed a bit different than I remembered.

"Good," Zaria repeated. She then scribbled down a few more notes and placed the clipboard back at my bedside.

"What... happened?" I asked.

"Your spirit core failed," Zaria said. "After opening you up, I found the thing torn apart by those metal cogs that kept some of your body together. The best thing I could think of at that moment was that you needed a new body. So, I ported your failing body into a mechanical one that worked better. I hope you understand."

"Am I still an Undead?" I questioned.

Zaria shook her head. "Nope, you are now an Automaton. Well, 95% Automaton minus the spiritual core and the brain. The brain we will have to convert soon, but... I know a guy who specializes in that procedure."

While I was sad for losing my prior identity as an Undead, I began to brim with happiness. People respect Automatons way more than Undead. Talk about an upgrade.

"So if I'm an Automaton, what's powering me currently?" I asked.

"Currently, a Hexon B25 drive unit, but in layman's terms, it's a small steam compression unit located in your abdomen," Zaria said, looking at the time. "Now, I'll answer all of your questions later after I see a few more patients. The shop has been quite busy as of late. If you want, I'll turn the lights off so you can get some shuteye.

"Sure," I said. Zaria began turning away when I had one question in mind.

"Zaria?" I asked.

The words felt odd to me, but it seemed like the natural thing to say after quickly mulling it over.

"I love you," I said.

She smiled at me. "I love you too, hun." She replied. Zaria then started to head toward the door and had another thought.

"Zaria?" I asked.

"Yeah?" She replied.

"Once I get fully healed up and stuff, you think we could stop by Weston's for another date?" I asked.

"Sure thing." She said as she smiled larger this time. "But get some rest first. Push the call button if you need something."

She dimmed the lights and left me to my own devices. I adjusted my position in the bed and breathed a sigh of relief. For once in my life, I felt cared for and loved by a person who accepted me for who I was, not what I was trying to be.

FORGET ME NOT

by J. Patrick Conlon

"Who's there?" Kyle ripped the door open.

"Oh, I'm terribly sorry. I was under the impression that no one lived here." Guenther thrust his hand into his pocket, a faint glow dissipating as his hand disappeared.

"I haven't been run off yet, so you can tell those flippers that I won't be chased off so easily."

Guenther raised both of his hands slowly. "I'm not with any house flippers."

"So you're another ghost chaser? Well, there are no ghosts here, only some cheap scare tactics that those blood-sucking ghouls think will frighten me away."

"Do you see any cameras or crew with me?" Guenther turned in a slow circle, leaving his arms spread wide.

"What's in the satchel?"

"Nothing much, here take a look." Guenther opened the bag wide.

Peering in, Kyle saw a bunch of small bags, each containing small collections of stuff he couldn't identify.

"What is all this gunk?"

"Not a camera nor any kind of recording equipment, so does it matter?" Guenther raised an eyebrow.

"Ok, so you're not a house flipper or a YouTuber. Who are you, and what do you want?"

"I'm here to help you get rid of the house flippers and ghost chasers. Isn't that enough?"

It was Kyle's turn to raise his eyebrow. "You want to help me out of the goodness of your heart? What do you get out of it?"

"Can I come in? I find conversation much better over a cup of tea, don't you?"

"I don't have any tea."

"I have some, and I think it will be just the thing to calm your nerves."

"I'm not nervous."

Guenther placed a hand on Kyle's shoulder. "Your bloodshot eyes say different. Let's just sit down and talk."

Kyle's shoulders sagged. "Just a cup of tea?"

Guenther gently turned Kyle around and guided him into his house. "Just a cup of tea and a sympathetic ear."

"Sorry, I don't have a teapot. Where are the tea bags?"

"This blend is my own and much better than anything Mr. Lipton could provide."

Steam rose in a steady stream from the saucepan as Guenther sprinkled a muddled mix of green, brown, and dark red items into two small tumbler glasses.

"It smells good, what's in it?"

"You are smelling the dried orange peel and cinnamon."

"What else is in it?"

"It's an ancient family recipe. I'd prefer not to say."

"I thought you said it was yours. Is it safe?" Kyle was leaning over the glasses with his eyes scrunched up.

"Well, I am the steward of my family, so they are one and the same. And this is much safer than you've been recently, I would imagine. Go sit down while I finish up here."

Kyle sagged into the kitchen chair, slumping forward until his head fell into his hands. "That tea smells very good, but I think I can smell more than just orange peel and cinnamon. You sure you won't tell me what else is in it?"

Guenther smiled. "I doubt you would know the spices even if I described them to you in detail." Upon seeing Kyle's face begin to tighten, he added. "However, I can tell you that nothing in this blend is harmful, and you can see I'm pouring a cup for myself as well."

With that, he carefully tipped the saucepan over, and water cascaded into the first cup. The scent of orange and cinnamon, which was discernible before, exploded into the room with such force that Kyle shot up from the table with a start.

"That smells great." Kyle's eyes began to glaze, and his cheeks flushed.

Guenther sat the steaming glass in front of Kyle and spoke gently, his voice somehow deeper and more resonant. "Now, don't touch the glass yet, Kyle. It is much too hot to handle yet. Just enjoy the scent and relax."

His words hit the younger man, and the tension melted from him immediately. "Who are you?" he managed to whisper as his eyes began to close.

"Since you won't remember this anyway, I'm a druid. A keeper of knowledge."

"A druid named Guenther?"

"I'm Italian. Druids weren't just Irish, you know."

"An Italian named Guenther?"

"It's not as long a story as you might think. Celtic tribes weren't just in Ireland but all over the Mediterranean as well." Guenther brought out a well-worn leather-bound book and a plastic ballpoint pen. "But don't worry about that now. Just relax and tell me everything that has happened over the last six months."

Kyle's eyes closed, and he began reciting the events of the last six months. The only other sound in the room was the occasional scratching of the ballpoint pen.

"It sure sounds like a poltergeist," Guenther muttered to himself as he sipped the tepid remains of his tea. Kyle snored lightly, his head resting on the table, cup of tea still mostly full. Guenther smiled. He would let him get some rest while he tracked down the spirit wandering around the house.

Guenther squinted in the dim light of the afternoon sun. He got up and flipped a switch on the wall. Florescent light filled the kitchen. He returned to the desk, flipping to the beginning of his notes in the old worn leather-bound book. Overturned chairs, doors slamming, car tires popping, and things generally going missing. The only thing that confused Guenther was that Kyle was never injured in any of these instances. Guenther had checked him over after the tea had finally sapped the last of the man's exhaustion. There wasn't a scratch on him.

"If he'd really been here for six months, something would have happened to him by now." He flipped to the final page in his notes.

Kyle describes several incidents where others were injured, mostly people who came uninvited. Solicitors, House flippers, and several ghost hunters. The injuries they sustained were mostly superficial and then usually from stumbling and falling to get out of the way of things *crashing to the floor.*

Guenther closed the book again and placed it back into his satchel and retrieved several small items. First, a small length of white ash. He turned it over in his hands, running his fingers along several places where the light brown bark had been cut away, revealing the stark white wood underneath. Next, a small ball of twine, then a folded pocketknife with some kind of horn worked into the hilt. Finally, a small plastic bag from a grocery store produce aisle filled with a bunch of fuzzy pale sage leaves.

Working slow and steady, he plucked several of the leaves and then, after licking each of them along their entire length, stuck them to the ash wand. He flicked open the knife and sliced a short length of twine, which he then wound around the wand, making sure that each leaf of sage was fastened beneath. Finally, he tied the twine to itself and cinched the knot tight against the wand.

"Well, this should be easy. This one doesn't seem nearly as violent as the one I tangled with in Belfast."

He glanced over at Kyle to ensure the man was still asleep. After several seconds passed and his breathing did not falter, Guenther rose from the table and began to make his way through the house.

As Guenther reached the third floor, the last of the sun's rays were fading fast as twilight gave into night. Striking a fourth match, he set the very tips of the sage leaves wrapping around his last piece of ash. The edges of the sage began to glow with a pale orange light.

Starting in the basement seemed like such a good idea ninety minutes ago, he thought to himself. Normally, spirits were drawn to lower places, so it made sense at the time. But now he was starting to think that Kyle had been correct. There was no poltergeist, only some pranks being pulled by the men that were attempting to drive the man from his home.

As he moved down the hallway, he came to the double door that Kyle had described as the master bedroom. He had said that nothing ever seemed to happen in that room, so that was where he spent most of his time. As Guenther placed his hand on the doorknob, the metal beneath his fingers grew frigid. The edges of the sage began to glow white hot, and the faint smell of the ash blistering beneath grew slightly pungent.

"Well, now, this is more like it." Guenther turned the knob and strode into the room, wand held before him. "I think it's time I introduce myself. I am Guenther Steiner, keeper of knowledge and secrets of the Celtic Druids. My legacy stretches back thousands of years, so don't presume that I haven't met your kind before." He swung the wand around the room, the light smoke from the sage beginning to swirl around him.

GET OUT.

The words slammed into Guenther's mind like a sledgehammer. His knees almost buckled under the weight. He swung the ash around himself in a tight circle, the smoke coalescing around his body. His head cleared for a moment, and he searched his surroundings. This room appeared much more ornate than the decidedly bachelor decor of the remainder of the house. A four-poster bed was placed against the far wall, curtains hanging from each post. The furniture was ancient compared to the IKEA standard upheld throughout the house as well. Guenther moved further into the room and looked at the bed itself.

GET OUT!

Guenther slapped a hand to the side of his head and his eyesight swam from the force of the repeated epithet. The mattress seemed to be undulating as his vision tunneled. He reached a hand out to steady himself, and as it touched the mattress, it rippled and cracked. He recoiled as roaches, centipedes, and all manner of insects poured from the cracks and swarmed towards him.

As he moved away from the bed, a coil of rope suddenly snaked around his neck, and he was yanked off his feet. Guenther began to flail and tried to scream out, but the rope was too tight. His feet were barely touching the floor as he kicked and struggled to get free. His vision tunneled as the wand tumbled to the floor, and his left hand fought to open the satchel slung around his shoulder. His right hand fought against the noose, allowing just enough air to get into his lungs to keep from passing out. Fumbling fingers finally swept the satchel open and dove inside. After several seconds that felt like hours, his hand clasped around the familiar bone hilt. He felt his right hand begin to ache as the rope sliced into it, tiny beads of blood seeping into the strands as he struggled with the catch. The knife finally snapped open with a click.

Reaching back, he swung wildly. It sliced through the rope easily, and he toppled to the floor. He ripped it from around his neck and chanted in Gaelic. The glow from the wand intensified and flew from the ground and snapped into his hand. He whipped it around, and the tendrils of smoke thickened. He snapped the wand down to his side, and they shot towards him, wrapping him in a cocoon of fog.

"Demon of wind and sound, spawn of chaos, be gone from this place!" Guenther pulled himself up to his feet. His wand flared, the blue flame intensifying into a brilliant white. He thrust his hand upward, and a blast of pure white light exploded outward in a ring that swept through the room. The swarm of insects flew apart as the light touched them. The cracks and rips in the bed disappeared as well. Guenther shook himself, and the smoke fell away from him and faded away. His eyes scanned the room, watching for any sign. After several moments, he turned towards the door and opened it.

YIELD!

The words slammed into Guenther's back and he was flung out into the hallway, crashing into the far wall. The door slammed shut behind him as he lay stunned on the floor.

"I think I need to have a further conversation with Kyle. That is definitely not a poltergeist."

Genther looked down at Kyle as he snored lightly, still firmly under the spell of the magic-infused chamomile that he had put into his tea. It was obvious that he hadn't slept in a while, but he did not outwardly look like it. If it wasn't for his eyes when he confronted him at his doorstep Guenther would not have known he needed rest. Something else was going on here. He didn't like having him awake for what came next, but he was sure that whatever was in this house was not your run-of-the-mill ghost or specter. He had not asked the right questions. He reached out his hand and gripped the sleeping man's shoulder.

"Dúisigh"

As Guenther spoke the word, a soft glow spread from his hand and across Kyle's shoulders. A faint shimmer rose from the sleeping man and drifted up to the ceiling. Kyle stirred.

"That tea was very good." Kyle blinked in the dim light. "What time is it? Did I drift off?"

"Yes, you could say that, Kyle." Guenther gently helped him steady himself into the kitchen chair, leaving his hand on Kyle's shoulder. "Unfortunately, this night is going to be a longer one than you are used to. I have a few more questions for you, and this time, I need you to be aware that I am asking you."

Kyle shook his head. "What do you mean aware? What did you ask me before? Where have you been while I was sleeping." He began to rise, his fists clenching.

Guenther tightened his grip.

"Reo"

As he spoke the word, Kyle's eyes grew wide, and he stiffened. His face remained frozen, but his stare was one of terror.

"Now, I am going to say this quickly because I don't want you to panic any more than you already are. I am a Druid, a keeper of secrets. I told you this before, but you were under the influence of my tea so you don't remember. I thought a poltergeist had taken up residence here but I just tangled with something in your bedroom that is unlike any specter I have ever seen. It has attached itself to you somehow and I need to free both it and you. But I need your help. Will you help me?"

Kyle's eyes darkened for a moment, then the resignation that Guenther was hoping for shined through.

"Leá"

Kyle exploded from his seat and banged his knee on the edge of the table. Only Guenther's hand prevented him from sprawling across the floor in a heap.

"What the hell was that? Who the hell are you!"

"I've just explained." Guenther began.

"No, no, no, you just said you're a druid. What does that mean?"

"I'm the keeper of knowledge for the Celtic people. I come from a long line of Druids that stretches back thousands of years. I can explain more if you'll come with me."

"I'm not going anywhere with you until you explain a few things."

The lights in the kitchen began to dim and flicker.

"If you don't come with me now, we will not be able to talk at all. Whatever it is that you have here is not happy with my attentions, and I will not be able to help you when it turns its' ire on you."

"I've seen the lights dim and flicker before. This doesn't scare me, and I think you are with the people trying to scare me out of this place. I don't care how much this place is worth to you. I am not leaving."

An empty chair on the far side of the table rose into the air and shot towards Guenther. Guenther had just enough time to throw his hands towards it and shout.

"Sciath!"

At the words, the air shimmered in front of Guenther. The chair smashed into the shimmer and burst apart, the pieces flying in all directions around the invisible barrier.

Guenther grabbed Kyle's arm. "We go now, or not at all."

Kyle jumped from his seat.

"Maybe a short trip out would be good."

Guenther ran, dragging Kyle behind him. Guenther needed his questions answered before he came back here, but it was obvious he needed to return quickly.

"Are you sure we can talk here?"

Steam floated above the cup of coffee as Kyle's eyes darted about the Starbucks.

"Who exactly are you worried about? The guy over there buried in his laptop? I guarantee you nothing we say will pull him away from pretending to be a novelist to impress the college girls that come in for their coffee-flavored milkshakes."

"But,"

"Okay, fine." Guenther folded his hands beneath the table and closed his eyes.

"Doiléir," He opened his eyes. "There, satisfied?"

"Satisfied with what?"

"Anyone listening in to our conversation will just hear us talking about a new business venture we're going into."

"A business venture? For what?"

"It doesn't matter. No one pays attention to anyone talking about new business ideas in a Starbucks. Now, I think we should talk about what you left out of our earlier talk."

"Yeah, about that. Why don't I remember anything about that talk?"

"The tea you drank had chamomile in it."

"That's it?"

"That's all I'm telling you about it right now."

"But-"

Guenther glared at Kyle. "I'll give you a full recipe after we've figured out what is in your house. It seems to be anchored to the house for now, but I'm not so sure that will be the case for long. I need you to answer a few more questions."

Kyle's mouth opened, then he closed it again and nodded.

"Right, first question. You said this all started about six months ago. You said it just started suddenly, and you had just moved into the house."

"Yeah, that's why I originally thought it was the previous owner trying to scare me out of the house because he was foreclosed on."

"And if this were a poltergeist that had always been there, that would make sense. But I have a feeling that this is not that."

Kyle took a nervous sip of his cappuccino. "What makes you think that?"

"First, whatever this is is strong. Much stronger than any poltergeist I've ever encountered. Now, second question. Where were you seven months ago?"

"I was in Greece, finishing a semester abroad."

"Where in Greece?"

"I was in Athens."

Guenther looked under the table and then stood up.

"What did that tell you," Kyle stammered, getting to his feet quickly.

Guenther ignored him and walked over to the front counter, grabbing a box from a shelf on his way.

"Will that be all today?" The girl behind the counter beamed brightly.

"Yes, thank you," Guenther replied, handing over a twenty-dollar bill. "Keep the change."

Kyle looked at the box in Guenther's hand. He could just make out the words Emperor's Clouds before Guenther stuffed the box into his satchel.

"I thought you made your own tea? What's that for?"

"Sometimes you have to improvise," Guenther said over his shoulder. "We need to get back to your house before something worse happens."

The sky around the house was much grayer than it had been when they had left just a few short hours ago. However, Guenther had a slight bounce to his step that Kyle could not fathom nor match.

"Does this mean you know what happened?"

"I believe it does. And you will be delighted to know that if I'm right, your luck is about to change forever."

Guenther put his hand on the doorknob.

"When we go inside, I need you to do exactly what I say when I say it. We are not going to have much time once we are inside. I only have one last question before we start. Were you wearing those shoes in Greece?"

"My shoes?" Kyle looked down at his feet. "No, I got this pair about a month ago."

Guenther nodded. "And your old pair are in the bedroom?"

"Yeah, I was going to use them for trail hikes when the weather got better."

"Good man. When we go inside, I need you to get those shoes right away and bring them to me."

"You want my old shoes?" Kyle's eyebrow furrowed.

"Yes, then don't do anything else, ok?"

"I can do that."

"Well then, let's get this finished, shall we."

Guenther twisted the knob, and the door swung open.

The inside of the house looked like a hurricane had blown through in their absence. Chairs were overturned, the couch was lying vertically against the wall, and there were paper shreds and various trash flung about the room.

"It was never this bad before. What the hell happened here?"

"I'm afraid this is my fault. I challenged her, and she does not take lightly to challenges."

"What the hell did you do while I was asleep!" Kyle grabbed Guenther's arm.

"We don't have time for this," Guenther ripped his arm from Kyle's grasp. "Right now, it's me she's focused on, so you should be able to get to the bedroom and back before she can act against you. But that might not last for long." Guenther shoved him towards the stairs. Get those shoes and meet me in the kitchen quick as you can."

Kyle returned with his old and worn sneakers to see Guenther leaning over the stove, ripping open a tea bag and dumping the contents into the same pot he had used to brew the tea they shared earlier in the day. His satchel was wide open, small bags filled with various colored leaves and powders that Kyle couldn't identify were strewn around it.

"Good, you're back. Place the shoes on the table and then get out of the kitchen."

Kyle placed the shoes in the middle of his kitchen table and then crossed his arms.

"I'm staying right here. I need to know what the hell is going on."

"Suit yourself. Just don't get in her way when she gets here." As he reached into another bag, a butcher knife was wrenched from the butcher block and spun through the air at him.

"Look out!" Kyle cried out and dove at Guenther.

"Sciath!" Guenther shouted again, and both knife and Kyle were flung against the far side of the room. The knife sunk to the hilt mere inches from Kyle's shoulder.

Guenther pulled a powdery pale yellow substance from a bag and threw it into the pot, then tore open another tea bag.

"What on earth are you doing? What the hell is that? I'm not going to drink any more tea, especially not any that you make."

"That is ginseng, and you're right about one thing. Neither of us will be drinking any more tea. This is for those." Guenther pointed to the shoes on the kitchen table.

"What?" Kyle started getting up when a plate flew directly at his head, forcing him to the floor. "This is crazy!"

"Hey, you wanted to stay." Guenther swirled a spoon made of ash around the pot.

"Well, I changed my mind." Kyle started to get to his feet again.

"Too late now, she's here." Guenther pointed to the table.

A dark, cloudy shape was flowing from the openings of both shoes and began to spin around itself. The air in the kitchen became hotter, and Kyle struggled to breathe. The cabinets flung themselves open, and pots, pans, and various boxes of food shot out and careened around the room.

YIELD!

Kyle was flattened to the floor as the force of the words hammered into him. Guenther buckled to one knee. He almost lost his grip on the pot, where small tendrils of white steam had just begun to float above its' lip.

Two bright red orbs appeared towards the top of the murky shape and flared.

Kyle screamed as Guenther surged to his feet and swept the pot off the stove, and turned towards the kitchen table. The shadowy shape above the table billowed out towards him, tendrils of black flinging themselves at him as if daggers. Guenther ducked low and flung the boiling contents of the pot at the center of the table. The hot liquid dowsed the sneakers.

YIELD!

The words did not carry any force this time as the shadowy shape exploded outward in a hail of shards. Kyle threw his head down and covered himself with his arms as best he could.

"That ought to do it." Kyle heard Guenther say as he slipped into unconsciousness. The last thing he saw was a tall, willowy figure holding a spear standing on his kitchen table.

The tall, armored woman looked down at the young man sprawled on the floor of the kitchen, a quizzical look on her face.

"How long have I been here?"

"Looks to be roughly seven months." Guenther dumped another

dustpan's worth of debris into the large black trash bag.

"And how long have I not known who I was?" She brought her spear behind her in a languid stretch.

"Hard to say. I confess I don't keep up with the pantheon as much as I used to." Guenther shrugged. "You guys don't exactly get much attention these days. Do you have any idea what happened to you?"

"Best I can figure, I fell into the Styx, but I can't really remember when."

"That would make sense. I'm glad we're not fighting now that you remember who you are. I don't relish a contest with you."

"Nor I you. What you may lack in my battle prowess, you more than make up for in knowledge." She looked around the room again. "Speaking of knowledge, how did you know it was me?"

Guenther pointed to the soggy shoes, still sitting atop the kitchen table. "When Kyle told me he spent his last semester abroad in Greece, I looked at his shoes and I knew immediately."

She looked at the shoes. A bright blue swoosh stood out against the white. "I don't see anything remarkable about them."

"Well, I wouldn't expect you to. But as a druid, you have to know these sorts of things."

"I feel like you aren't telling me the whole story," Nike raised her eyebrow.

"Well," Guenther began. At that moment, a groan from below him drew both of their attention.

"Saved by the bell," Guenther smiled. "You should get going. I'm sure Athena has been missing you. I'll finish up here and make sure Kyle doesn't remember anything he shouldn't."

"That is probably for the best," The goddess of victory raised her spear above her head and began to fade from view.

Guenther watched her disappear and then turned back to the chaos around him. This would take some doing to fix, but it wasn't every day you got to bring a goddess's memory back to her. He reached over to the table and pulled off the cup of chamomile that had been cooling there and turned back to the gently stirring form of Kyle.

"I think it best you get a bit more rest, young man." Guenther smiled to himself as he gently dribbled some of the tea into Kyle's mouth. "It would be better for all of us if Nike was the only one to regain any memory of today's events. Guenther watched as Kyle's eyes drooped closed and his breathing became slow and even, then turned back to cleaning the kitchen.

BEARS FACE DEFEAT

by Mord McGhee

Her eyes opened, peeling away webs and the crawling things which nibble incessantly at her physical corpse. The Sumer Lich, also known as the Plague Mage, Nimrod's Bane, Warwitch of Babel, Demon of Calneh, Accursed Ragwoman of Akkad, arose from yearlong slumber in the tomb ensorcelled beneath the stadium, for she felt, at last, the warmth of Friday night lights. The time to quench her penchant for varsity high school football had come under a blood-red sky for the season's home field opener.

The elder gods bestowed perfect football weather, and humankind answered the call with a goodly crowd of Bears loyalists. Across the field were the minions of the hated foe, the Bentwood Spartans. From the contest's onset, there was much violence, much anger, and much pain. In this, the Sumer Lich reveled. Victory was imminent for the Bears until the whistle blew with five minutes left on the clock.

The Sumer Lich screamed, drawing the dreaded yellow banner of the black and white striped judges. Two rows back, a voice cried, "Get some new glasses, Ref!" Then, at the Sumer Lich, "Bring it down a notch, Judy!"

The Sumer Lich felt magic swell within her, feeling an urge to tear the mouthy one into a thousand gory shreds and sprinkle her as crimson confetti over the Fifty-yard Line. She instead bit her lower lip until the taste of 10,000 years old embalming fluid filled her mouth.

"Your protest means naught, mortal," said Sumer Lich. She clenched her fists and shouted at the officials, "Take a pound of flesh if you will! We will be victorious nevertheless." And so, the Bears earned an unsportsmanlike conduct penalty charged to the home crowd.

The raucous Bears Pep Club chanted, "Judy sucks! Throw her out!"

The Sumer Lich, not actually named Judy, gnashed rotten teeth together. She descended into the foam cushion upon which a set of modern scrawls read: *Bears #1.* "Insufferable hounds," said she, "curse you to retch a thousand snakes with the rise of the sun for a hundred days forward." Though she could've cursed them as such, she did not. Because they too loved the Bears.

The Sumer Lich plunged her hand into a bag of concession popcorn, thrusting the snacks into the blackened, worm-infested hole which had once been a mouth. She looked at the blue and yellow uniforms of the Spartan soldiers and thought of flaying the skin from their bodies atop the endzone goalposts. A whistle shattered the mind's image, and she threw the bag to the ground, scrunching her nose.

"Stale," said she. "Ought to be ashamed to take money."

Action on the field resumed. Tank Jones dropped what would have been a drive-killing interception. The Bears Pep Club roared, and the Sumer Lich glared over her shoulder at them. "Fools," she scorned. "Repeat not the mistakes of your superior! You're no more than descendants of hairy crop-growers."

Whistles blew.

Timeout.

The Sumer Lich studied each side of the battle. The Spartans were plotting something vile. A player in the huddle uttered phrases she thought were of the dreaded Sea People's tongue, though she could not be sure. His helmet muffled the secret meaning behind his words.

"Tis he who sleeps on the roof who dies on the roof," she said. "Go you the way of the Akkadian."

"Come on, Tank," a rowdy fan behind her shouted. "Hold onto the ball!"

The Sumer Lich could see a future in which the football smashed the person's face into a blackened, bloated pool of blood and brains, upon which the ghosts of the Lost Tribe feasted. She shook the desire to make it happen and returned her attention to the game. An opposing player wearing jersey number 23 caught a pass as the ball kissed green. No whistles blew, no stop in play. Number 23 sprinted down the far sideline and added six points to the visitor's tally. The crowd bellowed outrage.

"Beware," the Sumer Lich quipped, drumming fingers as jousting knights. She cultivated a cruel smirk, the likes of which once caused the Emissary of Nubia's heart to implode within his breast. "Or as sure as Gilgamesh has slain Huwawa and the Bull of Heaven, perish thee in shadow and flame!" She then snatched up a can of diet soda and sipped.

Play resumed. Two minutes remained, as decreed in glowing numbers labeled "Q-4." On the field below the bleachers, rows of players squared off in an attempt to add an extra point to the Spartan's total. It was a curious break in battlefield intensity, yet it often produced intriguing situations.

The visiting squad's kicker faked a fall. Instead, he sent the ball sailing into the arms of jersey number 23. The home crowd erupted with decrees of "Fake!" The Bears failed. Further mischiefs followed in the form of what the voice in the sky called "an onside kick." The Pep Club chanted, "Cheaters, cheaters!" The crowd at large complained of "a celebration too long!" calling for "unsportsmanlike!" and "march them back, refs!"

Meanwhile, the Sumer Lich placed her soda onto the bleacher beside her foam cushion. "Know this Spartans of Bentwood," said she. "The Bears shall suffer not defeat. Not now, not ever! If the hearts of a hundred virgins must slake the throat of Tiamat, then so shall I carve them out of their chests with my own hand and with my own knife."

"Shut your piehole, Judy," a young boy among a flock of them squealed.

The Sumer Lich flexed her wrists, calling upon the dark mysteries of the universe. She felt the soft soul of a moth emerge in the sky, and she dominated its will. Downward it floated, and as the boys cackled like a gang of spring mallards attacking a solitary mate, she sent it straight into his throat. He gagged, choked. Clutching his throat, he wept. The others heckled and beat him with sharp jabs of fists. The Sumer Lich felt justified delight. Better than she'd known for eons.

Back within the contest, the enemy Spartans pulled off a ruse with the ball, which the voice of heaven said, "risky, but took a friendly bounce!"

Lamont Fleck dove to cover, yet the ball squirted loose. A six-foot-high pile of players ensued. The Sumer Lich, fingers still entwined in the ley lines made of magic, whispered a trickery spell so the ball should find its way back into Lamont's arms. To her surprise, Spartan number 23 rose from the stack, thrusting the prize overhead.

"Not possible!" said the Sumer Lich. She regarded her fingers as though they were Igigi revolting against her Annunaki hands. In a corner near the goalpost, the enemy's bards struck up a victory rhythm, pounding tightly drawn, dried animal skins, cast powerful breaths into long, thin horns. The visitor's bleachers cheered, dancers, whirling like spinning dreidels, shimmering hand-puffs shaking triumphantly.

The Sumer Lich sank onto her cushion. "This can't be happening," said she to no one. Below, the Bears rallied themselves with cries of "keep your head in the game!" and "takeaway time!"

Above, the hands of the gods painted **Visitors 8 Bears 21.**

The Bears' emperor limped to his left along the sideline, face frozen as a hardened warrior. He was a creature who had seen his fair share of the horrors of war, and he held his composure neatly wrapped within and out of sight. She thought he would make a passable priest in her sect if ever the day for fanatical worshippers returned. On the other side of the green, the Spartans' emperor locked his gaze on the Bears' emperor, and the Sumer Lich saw sparks fly betwixt the two adversaries. In a flash, the Spartans produced another score and added an extra point.

Visitors 15 Bears 21.

Spartan marching bards struck up a furious tempo, whipping their supporting cultists into a lather. One final minute remained, with the Bears facing defeat. Soon after, the Spartan kicker booted the ball deep into the Bear's reception formation. The voice of the heavens announced, "Paco Juarez on his own five-yard line. Whoa, what a hit!" and the boy flew off the ground, flailing unnaturally, then crumpled earthward again. A pile-up followed, and as Paco crawled to his feet, he looked at his shoes as if they'd grown wings. Enemy Spartans barked threats and promised Paco's imminent and early demise. The Sumer Lich relinquished command of the wind, desperately seeking a reason her magic did not part the field and afford the boy easy passage to a touchdown.

A deep rumble began beneath the bleachers, and the Sumer Lich shook her head. She scoured her surroundings for a sign. The sky mocked her by revealing no secrets. A whistle blew. The voice in the air announced, "Timeout Spartans, their second." Fighters of both teams formed tight circles. A second, violent tremor appeared, holding for five full seconds. Players broke rank, pointed at midfield, and then at the glistening torches hanging high above the stadium. Glittering dust fell around them. A shout from the crowd proclaimed, "Earthquake!"

"No," said the Sumer Lich, watching the fools flee. "That's not an earthquake." She sneered, catching a whiff of fire and brimstone that comes with new world magic. Ten young bards across the field had dismounted from the bleachers and were pounding the skins as a thunderstorm. All stood and stared, glued to the spectacle.

All except the Bears' All-State middle linebacker Shakespeare Green. He ran to his emperor, pointing to a dark cloud in the sky. Its shape fluctuated, sharpened into an angular visage of a human skull.

"Not so fast," said the Sumer Lich, wriggling her little finger. The cloud disintegrated; the horizon cleared at once. The open use of incantation brought attention unto the Sumer Lich, and one of the drummers glared at her with igneous red eyes. There was a brief struggle between the two until the Sumer Lich realized she'd fallen victim to a witch trick.

She broke the spell with the wave of her palm, chuckling with amusement. Play on the field continued. The Spartans had somehow taken the ball back and stood poised to score nary twenty yards from the endzone. The Sumer Lich looked back to the enemy bards. They were gone. The storm had passed, and the battle was set to begin anew.

Facemask to facemask, the Bears stood against the Spartans. "Blue, blue," called Tank. Shakespeare waved his arms like a crane and yelled, "Watch the pass!" The home crowd began a chant of "Defense! Defense!" The Spartan quarterback raised his right arm, and a referee tossed a dreaded yellow banner into the air. As it dropped onto the field, the voice in the heavens announced, "Spartan timeout, their last one, Bears' fans! It all comes down to this."

As the pause in action closed, the Sumer Lich wove her hands in intricate patterns. She spoke softly, "Behold the power of Sumer! Fear and despair upon you, from the breath of the great dragon and the sword of the spirit in the sky." The earth came alive, quaking violently.

Suddenly, something jabbed her in the neck below a jaw spoiled from lying under dirt for half of eternity. She saw a hand with a long, spidery finger as the source. Her spell broke, and the Sumer Lich gasped, reeled backward until the seat cushion fell between bleachers. It was the captain of the enemy bards.

"Don't know who you are," said the captain, fiery eyes twinkling with a cold burn that sapped at the Sumer Lich's essence, "but I like you."

The Sumer Lich recoiled, "How dare you!"

The captain let out a sound which was mostly chortle but partial growl. Those flaming eyes became starving serpents, suddenly seeing a rat beneath the leaves. It was time to eat. The captain's upper lip peeled back, revealing the long fangs of a wolf. A whistle blew. The Spartans had driven to the one-yard line and were mere feet from a deciding score.

Three seconds, two seconds...

"Hut, hut," the Spartan quarterback called his team to arms.

And in the home bleachers...

"You don't know who I am?" the Sorceress snarled. "To dare such impertinence, I should draw and quarter you, infidel!" The captain of the drum, face squirming with caged light, a prowess of which the Sumer Lich knew nothing.

"Do you see Darius?" said the captain, lips moving in a way that did not match the language the Sumer Lich heard. Here was the witch without question.

"What?" snapped the Sumer Lich.

"Number 23."

"Of course."

"He can't be stopped. Won't be stopped."

"Says who?"

"Me," said the captain.

"Make a point or else."

"Fine," said the captain. "Whatever, whoever you are, your team can have this one."

"Have this one?" the Sumer Lich glanced at the score. "Nonsense!"

The captain laughed, cruel and filled with disdain. "Like I said, you can have this one. But I promise to see you in the playoffs." The captain vanished with the wave of a hand, leaving a strong smell like smoldering plastic. The Sumer Lich threw every bit of magic she knew at the captain, but of his exit, she found no trace.

On the field, the teams were shaking hands. The Bears had won, holding off the Spartans in the end. "Indeed," said the Sumer Lich, weighing a plague to kill the people of Bentwood. Without doing so, she muttered, "We will see you in the playoffs, of that it's an unbreakable vow," and grinned.

AN AUDACIOUS, TRICKSY PLOT

by Kathryn Reilly

The Great Pixie Revolt began before anyone knew it was happening. On a Monday, the city's hustle and bustle unfolded in its usual manner: laborers labored, dealers dealt, managers managed, tinkerers tinkered, bargainers bargained, bums bummed, and watchmen watched. Essentially, everything appeared normal: except the pixies had been planning.

Their plan was vast and demanded quite a bit of coordination. By nature, pixies are a tricksy folk and generally don't enjoy meetings of any kind. They like to go about their lives helping or frustrating the larger folk. Sometimes they worked together, but mostly not. Those living in the cities, caring for the plants and animals that eeked out a living, evolved differently from their purely forested kin. Their wings were a bit thinner and sleeker now since they never knew when they'd need to dodge around a car or a falling bit of brick or sometimes even bullets.

The city pixies loved their homes, carved into crumbling brickwork or wood beams in forgotten row houses, rooftop gardens or community parks, potted plants, or sidewalk trees. But when the Mayor announced the second-largest park in the city would be demolished to welcome a multi-use space sure to bring in hundreds of new jobs, the Queen of the Pixies decided to take a stand.

So she ordered the pigeons to be tacked and their riders to deliver her decree to every local pixie. This took some time because pigeons can be stubborn, and there were thousands and thousands of pixies in the city. Of course, pixies can fly, but covering great distances can be exhausting, and why should they tire themselves when they can tire out pigeons instead? But after a few weeks, each rider returned with their designated pixies' signatures verifying they understood their required presence at her secret meeting. The Queen knew that any projects in the human world took much time to accomplish because of regulations and paperwork and the like, so she knew the pixies had some time.

Humans may be smart, but they'd never discovered that the large oak tree in the city's second-largest park wasn't a live tree. It was actually a realistically painted tree with millions of silk leaves that the pixies enchanted to change with the seasons: green for spring and summer, yellowish-orange for fall, and invisible or browned for winter. It was a large tree with a canopy that could engulf several small buildings. Humans loved it because all the wildlife stayed away; it didn't offer nuts to squirrels or insects for woodpeckers or songbirds or shelter to any living thing. That the humans never questioned the absence of life and activity around the tree placed them in the clearly lacking intelligence category.

However, their Queen, as intelligent as she was creative, billed the revolt as the most audacious tricksy plot in all the fae's history. Not even the fairies or brownies or trolls or ogres could claim bragging rights to such a devious plan to take from the humans. They simply needed to pull it off.

There's nothing better a pixie likes than a plan with a bit of mayhem.

So several weeks later, on a Tuesday evening, the pixies arrived early and chattered among themselves. Their Queen hurried underground from her royal residence twenty feet away to avoid detection. As she emerged and fluttered to her throne, the pixies waited to hear the Queen's decree. When Queen Caoimhe spoke, her musical voice filled the room as she laid bare her plan. As one, the pixies cheered at the impossible possibilities of the plot. They flew from their gathering place determined to fill every bucket they owned with good soil in preparation. The skies filled with pixies flying every which way to find a seed from a plant they loved and tucked it safely into the secret pockets that all their clothes boasted. After all, pixie clothiers were some of the best fae garment designers in the realm. Their hidden pockets were so well designed that sometimes the wearers couldn't even find them.

Humans attuned to their surroundings certainly noticed the pixies, but it didn't occur to them to consider why, suddenly, pixies were everywhere in the city.

Night settled in the city, and the pixies waited early until the late hours when the streets emptied. They sat down near their assigned areas hidden by trees or flowers or waters or bushes or grasses or cracks and called their magics until they bubbled and raged and demanded release into the world.

At two a.m., when the humans were (mostly) sleeping, the Great Pixie Revolt began.

Aoife dumped her bucket of soil into the sidewalk's crack with relish. Then she looked at the rest of the crack and realized she would need a lot more dirt. Pixie buckets were small, well, because pixies themselves were tiny. Smaller than fairies and even brownies, no one would suspect the havok the pixies were about to unleash on the city under Queen Caoimhe's command. She looked to her right, catching Cara's eye, and gestured toward the tiny pile of dirt and the very long fissure. Cara nodded, frowning. Aoife looked to her left and tried to catch Padraig's eyes, but he was watching the night clouds.

"Padraig!"

"What?"

"We've got to go get more dirt. We're going to need lots and lots more dirt."

"Do you think Queen Caoimhe realized just how much dirt we were going to need?"

"Doesn't matter, now does it? We agreed to the plan. It's actually a really good one. So we need to fly off and refill and refill and refill and refill and re–"

"Aoife! Why don't we work smarter?" Cara asked.

"How so?"

"Well, why don't we wake the pigeons or ask the cats?"

"That's a really lovely idea, Cara!"

"Why thank you!" she replied.

All three flew upwards under the falsely lit night and saw Bella stamp her foot in frustration.

"Bella!" Cara called, "we're going to get larger buckets and pigeons or cats to help us carry them. Work smarter, not harder and all that! Would you like to come along?"

"Yes," Bella screeched. "I don't want to spend all night hauling dirt. I want to look at the stars or the moths or chat with a bat or smell a moonflower. The lovely lady with the overflowing balcony on 43rd Street grows the most beautiful, most heavenly-scented moonflowers."

So the four pixies flew towards the closest pigeon roost, gathering others along the way. Soon, they had pigeons tacked and old soup cans with a threaded makeshift handle that was easy to loop around the pigeon's feet. More pixies followed their lead, and soon pixies everywhere in the city were riding pigeons or cats, rats or dogs, bats, mice, raccoons, or even owls balancing makeshift containers of dirt in old cans, takeout containers, shoes, coffee and soda cups, chip bags, or whatever thing with walls they could find, fill, and carry.

By 3 a.m., phase one of the revolt was complete: every crack, pothole, and ditch in the city had been filled with dirt from outside the city's limits. If there was a crack in the sidewalk, in a building, or on the street, it was filled. Every pothole in every street and alley and parking space was filled. Every ditch between the road and its boundary, every depression in every roof, was filled.

The pixies moved on to phase two.

In the middle of their assigned dirt, they hilled the soil with loving hands and removed their seeds. Thousands of pixies had brought thousands of different seeds: white oak and willow and holly and paw paw and walnut trees; wild bergamot and hyacinth and spiderwort and turk's cap lily flower seeds; moss and fern and pussytoe and vine seeds; big bluestem and northern sea oats and Virginia wildrye and tall fescue grasses; spicebush and inkberry and buttonbush and chokeberry shrubs.

They covered their seeds with their last bit of dirt and watered them gently. Then, releasing their magic, they began to sing:

The earth she gives
The earth she takes
He who lives
He who breaks
We plant each seed
To life succeed
Our magic brings
Eternal Springs

As one, the pixies' voices rose above the electronic hum and sirens of the city. And while it didn't wake the humans, it did shift something in the world they shared. The seeds quivered, and roots yawned, breaking through the thin shell and digging deep into the hilled dirt. When they reached the manufactured pavements or rooftops, the pixies sang louder, coaxing them to break the barrier and seek the soil below. With the magic strengthening their roots, they did.

Stems stretched skyward, and branches and leaves yearned toward the sky, reaching, reaching. The pixies' chorus rose sweetly in the night and the nocturnal creatures stilled, listening and watching the magic unfurl.

By daybreak, full-grown trees erupted from sidewalks and alleyways and roadways. Mosses covered blacktops and parking lots and sweetly snuggled tree roots. Heavenly-scented flowers bloomed in sidewalks and in gutters and in trash cans (some pixies had taken their extra dirt and filled the receptacles whenever they could). Greenery exploded as far as the eye could see.

The humans woke to find roots curling down their condo walls and leaves brushing against their apartment windows.

Revived, the earth was.

The Mayor's phone began ringing incessantly. No precedent existed in the history of the Mayor's office for dealing with such an issue. The Department of Public Transportation called to say that the roots had penetrated every subway tunnel and had gone straight through the tracks back into the earth. The Department of Education called, stating that school buses and subways couldn't transport students, and even if they could, the school buildings were besieged with flowering vines. The Mayor stood befuddled, not knowing who to call or where to begin.

While no humans were physically injured during the city's transition, many of their homes were now uninhabitable. Unless, of course, they enjoyed living somewhat outdoors.

Some more aggressive humans grabbed their pruning shears or other sharp objects and attempted to harm the plants. The pixies boxed their ears, sent wasps after them, or had the plants themselves restrain them. Angry constituents began demanding action on the Mayor's behalf; they demanded to know his response.

The Mayor panicked and turned off his phone.

Queen Caoimhe arrived precisely at noon with tea and knocked upon the Mayor's door. Her pixies in waiting (because it was an honor to serve the Queen regardless of gender) flew in, bustling about setting up the tea. He stood in silence and watched as they arranged the room; the Queen sat down on a throne carefully arranged on the table and motioned for the Mayor to sit. He did. Several others turned the Mayor's computer on, repositioned its camera to center on the Mayor and their Queen seated at the lavish conference table, and activated a live broadcast. The Mayor looked at the camera and immediately straightened his tie.

"Mr. Mayor."

"Queen Caoimhe," the Mayor returned, flashing very white teeth.

"I'm sure you realize by now that the pixies have nurtured this city closer to its original origins. While we tried to honor the native plants to assist the local ecosystem best, there are some personal pixie favorites thriving in the mix."

"Yes, I do see this," the Mayor answered, gesturing to the rather large grapevine now residing on his office wall.

"And do you know why this extraordinary event has occurred in this city?"

"No, I do not, though I would like to understand and work towards--"

"Mr. Mayor, this revolutionary event has occurred in your former city because you don't understand boundaries. For the past several decades, your city has continually expanded, replacing the earth with pavement and sidewalks and roads. You've replaced trees with buildings. You've replaced shrubs with statues and trash cans and fire hydrants. You've forced the mammals and birds and insects and amphibians to fight among themselves for sustenance as they are reduced to smaller and smaller spaces. Spaces, sir, that are incapable of supporting such high amounts of life. And you most recently announced, proudly, disgustingly so, that the city, under your authority, would be demolishing the second largest park to build more buildings."

"My former city? I am still Mayor here, and that project is essential to our city--"

"My city Mr. Mayor. And our city? Do you include the pixies in that statement? Beings tied to the very nature you've been obliterating. Did you perchance forget that my home, my court, is located in that same park? Your predecessors negotiated our presence in this city to aid its maintenance of green spaces; green spaces, as you know, are essential for human physical and mental health. The pixies have always abided by our negotiations with humans. As you did not think it pertinent to discuss your plans with me, I simply extended you the same courtesy. I am a kind and, more importantly, capable Queen. Humans may continue to reside in our city. They may continue to work and thrive here. We do so love the coffee and bakery shops, the dance halls, the theaters, the universities, and the music venues. Such creativity in all these places. However, the trees and shrubs and grasses and mosses and vines and flowers all stay."

The Mayor's mouth dropped and moved silently, but no intelligible words formed.

"Very well then." Queen Caoimhe turned straight to the camera and spoke clearly in her chime-beautiful voice: "Too long have humans taken at the expense of all others living in our city. A well-planned city should have metal and greenery. Instead of fixing homes that broke, you abandoned them and destroyed the land to build new ones. This approach is unsustainable. All lives are equally valuable; no being is more important than others. You are welcome to stay as a member of our city community, or you are welcome to leave. If you would like to go, goddess speed, but know that you are marked. The leaf tattoo located just below your left ear is permanent and will alert anyone anywhere you go, human or fae, that you are of this city and you left. I encourage you to stay and live better, live more sustainably. My court resides in the large oak tree in the northwest corner of the second largest park, which will not be demolished--now or in the future. If you would like an audience, you may petition my court to be seen. I wish everyone a very nice day and good health. I hope you will go outside and smell the flowers, let moss tickle your bare feet, and breathe in the finally crisp, clean air."

And with that, the Great Pixie Revolution achieved its objective without a drop of blood spilled.

By noon the next day, owls and hawks and skinks and even an alligator arrived bearing royal communiques from across the fae realms asking just how Queen Caoimhe managed a successful urban revolution in less than twenty-four hours. The Queen simply smiled, sat before a beautifully crafted clay pot on her table, hilled the dirt before her, and coaxed a chocolate cosmos to full bloom.

A WIZARD FOR THE TUNNELS

by Colin Anderson

"Tremendous view. I could look out this window all night." Narjiff declared, gazing over the shadowy city skyline. The view from Southside Tower, spectacular at all hours, showed most majestically just after dusk. Rarely would Narjiff have the opportunity to enjoy the view from his office at such a late hour. Typical business would usually conclude in the early afternoon allowing him to escape the evening chill. Today's business, however, kept Narjiff in the office past sundown. An important client requested immediate contact, and the possible information collected proved a meeting was much too lucrative to delay.

Narjiff turned to his client, who sat comfortably in one of the luxurious leather guest chairs. "Mr. Snyder, I trust you've *procured the reagent* for the ritual we have discussed."

"You mean this thing?" Snyder grabbed a briefcase from between his feet and tossed it on the desk. "You mean this thing that took four goddamn weeks to find in *my* goddamn city? Yeah, I've procured the reagent. And I gotta tell you. I don't see it. I don't see how this is gonna work." He exhaled an irritated chuckle and continued. "And it better work."

Narjiff absorbed Snyder's aggression in stride. "It will work, Mr. Snyder. I can explain the process again in more detail, but it would seem a more prudent use of time to simply show you at this point. Did you adhere to the storage specifications?"

Snyder chuckled again. "Yep. Just like you said." He then unlatched the briefcase and opened it. "This is it. We good?"

Narjiff looked over the contents of the case, quickly taking inventory.

A clear glass box housing a radiant blue crystal sat snugly in a cutout in the middle of the briefcase. "Yes, very good, Mr. Snyder. Very good indeed. This certainly will work." Narjiff shut the case with satisfaction.

"What I don't get is why did I have to go get this? Ain't you a cam? Can't you go invisible? Pop in and take care of business?" Snyder suggested inappropriately. "You guys can steal pretty much anything you want. What I'd do for one of you on my crew...."

Narjiff sighed. His work introduced him to the unscrupulous, the unsavory, and just as often, the uninformed "No, I'm not a chameleon. Not all *lizzies* are cams." Narjiff winced as he uttered pejoratives to bring the conversation to his guest's level. "And, as we agreed, payment for our arrangement is not limited to the percentage of the proceeds. I suspected, correctly it would seem, that you had the means to accomplish the task I asked of you. And here we are. Before we begin, perhaps you can make that payment. Tell me about the palace. Where is it? How was it in there?" Narjiff returned his attention to the skyline view as he awaited details.

Eager to gauge the success of the ritual, Snyder begrudgingly began his story. "Yeah. The palace is east by the river. Near that scrapyard at the port. Took some time to find because GPS is crap out that way. But that's probably why it's a good spot. Needed a couple of weeks to pinpoint the entrance, but once we did, the key lit up like you said." He paused and surveyed the room. "You got anything to drink?"

"Yes, of course." Narjiff opened the bottom drawer of his desk and selected a bottle and glass. "Will bourbon do?"

"Yeah, great," Snyder affirmed. Narjiff poured the bourbon and handed the glass to Snyder. He then selected a bottle of nectar from the drawer and poured himself a drink. Snyder raised his glass and nodded, then proceeded to tell his story. "So there wasn't much to plan. We didn't know what would be inside, and you couldn't tell us anything. Plus, I haven't really dealt with them before. Figured they didn't do too much during the day, though."

"I certainly would have shared more if I knew what to expect," Narjiff interjected, "but I knew it would be difficult, and there were many unknowns, although I agree working in the daytime would likely yield the best results. I did tell you that. I'm sorry I couldn't provide more information, but I just don't know enough. Learning this information is very valuable to me, though, hence the lower percentage we negotiated. Please, tell me. Go on."

"Yeah, yeah." Snyder continued. "Well, we got ready out front at nine or so. We had workin' clothes just like scrapyard guys. Just in case anyone was watchin'. I made sure each guy on the team had a copy of the key app. Everyone spread out, worked different sections. Did it on Saturday when there wasn't an actual crew workin', paid off the supervisor just in case, though. Don't worry; I told him we were just lifting some scrap. I used to have a crew doin' that a few years back. It's common. We lighten their load a little bit, and the supervisor gets a few bucks in his pocket. So, we really didn't have much to worry about as far as being caught pokin' around. Took a few hours. At about noon, one of my guys said his key got a hit and let us all know. Turns out that was it. Brushed away some light scrap and found it. The door looked like a big metal refrigerator door, like the walk-in kind, but it was angled downward; it wasn't straight up. We could hear the lock clicking, I guess because of the key. Opened up, no problem."

"It was easy enough opening the door, then?" Narjiff asked, seeking confirmation. "You have your phone with you? The key will have collected some additional data."

Snyder nodded, "Yeah, I got my phone, and that's right. The door opened right up to a stairwell. We took the stairs down, and goddamn did it stink." Narjiff took a seat in the second guest chair and leaned forward, listening intently as Snyder described his team's descent into the palace. "We didn't see anybody there when we got down the steps, but it stunk. Stunk like they didn't take the trash out for a long time. We got the light on and saw there was shit rotting all over the floor along the walls. Big, long table in the middle of the room with nothin' on it. But, there was a door in the back of the room, so we went over that way to try to figure the place out more. The door opened up, and twenty of 'em came out before we got halfway there."

Narjiff frowned as he anticipated the blame.

"So," Snyder delivered as expected, "the info you gave us... again, it was a little on the useless side. It was like these Rats knew we were coming, or they were expecting unwanted guests. Well, not like they knew I specifically was coming, but they knew someone was coming. We got ready for a fight, guns drawn, they had... whatever the hell those stick things are."

Narjiff stood and began pacing as he interrupted. "Surely, the confrontation wasn't too much to handle. You made it here, and you look like you haven't seen a fight."

Snyder nodded with an eye roll. "Some of my guys aren't the most reliable. Can't say I blame them seein' as we were outnumbered big. They gave up pretty quick, and the Rats sat us down at the table. Things settled pretty quickly after that, and they at least lowered their weapons. Cooled off. Like I said, they were expecting someone. They were showing a little force first, set the tone. But, after everyone calmed down a little bit, some big Rat boss came out. They all shut up and stood back. So, yeah, they weren't really lookin' for a fight. They were lookin' to talk."

Narjiff stopped pacing, his back toward Snyder.

"So the Rat boss." Snyder began, taking a subtly more aggressive tone. "The Rat boss told me some stuff. He *was* waiting for someone. He was waiting for you or whoever you would send. Yeah, turns out they knew you were looking for them."

Showing concern, Narjiff interrupted and reminded Snyder once more. "I did say that the information was most valuable to me. Learning what was down there. I told you that when we agreed to terms."

"Yeah, you did," Snyder confirmed. "But, you knew that this was a bad situation you were sending me into. And it turns out I was a bit outnumbered. Maybe we could have fought our way out, but I don't think many of us would have made it. And I certainly wouldn't have been able to grab that." Snyder nodded toward the briefcase.

Narjiff sighed. He knew what to expect next and helplessly offered an excuse. "I didn't expect this level of resistance, Mr. Snyder. I would not have asked you..."

Snyder continued his story as if Narjiff wasn't speaking. "That Rat boss, he started asking questions. He wanted to know where YOU were.

So, I told him about your office here. Then he wanted to know if you had security or bodyguards. So, I told him you didn't. Then he wanted to know what our arrangement was, how much your take was. So, I told him. Then he made an offer. A pretty good offer. Well, any offer would have been a pretty good offer in that situation, but he made a solid gesture. And, seeing as you put me in the position I was in, I sure accepted. Now I get my returns fixed, and I get paid to clean up the loose ends."

"Fine," Narjiff interjected. "Just tell me, before you do it, was the crystal already in the case when they gave it to you, or did they put it in the glass? I have to know if this was even worth it in the first place."

"Man, the weird shit you Lizards and Rats are mixed up in." Snyder chuckled, shaking his head. "Ok. It wasn't in the case. They got it from the back room they ambushed us from and put it in that glass box before they sent me away with it. Said this is what I needed for the ritual, and you'd know it would work. I hope this means it was worth it." Snyder cracked a sarcastic grin.

Narjiff roared a defeated laugh and buried his face in his claws. The office door swung open, and three Rats armed with shock rods stepped inside. Snyder held up his hand, signaling them to wait, and they complied.

"We're not quite done yet, though, are we? You're still doing the ritual. That's the whole goddamn point of all this." Snyder demanded. "I've still got money for you to fix."

"Why not?" Narjiff stood and threw up his arms. "Let's do it now."

Narjiff's concession instead served as a command, and every wall in the office swirled and churned as his Chameleon guard, a dozen strong, dropped camouflage and stepped forward. They shredded the Rats into puddles of meat and blood before a single shock rod was raised in defense. Snyder jumped from his seat, shattering his glass on the floor. Quickly realizing all avenues of escape were blocked by sharpened pikes at the ready, he stoically regained composure and once again took his seat.

Satisfied with his guard's swift victory, Narjiff turned his attention to Snyder. "Your phone, Mr. Snyder. Please give it to me." He asked with a politeness quite unnecessary.

"I'm sorry, I didn't mean..." Snyder started begging forgiveness for his greed and overreach before Narjiff cut him off. This time sternly.

"Give me your phone," Narjiff demanded, claw extended.

Snyder, shaking, nervously pulled his phone from his pocket. Narjiff took Snyder's phone, and the Chameleon guard captain took Snyder's head. The decapitated body slumped back in the chair and bled heavily onto the floor.

"What shall we do with the bodies?" Chyz, captain of the guard, asked as he wiped his blade clean across the jacket on Snyder's corpse.

"Leave them here for the Rats to see," Narjiff instructed. "They'll be here soon enough. Nice work with this, always appreciated."

"Of course." Replied Chyz. "This should be what we needed, right?"

"Assuming Mr. Snyder spoke the truth, they have a wizard," Narjiff answered with an elevated mood. "And we know where the palace is. And with this," Narjiff held Snyder's phone up, "we will have a fairly accurate map of the structure. We'll have that wizard by next week. And then, well," Narjiff gestured across the skyline, "then we'll have the rest."

"Very good." Chyz nodded. "Which office are we using next?"

Narjiff took no time deciding. "Let's use the one out in the west side. They haven't been there yet. It gets a lot of sun, and if all goes well, we shouldn't have to move again. This place was too cold. We can set up there tomorrow, but first, let's accept Mr. Snyder's payment before getting out of here."

Narjiff took the glass box from the case and gently set it upright on the desk. Holding both sides of the box, he carefully separated the bottom, which served as a pedestal for the crystal from the rest of the container. The crystal's radiance showed much brighter as it was exposed.

Narjiff logged into his accounting system and attached sensors from his laptop to the crystal. With a click of the mouse, the ritual began. Narjiff stared intently at his laptop screen. He watched the tax return preparation, including merging falsified charitable deductions with declared income, process, and flash on the display. When a notification arrived declaring the audit clean, Narjiff transferred the agreed-upon percentage to his account and left the rest of Snyder's money in the return deposit account. Finally, he disconnected the crystal, now dull and emitting no light, smashed it to dust with the briefcase, and swept the powder into a waste bin next to the desk.

One step closer to success with confidence growing in stride, Narjiff signaled his Chameleons to follow as he left the Southside office for the last time until his victory was sealed.

THINGS CAN ONLY GET WORSE

by DJ Tyrer

1997. Not long after Tony Blair had swept to power to the refrain of *Things Can Only Get Better,* an event Paul Starling found bemusing, never having been taken in by the man's smarm. He could only imagine the voting public truly were credulous. Or, perhaps, the man had managed to cast a spell over them – Starling was familiar with such things and found it the more credible alternative in his mind. Paul would recall the period as one of low spirits for himself and all the others who loathed the man's vacuity and disrespect for tradition. But, the period truly stuck in his mind for another reason – it was when he was asked to investigate the curse that seemed to have fallen upon the inhabitants of a tower block in East Ham.

A woman named Elizabeth Manning had called him – how she'd obtained his name and number, she didn't say – and offered him a modest fee to look into a curious matter. With a small private income, he wasn't much attracted by the offer of money, but the case...

"Two dozen people died of fright?"

"That's correct. Out of a hundred-and-fifty-odd inhabitants."

"Intriguing..."

It wasn't his usual fare – he was more used to investigating the mysteries of old houses, not modern blocks of flats – but it promised to be an interesting case if there was anything to it.

"I'll help you."

Aneurin Bevan House would have been just like any other dreary, decaying concrete abomination, home to the hopeless and disaffected, had it not been for the disturbingly high death rate of its inhabitants.

Not by drugs and violence, nor cancer and asbestosis, nor even a rash of suicides that might have seemed explicable given the lives the inhabitants were forced to lead. No, death by fear. More than a tenth. Even the dullest council official couldn't fail to grasp something inexplicable was happening, and only the lack of an obvious cause coupled with the fascination with the recent election had kept the press from running with wild theories.

"We need someone with your knowledge and experience to undertake a low-key investigation of events," said Ms Manning, as she styled herself in a manner he found quite vulgar.

Starling was silent for a moment. "Very well."

"Could you meet me in my office tomorrow at ten?"

"Yes."

"Good. I'll give you all the information I have when I see you. Then, I'll conduct you to Aneurin Bevan House. I have established a, ahem, cover story for your presence. If anyone asks, we'll say you're carrying out a survey of modernist architecture."

He resisted the urge to snort. To anyone who knew him, the story was implausible, but it was plausible enough to the casual observer, given his monograph on English Churches. To the uninitiated, architecture was architecture.

Paul arrived early the next morning. He found Ms Manning was his opposite: Where he was tall, she was short; where he had dark hair and grey eyes, she was blonde with bright blue eyes; and, where he was slouched and slightly ruffled in appearance, she was ramrod straight and impeccably dressed.

"Sit down, Mr Starling."

It was like being back in school. In fact, he found her no-nonsense attitude a little intimidating.

"Here." She passed him a pile of files on the building and the deaths. There was nothing in the latter that provided any illumination.

Leafing through the files, he could find nothing concerning the building itself, nor the site's past, that might explain the deaths – no stereotypical legends of satanic cults nor any hints of magical or sacred aspects to it.

"There's no evidence of any similar deaths until just after electioneering began." He gave a sniff. He resisted the urge to make a political comment. "In short, whatever is causing the deaths is of recent origin."

Ms Manning nodded, slowly. "But, we're still no clearer as to what."

"If there are any clues," he said, "they'll be in the block."

She stood. "Well, let's head there now."

"Sure." He wouldn't have dared disagree.

Aneurin Bevan House was a short drive away.

As he climbed out of the car, Paul looked up at the building.

From the outside, the towerblock looked totally normal, a standard 1960s abomination against good taste.

"I wouldn't want to live here," he said.

She shrugged. "Me neither."

"Still, it looks no more likely to inspire despair in its inhabitants than any other such block. A spate of people losing the will to live hardly seems likely. Nor can I sense anything strange about the place. Yes, it has the usual 'slightly-off' aura to it and the taint of bad emotions – hatred and despair – that such housing estates tend to have, but no more than anywhere else. No emotions strong enough to warp the spiritual fabric of the building, nothing alien, nothing deliberate."

He looked up at the building and sighed. "If I knew nothing about what is happening here, I wouldn't have guessed it."

"So, you don't know what's going on?"

"Not yet. Whatever caused it is either gone or has concealed itself..."

"So, it could still be here?"

"Yes. I'll have to investigate further to be sure."

She looked at him. "How does this work? A séance? Or do you use machines? Magnetometers or something?"

He almost smiled. Clearly, she'd done some research.

"No, not quite. I'm... a mystic, you might say. I do things the old-fashioned way; no gizmos for me. But, no spiritualist hokum, either. I'll examine the building in person, then, if necessary, I'll explore it in the spirit."

Her eyebrow rose. "In the spirit?"

"Astral projection."

"Astral what?"

"Astral projection. I detach my spirit from my body and let it roam through the spiritual dimension."

"Oh."

He couldn't tell if that was an 'oh' of disbelief or one of understanding, but she didn't query him any further as they went inside.

There was a stale smell. Urine. Mold stained the concrete where the walls of the passageway met the ceiling.

"Lovely..."

As they wandered through the corridors of the block, they only saw a couple of the building's inhabitants, people with the blank expressions of those for whom life held no interest, who passed in silence.

The hallways and stairwells – the lifts didn't work – were grey and defaced with graffiti, exactly as he'd imagined.

Ms Manning paused outside a door.

"We can go inside. This flat is one of those belonging to those who died."

Denuded of furniture, it was as grey and bleak as, if a little cleaner than, the public areas of Aneurin Bevan House.

"Hmm, you do the bare minimum, right?" He guessed the inhabitants lacked the money and inclination to decorate themselves.

The woman's eyes narrowed a little, but she didn't respond, and he proceeded to examine the flat. When he was done, she took him to another empty one to look at.

Paul shook his head. "There's nothing obviously wrong with either flat. Again, without knowing something happened here, there's nothing to alert me."

Even a cursory look into the twilight world of spirit had revealed nothing. Buildings like this were naturally lacking in spiritual resonance, and this one was no different.

She looked at him.

"I'm going to explore the building in the spirit. While I'm doing that, my body will remain here in a... comatose state. You do not need to do anything, Ms Manning. In fact, please do not do anything, even in the unlikely event that I spasm or seem to manifest wounds upon my body."

"Wounds?"

"Harm to the spirit can be reflected in the body."

"Oh."

"While I'm out of my body, you can do nothing to help me and might even harm me, so leave well enough alone, please."

"Er, sure."

He sat down in the corner of the empty room and propped himself up against the wall as he prepared to let his mind and spirit drift free from his body. Normally, he would put on a bit of a show when doing this for someone – people seemed to be reassured by an occult display, compared to his just slipping quietly away into a sort of trance – but he didn't think that she was the sort to need such trappings. In fact, he guessed such theatrics would likely only stoke her doubts.

Carefully, he slipped his rimless glasses into his shirt pocket in order to avoid them sliding off his nose. He closed his eyes and willed himself free of his physical form.

He might still have been in his body, except he could see the shadow of it at his feet.

Here, where the spiritual plane was close to the physical world, illumination was largely reliant upon the presence of life, and the empty flat had precious little of that. Frequently, even in such buildings, there would be mold to provide a low glow, but there was only his body and his companion to give off the aura of life energy and a little light from the sun through the windows. The flat was sterile.

Something was very wrong, but a close examination failed to make it any clearer.

Discouraged, he slipped back into his body and opened his eyes.

Ms Manning looked at him quizzically.

"This will take more effort than I expected," he said as he stood with difficulty. "Would it be alright if I spent the night here?"

She was silent for a moment, then nodded.

"Here." She handed him a key. "I'll be by at nine in the morning to collect it and get your report. Please, try not to die – that would be inconvenient."

"I'll try not to." He grinned.

"Good. Will you start right away?"

"No, I think I'll have something to eat first." The evening was drawing on.

Ms Manning nodded. "I know a nice restaurant if you'd care to join me."

"Um, sure, why not?"

It was, indeed, a nice restaurant, and he didn't feel entirely at ease in it. Although he was quite well-off, Paul had a preference for dining simply on his own – he was a passable cook and was entirely happy with a takeaway or microwave meal when he was too busy to take time out to deal with fresh ingredients. Restaurants weren't really his things, especially as Ms Manning, or Liz, as she was now insisting he call her, was eagerly engaging him in small talk. A closeted academic by nature, he wasn't very comfortable around women.

"You're really not at all what I expected, Paul," she said as they finished eating.

"Oh? In a good way or a bad way?"

She laughed. "I don't know. Different. I expected something more... Aleister Crowley. You're... quite normal."

"Thank you." He straightened his glasses.

"I'll drop you back at the block," she said.

"I need to visit my car first – there are a couple of things I need from the boot."

"Oh, sure."

It didn't take long to collect what he needed, chalk and candles in particular. Then, she dropped him off at the front entrance to Aneurin Bevan House.

"I'll see you tomorrow," she said as he closed the door. "Be careful."

"I will."

The 'Out of Order' sign was gone from the lift door, but he headed for the stairwell, regardless. He'd read stories of people being trapped in lifts that malfunctioned and would rather take the six flights of stairs to the flat he'd be spending the night in. Paul wasn't the fittest of people, but he was a pretty active walker and didn't find it too tough going.

Once back inside the flat, he began preparing for the ritual he intended to perform by sketching out a circle in chalk and placing candles and other items taken from his briefcase about it. With nothing else to go on, he'd have to attempt to see what had happened here for himself, and that was no conjuring trick to perform on a whim but a difficult and demanding task.

Once everything was in place for the ritual, he began to chant in Latin and performed the necessary oblations it demanded. Such rituals took time and effort, and the slightest error at any point risked causing the entire ritual to fail – not only wasting his time but putting him at risk: Magical workings of this level required a great deal of energy, and its mishandling could have all sorts of unpleasant side effects. Inept mages seldom survived for long. There was a similarity to computer programming, except mistyping code seldom had the potential to kill the programmer.

An hour passed, and he was ready.

He leaned forward to stare into a shallow brass bowl filled with water that sat on the floor before him at the centre of the chalk circle.

The water appeared to ripple and swirl, although there was nothing to stir it, and an image formed upon it, flowing up from the bowl into his mind. It was an image of the flat in which he currently sat at the time of its inhabitant's death.

The flat was barely furnished, even then, and he had no trouble recognizing it. He could see an armchair in the lounge and a unit with an old TV and video player on it opposite, a folding TV table, and a little shelving unit with video cassettes upon it. An elderly man sat in the worn-out armchair, dressed in a baggy, greyish tracksuit that matched the color of his straggly, rat-tailed hair, watching some dross on the television.

The scene was totally normal. But Starling knew that was about to change: He was reviewing the events of the man's death. Had he been watching events unfolding solely in the mundane world, Starling would've been able to see nothing more than a peculiar look of surprised terror appear on the man's face before he keeled over dead.

But, the vision also showed the spirit world, and there, something like a dark cloud or fog oozed into the room through a wall; spirits were unconstrained by the impediments of matter. Starling didn't recognize the type of spirit; there were an infinite number out there, many of them unique, but he could palpably feel the menace, the evil, exuded by it.

In the room in the present, he shivered.

He watched as a series of ropey extrusions flowed out from it and attached themselves to the aura of the reclining man at the moment he registered shock. The colors of the man's aura darkened and faded as it sucked the life force from him until his aura was gone and the man was dead.

Bile rose in Starling's throat, and he swallowed hard but continued to watch as, in some manner, he didn't understand, the spirit erased the lingering traces of its presence and what it had done. There would be no echo of the horror it had perpetrated.

Drawing away from the vision, he found himself back in the empty room, its sheer mundaneness disturbing now. That it could erase its presence was a worrying development, but the act also implied intelligence rather than the more usual primal urges that drove most predatory spirits.

"Bad..." he murmured as he sat back from the bowl.

Facing a calculating foe such as this was more like attempting to hunt down a human serial killer than trying to trap a wild animal. Unless, like some murderers, it was driven by some agenda that could be discerned and predicted. But was it?

He sat in silence for a time, the candles flickering about him, slowing his breathing and focusing his thoughts, then stood and crossed to where he had left the files Liz had given him.

Amongst the information he'd earlier asked for was a diagram of Aneurin Bevan House. Carefully, he compared the locations of the deaths within the building. It took a while, but eventually, he spotted the pattern. Looking at it in cross-section, he realized, the locations of the deaths – some of which had occurred multiply in the same flat – described a pentacle; only the point of the uppermost arm remained unfulfilled.

Starling considered the dates of the various deaths. Initially spread out, they were growing closer and closer together in time. If he was right, the next attack would be the following evening.

That gave him a little time to prepare, but first, he needed to sleep, the ritual having left him drained, and he did so until Liz's knocking at the door woke him at nine.

"Good to see you're fine," she said when he opened the flat's door. "Although, saying that... you look rough."

He shrugged and let her in.

"Coffee?" She held up a flask.

"Thanks." He took it and poured himself some.

"How did it go?"

He considered for a moment. "Good, I guess." He took a sip of the coffee. "I know what's going on – and I know where and when the next death is likely to occur."

Starling showed her the diagram.

"See? We need to get whoever lives *here*," he jabbed his finger at it, "out so that I can deal with it."

"Um... Sure, I'll buy it... We could tell them there's a gas leak or something. But what's causing it?"

"You wouldn't believe me."

"Really? I'm believing you enough to go along with tricking someone out of their home for a few hours... I've trusted you this far, haven't I? Trust me in return..."

"Fine. It's a spirit. It... drains the life force of its victims. I cannot be certain exactly what it is or why it is doing this, but I am certain it is evil and is conducting a ritual of some kind..."

"And that's bad, right?"

"Well, let's just say that things can only get worse. It has to be stopped. I *will* stop it. I just need you to get me into that flat and its inhabitants out."

"Right. But, you are sure you can stop it?"

"Yes." It was a lie, but he didn't want to alarm her. "I have no little arcane ability, myself, and I have my own spirits I can call upon to battle it. Tonight, its evil will be brought to an end."

"Good. So," she smiled, "how about breakfast?"

"Yes, that would be good."

This time, it was just a local greasy spoon, empty of customers, so he didn't feel nervous about eating there. Liz didn't make much small talk, and her eyelids were drooping; she was obviously not a morning person. After a fry-up, they discussed their plan of action over a cup of coffee, finalizing on her suggestion of a gas leak.

"I'll handle it," she said, her tone certain. "When do you need them out?"

"By six o'clock, at the latest. Earlier would be better."

"No problem."

True to her word, she had cleared it and its neighbors by half-five, and he was inside before six.

"Can I do anything?" Liz asked.

"Yes – leave!" He laughed but wasn't joking. "This will be dangerous, and I don't want you anywhere near here."

She nodded. "Fine. I'll put warning tape across the corridor by the lifts, discourage people coming this way." She took a deep breath. "I'll see you in the morning..."

There was a note of doubt in her voice, but he brightly affirmed that he would.

After she'd gone, Starling prepared himself for the coming battle.

Taking out his chalk, he drew a warded circle in the middle of the room, where he could leave his body whilst he battled the spirit. Such wards weren't unbreachable but were better than nothing if things went awry.

That task done, he set about summoning the spirits that would assist him. The first three required little effort, three small and almost-formless shapes with just eyes and a mouth in them, *demi-spirits* formed from his own mental energies, named Winkin, Blinkin, and Nod. Although weak, they were utterly loyal.

Then, he drew a circle of summoning about a large candle and called forth a trio of fire elementals from the dancing flame. The spirits took the form of fiery salamanders that moved sinuously about the room. He hoped that such incandescent beings would be effective against the dark spirit he faced.

Finally, he erased the circle and drew a fresh sigil.

"Come to me, guardian of this place. Come to me; your people need you."

There was no hearth in the modern building, but the gas boiler served much the same purpose, and from within, it tumbled out a short, stocky figure in overalls, a miniature maintenance worker; this was the spirit of the building itself.

It looked at him.

"An evil spirit is harming the inhabitants of this place. They need you to protect them. Will you fight for them?"

It nodded.

"Thank you."

Starling would've liked a few more, just be sure – the spirit seemed powerful – but there wasn't time... He could've called upon Arabella for help, but there was too great a risk. He'd gamble his own life but not her existence.

He lay in the middle of the warded circle and waited, his three *demi-spirits* dancing about his head like over-eager puppies. The salamanders circled the room like fiery guard dogs, and the spirit of the place waited, arms crossed by the front door, as if daring the spirit to enter the flat.

Then, he sensed it. The spirit was coming, a nauseating sensation on the edge of his consciousness.

It flowed into the room like dark smoke, a palpable sensation of *wrongness* oozing from it. Doubtless, it received a nasty shock to discover not an oblivious, mundane family waiting to fall prey to it, but a mage and his spirits, yet he felt no wavering in its will to act.

"Sic!"

Starling slipped from his body and led the charge.

Winkin, Blinkin, and Nod were of no real power compared to the spirit, but could chip away at its defenses whilst it concentrated upon the more powerful threat of the salamanders. The spirit of the block fought tenaciously and kept Starling safe from the entity's attacks.

Although he hadn't shied away from leading the attack, Starling now hung back. Not very skilled in such spiritual battles, he preferred to lend his support than take an active part in the fighting, relying upon the elemental fire to cleanse the evil.

Flames danced about the room as if the gas pipes had ruptured.

Had there been an observer upon the physical plane, they would have seen nothing save Paul Starling laying, occasionally twitching, in the middle of a chalk circle, but in the spirit, a terrible battle raged with whiplashing tendrils of darkness and coruscating waves of flames spewing back and forth.

Shadowy tendrils seized one of the salamanders and tore it apart in a shower of sparks.

They pressed on. Suddenly, Blinkin was swiped out of existence.

Starling gasped as he sensed the shock of its destruction.

Focusing his will, he resumed the attack. They had to do this.

The remaining salamanders tore into the shadow, shredding it like mist before the bright light of dawn.

As the final fragments of darkness vanished, the oppressive feeling of evil that had accompanied it faded, and Starling knew they had won.

He drifted back into his body and let sleep claim him.

Starling woke in the early hours, feeling as if he'd gone ten rounds with Mike Tyson. He'd manifested some cuts and bruises as a reflection of the wounds sustained during his spiritual struggle, but he was essentially alright.

The spirits were gone except for the little maintenance worker.

"I hope we destroyed it," he said, then yawned. "Still, if we've driven it off, we've probably stopped its vile ritual."

The guardian spirit nodded at him, then headed back towards the gas boiler.

Slowly, painfully, Starling stood. He'd make certain to unravel any remaining threads of the ritual, just in case.

The raging battle had had no effect upon the physical world, so all he had to do was clean up his chalk markings from the floor. When he was done, he collapsed onto a chair and fell asleep again, only waking when Liz arrived.

"Is it over?" she asked as he opened the door.

He nodded. "Yes."

"Good." He thought he caught a hint of disappointment in her voice. She followed him in. "You look terrible."

"Well, at least I've still got my ear."

"Sorry?"

"Uh, private joke. I'm fine. It was a nasty fight, but I got there in the end. I've just got a little tidying up to do, a few loose ends, but that can wait a while. In the meantime, you can let the people return to their homes..."

"Sure."

She helped him pack the last of his accouterments up; then they headed for the lift. A little warily, he joined her in it. Given the way it creaked and groaned, he rather wished they'd taken the stairs.

As they rode it down to the ground floor, she looked at him and said, "Would you like to have dinner this evening when you're done?"

Her smile told him she was probably interested in more than a meal.

"Sorry, no. After a quick coffee and a sandwich, I'll be heading home to Buxton."

"Maybe I could call you...?"

"Sorry." He shook his head. "I'm already in a relationship."

She sighed. "Oh."

He hoped she didn't press him for details. Some things weren't easy to explain.

She gave him a half-smile but said nothing as he turned and walked away, glad to leave the tower block behind him.

TROLL IN THE MACHINE

by Johnny Guzman

Troll: A being in Scandinavian folklore, including Norse Mythology. Dwell in isolated rocks, mountains, or caves. Rarely helpful to human beings.

Internet Troll: A person or persons who starts flame wars or intentionally upsets people on the internet, done by posting inflammatory and digressive, extraneous, or off-topic messages in an online community, with the intent of provoking readers into displaying emotional responses and normalizing tangential discussions.

"Prudence, this trip had better be worth the aggravation I am forced to endure..."

Not that this was her fault, of course. In fact, the trip was quite uneventful, save for the usual uncouth riff-raff that deigns to accompany me. A long train ride to the lower village can be very adventurous, as I am quite unfamiliar with doing so after all of this time. But sadly, the brief moments of respite are commonly interrupted by the caterwauling of juveniles, carrying on about some online chicaneries that I dare not inquire about.

"Yo, I got to the mid-level floor with my Deeps, scoring mad damage before the Tank forgot to pull!"

"Ah, man, we coulda cleared that if the mage didn't run outta mana! Such an easy fight!"

These children speak a language that is familiar yet completely foreign to me. There is nothing to be gained from listening.

Or at least, I believed so until I heard one of the urchins mention a familiar name.

"Yo, you see what happened with Fenrir-Slayer, man? Admins are trying to boot him!"

"For what?" questioned urchin No. 2. "Not his fault he's so OP!"

"He's been trolling the boards trying to get guys to click some link. Admins say it's spam, but Slayer said it helps with Deeps and Strat. Called N.S.O. or something."

"You click it yet?"

"Probably later. Can't be that bad if it's helping the Slayer out, right?"

I pulled my notes from my side lapel to give a quick read of a letter sent by my niece, Prudence. In it, she mentions a friend named Bryan Kinny.

According to her letter, Bryan is a normal individual leading an everyday life. I suppose that's what we all believe is true in our lives, and for the most part, it is. But there are times, of course, when normalcy has to take a back seat to the unexpected.

Per my notes, Bryan leads a simple enough existence. At 24 years old, he makes a living taking customer service calls at home, working for a computer software company. In his spare time, he plays a popular online game, "Norse Kings and Conquests," as a character called the "Fenrir-Slayer." Now, that is a title I could not help but roll my eyes at, both his title and the name of this game.

Apparently, he is what is termed a "shut-in," preferring to order food from home rather than venture out to a restaurant and socialize. Any communication he has is through the online game or through voice chat applications. Well, that doesn't seem very fulfilling, I have to say.

Prudence makes mention of things I have no idea of what she is referring to. A level 100 Varangian, with high-level Aesir armor, equipped with the rare Gungir spear, obtainable in a 24-man raid, and both revered and feared in the player versus player zone known as Ragnarok.

Exactly what are they teaching these children in school nowadays?

It goes on to say that he had completed his fifth victory in a row in something called a "Battleground PvP." As per her notes, there are three classes in the game: the Aesir, the Vanir, and the Jotnar. Of the three, the Jotnar are considered the weakest due to the fact the class is composed of Dwarfs or Elves. While useful in other gameplay, they are commonly weak in a PVP setting.

A very banal description of Norse culture, I have to say. Plus, I've known many a dwarf and an elf that were quite strong, as well as very capable in battle. But I suppose I speak of times long past.

I arrived at her second-story apartment with a nice view of the city. Of course, that meant climbing stairs, which, at my age, I don't exactly look forward to anymore. But, I am not so broken down as to allow this trifling to best me!

...Although I suppose I should pace myself. For practical purposes, of course.

After completing the hazards of the incline, I make my way to her apartment door, where I give a slight knock with my forefingers.

"Uncle Bob!" greeted Prudence as she opened the door. She was wearing her college sweatshirt. A smart one, she is. Most likely, she takes after her mother.

"Prudence, it is wonderful to see you again," I stated, accepting her warm embrace. "I am somewhat surprised you called me so suddenly. Is there aught amiss?"

"Oh, no, I'm fine, Uncle Bob," replied Prudence. It's, well... "

"Hey, Prudy, I'm sorry to bother you, but," began a young man behind me before glancing in my direction. "Oh, snap, I didn't know you had company." His speech pattern belies an individual who does not rest for long periods of days, as he appeared disheveled, with dark circles under his eyes. Whether from staring at a screen for hours in a day or from a lack of sleep, who can say?

"Don't be silly, Bry! Come on in you two!" as she gestured over to the couch. Prudence was always a polite one, a credit to her parents for raising her properly. I noticed immediately that he stood a foot taller than her, with a bit of a gaunt frame, similar to a cartoon character I recall seeing, the one with a dog that solved mysteries or some such. "Bryan, this is my uncle..."

"Robert," I interjected as I rose to extend my hand to greet him. "Robert Aldurson. Very nice to meet you, Mr..."

"Oh, it's Bryan, " he responded as he accepted my hand in greeting. "Bryan Kinny. Sorry to interrupt your visit."

"Not at all, my boy!" I replied as I released his grip. *Strange, I surmised. There is an odd flow to his aura. It's as if it has been corrupted.*

As he sat, I couldn't help but notice his inability to sit still, as he was constantly fidgeting around, his knee practically bouncing off of the cushion. "You okay, Bryan?" asked Prudence.

"Sorry, you wouldn't happen to have another surge protector, would you?" Bryan asked, barely glancing at her. "I got a situation I'm trying to fix, and, well..."

"You don't want to blow up the building by plugging more cords into the wall," Prudence replied with a touch of melancholy. Clearly, this wasn't the first time he had requested this. "Let me check in the back and see what I got. Keep Uncle Bob company for me while I look, okay?"

"Um, okay," replied Bryan. He clearly wasn't enthused by the request, but I tried not to take it personally. He glanced over in my direction and took notice of the medallion I was wearing.

"Um, what's that symbol?" asked Bryan, breaking the silence between us.

"Oh, this?" I asked, clutching the sigil around my neck. "It's a symbol of protection. An old family heirloom passed down for generations."

"Oh," he responded, a touch of melancholy in his voice. "I thought it was some kind of code I saw."

"A code?" I asked, piquing my curious interest.

"Yeah, it looked like this symbol I keep running into online," His eyes opened up a bit as he told his tale. "See, I play this game online. It's called Norse Kings and Conquest..."

There was that title again, and I couldn't help but chuckle at the name. "I apologize," I quickly offered, composing myself. "Please, continue."

Unfazed, Bryan pressed on. "Um, yeah, so I've been getting harassed by this guy online. I mean, I guess it's a guy, I don't really know, but anyway, this guy, he did something to my avatar, I play as the Fenir-Slayer, have you seen my streams?"

"Streams?" I asked. "Do you have a garden or some such?"

"What?" He glanced at me as if I had asked the most incredulous question possible.

"Disregard what I asked," I countered, hoping to return to the point of conversation. "Please, continue."

"Yeah, so anyway, I fought this guy online, and he made me look like an idiot! I don't even know how he pulled off a move with a level-one weapon! He stole.." He stopped, realizing he might have been a bit too forward. "Um, sorry, I didn't mean to get like that."

"It is no concern, " I countered. "You said this, 'Guy,' as you stated, has been causing you distress?"

Bryan took a breath and then continued. "Yeah, um, so what happened, I was doing PVP, and I just got this weapon you win after you fight the big snake..."

"Jormungandr," I interjected.

Bryan looked confused. "Huh?"

I had to give a slight sigh before continuing. "You indicated it was a giant snake in a game based on Norse legend," I replied. "His name is Jormungandr."

"Oh, um, I guess," he responded, clearly not impressed. "So, anyway, I was getting ready to whoop up on that internet troll..."

"Internet... Troll?" I asked

"Um, yeah," He continued. "That's what we call people who like to mess with people online. And this one that keeps messing with me. He goes by Alviss. He went and hacked into the game and locked me out of my account!"

Aside from some of the terminology I was struggling to understand, I took a moment to ensure I heard the name correctly. "I'm sorry. You said his name is Alviss?"

"Um, yeah?"

"Apologies," I began. "It's just that I knew an Alviss. His name meant 'All-Wise' in the old Norse tales. Such an odd name for one causing all kinds of trouble for you."

Bryan looked stupefied. "Um, you kind of know a lot about Norse stuff, Mr. Adlurson."

"Well, I do consider myself a bit of an expert on the subject," I replied. "Tell me, are his attacks related strictly to the game alone?"

"It was," replied Bryan, "But then he started messaging me online, even when I'm at work." His hands clutched his head as if something were trying to escape. "I tried blocking him, but he keeps bypassing the block encryptions!" He looked up as if embarrassed by the sudden outburst.

"Yeah, so I'm putting in a new firewall to try to keep him out, but I ran out of outlets. That's why I was asking Prudy for another surge protector."

"Which I just found," interjected Prudence, re-entering the living room. "Sorry, didn't want to interrupt while you guys were talking."

She handed the device to Bryan as he stood up to accept it. "Thanks, Prudy. I owe ya. Sorry to take up your time. I'll get going now."

"A moment, Mr. Kinny," I started, standing up as well. "Perhaps I might be able to assist with your problem. Especially since the subject matter appears to be something I'm very familiar with."

Bryan nodded in agreement. "Um, okay, sure. I'm just across the hall. I'll see you in a bit then."

As he left the apartment, I glanced over to my niece. "Is this the reason you asked me to visit?" I asked her.

Prudence gave that mischievous smile of hers and shrugged her shoulders. "I figured you might be able to help him out. Especially since it might be involving a certain someone you and Dad kinda know." She grasped my hand and placed several familiar objects there. "Here, you'll probably need these for whatever's in there."

I truly love my niece, but clearly, she embraces her father's love of adventure. "Prudence Thorsdotter, what have you gotten me into this time?"

As I entered the dwelling, I couldn't help but wonder how a grown man could possibly live in an environment such as this. Pizza boxes stacked in a corner, some of which I believe still have half-eaten pizzas inside. Barely any furnishings, save for a couch, a television with a game console attached, and a desk in a corner, which you would be forgiven for missing, as it appears to be swallowed alive by computer monitors, consoles, and wires jutting out of every corner.

I believe this location was the inspiration for many science fiction movies, specifically the one about the fellow in the trenchcoat.

"So, I just need to download this app, and we should be all set," replied a voice from the computerized monstrosity, as Bryan Kinny was already typing away frantically on his keyboard. "I got this program that should purge the viruses out and get my game back online."

"I have to say, Mr. Kenny," I replied, approaching the desk ever so carefully, lest those tendrils attached to the desk were to become sentient and lash out at me. "This seems like a great deal of work simply to play a video game again. Why not just delete the entire program and start fresh?"

"And lose all of my gear and weapons?!" he remarked as if the concept was the most ludicrous statement ever uttered in existence. "What are you kidding me?! Naw, man. I spent way too many hours grinding to get that gear. I ain't losing out on that!"

As he continued to work, I carefully placed the objects Prudence provided for me in certain locations around the dwelling, careful not to arouse suspicion. As I approached the desk, I noticed on the screen the application he was using. The initials NSO were present on the folder icon. The icons were wrapped in the image of a serpent, and I immediately recognized the symbols. It glowed ominously, as if preparing to explode.

"Now, to finish the connection," Bryan said as the mouse icon hovered over the link.

"Wait, Mr. Kenny," I tried to warn, extending my hand out. "I advise exercising caution. That program does not appear very safe."

"It's cool, Mr. Aldurson, I got this," assured Bryan as he maneuvered the arrow over the icon and clicked "Enter" on his keyboard.

The folder changed form, appearing as the letter "O," but not in the Western text, as a tail is shown on the letter, much like in the orthography of the Old Norse language. I gasped as I suddenly realized where that symbol appeared. It is in the text spelling of Nidhogg.

"Mr. Kenny!" I exclaimed, grabbing his shoulder, "Move away from that screen, NOW!"

But it was too late. The cables surrounding the desk became sentient, rising, coiling around him, until the end appeared to form a snake head, preceding to bite his shoulder. Bryan yelled in pain, his eyes glowing as a flashlight, convulsing until settling down. I attempted to pull the cables off before getting knocked over by the snake's tail.

The cable snake then turned the body of Bryan to me, and spoke, but not in his words.

"Well, well," he said, sounding tonally different. "I wondered when you would show up to spoil my amusement!"

"I know you," I replied, slowly rising to my feet. "Mr. Kinny mentioned he encountered an 'Internet Troll.' Apparently, he did not believe he had encountered an actual troll. Now did he... Ondskap?"

Bryan cackled against his will. "Oh, he shows off the wisdom of Odin all too well! But then, the wisdom is somewhat hereditary for the son of Odin. Right... Baldur?"

I dust myself off as I stand upright. "I prefer Robert Alderson, thank you. This is not Asgard, after all." I look around to see that the cables start extending out of the apartment window in an attempt to reach other ports in the building complex. "Such a juvenile play here, Ondskap. Sneaking into a children's game and creating your own narrative? Did the Frost Giants chase you from Jotunheimr again?"

"Children's?!" Ondskap remarked, "Have you seen the language used in this world? Not exactly fitting for children, I would say. No, in fact, it was quite easy to come in contact with these fools who amuse themselves by masquerading as Aesir, Vanir, or even Jotunn! Their false bravado was quite easy to manipulate!"

"And so now," Ondskap continued. "I will have Nidhogg use this vessel to infect every one of these mortals who are fool enough to believe themselves above their station, until everyone on Midgard will help to bring forth Ragnarok again!!"

"Foolish troll," I growled as I clutched my rune pendant. "Did you really think I would allow this to happen?"

I chant the incantation of the Aesir. The objects I placed in several locations began to glow brightly until a circle formed around the desk. The runic symbols of the Old Norse glowed around the circle, ever brightly around the cable serpent known as Nidhogg. The snake released his bite and recoiled as Bryan fell to the ground.

"NO!!" Bryan cried in Ondskap's voice. "How is this possible?!"

"N. S. O," I began. "Nidhogg. Svafnir. Ofnir. All familiar names of the serpents of Asgard. Which in a game designed to emulate the theologies of Norse culture was not too difficult to decipher." I press forward while maintaining the seal. "You clearly were not very creative, Ondskap. Once Mr. Kinny mentioned to me that the person he encountered in the game was named Alviss, well, it was easy to figure out who was manipulating things. Your master still harbors that grudge against the All-Wise, I see."

Bryan's eyes start to flicker as Ondskap's control begins to fade. "This is not over, Shining Prince! The master will return! And soon, all of Midgard will fall before his might!! You will see...!"

The glow ceased as Bryan dropped to the ground, regaining his control. "Aw, man," he began, shaking his head. "What... what happened?"

I once again extended my hand to him. "It is quite alright, Mr. Kinny. I believe the ordeal is now over."

"The or-what now?" he asked, accepting my hand up before glancing over at his desk. "Aw, Man!! What happened to my desk?!"

Unfortunately, using the runes does involve expelling anything in the circle, which leaves a bit of a charred mess behind.

"It appears your 'surge protectors' were not very effective," I quickly offered, attempting to cover for something that could not be properly explained. "Luckily, your fire extinguisher was close by. Otherwise, you might have burned the entire complex down."

As Bryan ambled over to the now destroyed workstation, I took the opportunity to slowly make my way out of the apartment and back to Prudences' dwelling, where she greeted me with a cup of that delectable broth she calls "coffee."

"Nicely done, Uncle Bob," she responded with that warm smile of hers. "I guess Bryan shouldn't have to worry about any more problems with his game."

"True, although I do not believe he is in the celebrating moment at this time," I replied, as a faint wail could be heard behind me. "Furthermore, it appears thanks are in order for advising me to prepare the runic enchantment as well." I held up the letter she had written to me. "It was very effective in keeping Nidhogg contained."

Prudence procured several runes in her hand and beamed. "Well, you did teach me to anticipate the unexpected, after all!"

"Still," I surmised, glancing over to Bryan's apartment. "We're going to have to be on alert now. Ondskap's not smart enough to utilize the power of Nidhogg, Svafnir, or Ofnir. I have a feeling we're going to keep a close watch for his 'Master.'"

In a high-rise building used primarily for corporate interests, a man sits in a corporate chair overlooking the city. Three snakes slither to each side and climb over the shadowed figure. He strokes them as if they were common house cats and stares out into the city.

"Ah, Nidhogg, Svafnir, Ofnir. Welcome back. Yes, I see Ondskap failed at his task." He appears to focus on a specific building in particular. "Be sure to send that boy another console of the game, would you? A 'courtesy' for being such a valuable player in the gaming community."

The snakes retract out of sight and appear in front of his desk as three women, all hidden in the shadows, their eyes glowing with a sinister red hue.

"Of course, Lord Loki," the three women reply in unison.

"Now, now, we're in Midgard, after all," he corrected. "In this world, I am Edward Laufey, CEO of NSO Industries. Do try to remember that, won't you?"

"Of course, Mr. Laufey," replied the women in unison, disappearing into the darkness and leaving Loki alone with his thoughts.

"You stopped me this time, Son of Odin and Daughter of Thor," he sneered, his hand bending the handrest. "But there are so many more Trolls I can send out into the world I created. Mark my words... I will bring about the end of Asgard and Midgard."

Loki smiled with his devilish smile. "Ragnarok will come again. Of this, I promise!"

TALL, DARQ, AND DEADLY

by Jay T. Levy

"What'd ya say, Honey?"

I barely heard Jeff as the wind blew through my dark purple hair. Last week, it was green. Next week, who knows?

Salt-filled ocean air wafted on the breeze from the open car window. God, I love the summer and its aroma.

"I don't know why I crave night air," I repeated louder over the wind. Lights zoomed past as we zipped along Coastal Highway. "I like stars and shadows. They've always called to me, I guess."

"Cool." Jeff nodded and moved his hand through the wind outside his passenger window in a wave, passing over the empty outlet stores and parking lots. At this time of night, only the bars and pool halls were open. While fun, tonight wasn't about drinking and shooting pool. The funny thing was, Jeff couldn't go drinking with me even if he wanted, being only nineteen.

Seemed every year these guys kept getting younger.

Jeff was the arcade manager. Every summer, the employee changed. He looked good in his tight jeans and old-school band t-shirt and smelled great, even if it was the cheap, knock-off stuff. There was something about him I couldn't resist.

The hot weather brought so many strangers to the coastal beach towns and, with them, so many fleeting good times. Most of my summer boyfriends lasted weeks if that.

I pulled my boxy, used Kia into a little space for compact cars. It put us right at the entryway to the boardwalk and the beach behind the dunes.

I knew where tonight was going and had on my shortest Daisy Dukes for easy access. My hair was down my back, and my ponytail stopped at my ass—a part of me that got so much attention. Over the years, I've heard all the cat calls but stopped paying attention.

It was difficult, however, not to notice eyes at my chest. Just above my cleavage was one of my many tattoos, the Superman "S" shield, with 'Respect' in script underneath. The "S" was my personal shield, a reminder to be strong whenever I looked in the mirror.

I shifted the car to park and noticed Jeff's excited smile. I guess he knew where this was going, too.

"Right here, Honey?" He eagerly tugged at his belt buckle and zipper. "Right now?"

"No," I cooed in his ear. "It's late, but there's still a chance of being seen right here."

Disappointment flashed in his eyes.

"Look," I pointed out the window, "the boardwalk ends up ahead. We're going there. No one patrols this late. I've been around here long enough. I know what times work best."

A tattoo on my forearm caught my eye. 'Andy' with two dates—one for birth, the other for death. Andy was my son, who only lived three days. I was just another statistic—a teenage drug user with a baby a few days delayed from being stillborn. He never had a chance. I still can't believe I carried him to term. Sometimes, the hunger for a fix gnawed. And luckily, I've never gotten pregnant a second time.

Andy was ten years ago. Jesus, did I really piss away that much time? I'm twenty-seven now. Where did my time go?

When Jeff got out, he came over and took my hand like we were some kind of high school item. I laughed.

"What's up?" Jeff withdrew his hand. "What's funny?"

"Only you. It's cute. I don't get 'cute' from dates much anymore." I lied. They were all the same. I took his hand and entwined my fingers.

Jeff was in town with some friends, a lifeguard, and two waiters. The four had rented a house for the summer as a last hurrah before separating to different colleges. I hadn't known him longer than a week. But when

I saw him, I knew I had to have him. For days, we flirted—until finally, he admitted to having fantasies. It must have hit me at the right time, with me in the right mood since we found ourselves a few hours later at my favorite late-night spot.

We held hands, crossed the street, and headed to the empty boardwalk. We strolled along the boards and felt the wind from the ocean. The moon was bright overhead, seeming both romantic and dangerous. Jeff gripped my hand with a nervous tightness.

Like children, we removed our shoes—his big black boots, my flower-printed, hemp-rope sandals—and held them tight as we leaped over the side and landed on a sand dune. It may have only been a drop of six or seven feet, but it felt wonderful, the night air and that momentary sense of freefall. The sand felt gritty but soft between my toes as I stood in the moonlight and inhaled the saline air. I love the night.

We snuck under the boardwalk, where mottled shadows and moonbeams shone through the cracks and painted us like zebras. I lay back, wide-eyed, looking at him, and laughed at the confusion in his movements. It seemed Jeff didn't know where to begin.

"Am I your first?" I smirked.

"Yes," he whispered, but, in truth, he didn't need to respond. His face said it all.

I waited on him to make the first move, wanting to see what he came up with on his own. With his hormones, I'd be a fool to think he didn't fantasize about women. Would he be gentle, or would he pull some X-rated shit he saw in a movie? Touching me, his hands shook with a nervous jumble. He started at my foot, then worked his way toward my knee, my thigh. I couldn't help it; I uttered a soft moan.

Suddenly, a commotion echoed off the ocean's crashing waves.

"What was that?" Jeff stopped and rose to his feet. The effect took his hand away from my leg, and I didn't like that. "That noise—it sounded like a roar."

"It's just dogs playing," I whispered, annoyed. But I'd heard it, too. "It's stopped now. It's probably nothing."

I sighed. Jeff had somehow lost interest in me and looked around the beach. I sat up on my elbows and feigned indifference, not wanting to care. But the breeze caressed my shoulders and sent a sudden cool shiver down my spine.

The sounds started again. These weren't the playful noises of someone's pets at play. Suddenly, I heard feet running on the boardwalk overhead. It got closer and stopped right over our heads. The boards creaked, and someone leaped over the rail, landing in the sand. Jeff gasped and fell on his ass. I was already on my elbows but admired the stranger's style, landing gracefully like a cat. The man's black trench coat fluttered in the ocean breeze as he turned and looked right at us.

"They're getting closer." He looked both left and right.

The barking intensified.

His skin was pale like moonlight, and his long charcoal hair matched his coat, clothes, and boots. His jaw was a grimace of power, with an edge of nobility in his features. I heard danger in his voice and a sharpness that made my heart flutter.

The roar-bark continued, louder and closer.

"They're after me," he continued as if choosing each word to say. "You two should leave." He pointed away from the beach, and his long finger gleamed in the moonlight. "Be smart. Go now."

All his fingers were slender and long, like knives or thick ice picks. I couldn't tell if they were metal, or ice, or something else entirely.

"Who..." I stammered, both excited and nervous. "Who are you?"

"Marq." He eyed me looking at his fingers, and put his hands in his pockets. "With a Q."

When he moved away, I saw the dogs approach. Their black fur bristled, teeth were bared, and their ears were flat to their heads.

But these were no dogs. I may not have graduated, but I've seen enough National Geographic to recognize a wolf. Only, I've never seen one wearing a red bandanna around its neck and with a scar across its muzzle, which gave it a perpetual sneer.

The other wolf had an eye-patch. For real. An eye-patch.

With the breeze as strong as it was, I was sure my scent carried upwind to the pair. I hoped Marq would look our way again. Either way, I figured Jeff and I were going to become a part of this situation no matter what.

But the wolves never looked at Jeff or me. They flanked Marq and growled in their deadly circle around him. The way they moved—they'd done this before.

Marq kept his elbows close to his sides and spread his fingers wide. He looked stolid and unfazed. "Come at me."

The wolves circled, then jumped in unison.

Marq smiled and twirled, thrusting his arms outward, one hand per wolf. With the twirl of his jacket and his lithe movements, I wondered if he wasn't showing off. I would if I had knives instead of fingers.

But Marq failed and missed contact with both animals. Eyepatch grabbed his leg, and the other collided with his chest. He grunted as the wolf's jaw locked onto his shoulder and knocked him into the sand.

Eyepatch used the momentum of the fall to rip off a large chuck of flesh and spit it out. The hunk melted like ice in the sand, pooled into a puddle of inky shadow, and oozed below, leaving no trace.

Marq yelled a warrior's cry and stabbed the wolf locked onto his shoulder in the ribs. He dug his knife-like fingers into its side up to his third knuckle, and the wolf let go and howled, sounding more like a human's cry of pain than I'd expected.

Eyepatch grabbed Marq's leg again but caught him by his pant leg rather than flesh. Marq tried to kick the wolf's muzzle but missed and provided the wolf with an even better target. It latched onto Marq's ankle instead. Such tender skin, Marq's pain must have been excruciating.

I crawled forward, feeling sorry for this moon-skinned stranger. He was being attacked, and I wanted to help.

"What're you doing?" Jeff asked, his voice a horse, fearful murmur. "Are you crazy? Don't go out there; you'll be killed!" He grabbed my ankle and held it tight.

"Back off," I said, angry at his touch. He let go but did have a good point. What could I do? And why, suddenly, did I want to?

Marq un-sunk his buried fingers, pulled back, and slashed at the wolf again, raking it across the eyes. Blood splattered in wide arcs from his glowing yet blood-covered fingers. The wolf howled and fell off, hitting the sand face first. It shook and rubbed with its front paws. Normally, that'd be cute, but not with the blood and whimpers of pain.

Marq kicked at Eyepatch and hit the side of his jaw. The wolf growled but let go and circled, preparing for another attack. Marq got to his feet, clearly favoring one leg. He slashed, but the wolf dodged, then leaped at Marq's uninjured shoulder.

Marq stepped closer and threw off the wolf's aim. In the split-second confusion, he stabbed the wolf in the throat, closing its mouth and cutting off its battle snarls. Spinning gracefully, Marq unburied his fingers, dropped the corpse, and turned to the other beast.

The wolf with the sneer was blind and now nipped frantically, trying to find something to bite. Blood dripped down its snarling face and sprayed the surrounding, churned-up sand.

Marq spiraled and, with each turn, struck the wolf with his knife-like fingers. He stabbed it in the sides over and over again, switching his location to throw off the blind wolf. Quickly, it dropped and lay panting and bleeding.

Marq swiftly fell to one knee and drove his fingers into the beast's neck. Was this mercy? Or would it have been more merciful to stop and forgo the killing?

For several long moments, Marq remained still, silent on one knee, almost as if praying. He hung his head, breathed heavily, and cradled his injured shoulder and arm. Dark-hued blood dripped over his body, only to pool beneath and ooze into the sand, unlike the wolf's blood. It clumped next to their bodies in puddles as it oozed slowly from open wounds.

When Marq rose, his blood loss had stopped. He turned and, with no apparent difficulty, picked up each wolf corpse by the tail and dragged them across the sand. It looked humiliating—their paws sprawled to their sides, their mouths open and bleeding. Marq slid them over the sand like undignified sacks of spuds, and he didn't show the slightest grimace of discomfort or pain. It was like he didn't have any wounds, nor ripped or tattered cloth either.

Marq entered the water's edge until the waves crashed against his knees. He went slowly and carefully like the moving salt water gave him reason to pause. Marq showed more fear to the waves than with the two beasts who had attempted to eviscerate him. Imagine that. He spun and released one, then the other. They soared through the air without a sound and dropped into the water far enough away that I didn't hear the splash. Sticking his long-fingered hands in his pockets, he turned again to slowly stroll back towards the boardwalk. He passed the swarth of crimson-stained and disturbed sand and paid attention to none of it; he looked directly at us instead. Marq wrapped himself tight in his long trench coat and held his head low as if bundling against the chill ocean air.

"You should have left." Marq was close enough to see him clearly.

Jeff whimpered like a scared child.

"Shut up," I whispered to Jeff, but I dared not to take my eyes off Marq. I couldn't tell if his expression was apprehensive or amused.

"You shouldn't have seen." He smirked. "Now what?"

"You tell me, Mr. tall, dark, and deadly." I smiled.

"You're crazy," Jeff mumbled. He crouched in the sand and cradled his arms around his chest. He shook, and his teeth clattered. He was terrified.

Why wasn't I?

Marq approached us, and I could see his eyes more clearly. His were the most brilliant emerald green that I've ever seen. Then he smiled and winked. His grin spread unnaturally across his face like a rubber band yanked the corners of his mouth to his ears. His mouth was full of pointed teeth but still pieced together in a devilishly toothy grin.

Wide-eyed, I took a curious step forward. I had now left the safety of the sub-boardwalk and stepped into the clear moonbeams of the night.

This surprised Marq, for he dropped his own smile, narrowed his gorgeous eyes, and held up a single finger, pointing it directly at my "S" shield. He didn't touch me, but I dared not waver my eyes to the knife-like finger. I kept them on his face and his eyes.

My god. What was I doing?

"He'll kill you." Jeff again. Not a mumble, but I could barely hear him. The blood pumped in my veins and filled my ears.

"I don't know what you, or your lover, think you saw. But you best forget. If not, this will happen to you both." He removed the pointing finger from my chest and rammed it through the palm of his other hand. With a spray of black blood, he removed the finger and showed us the hole, even putting it up to his eye to peek through it.

Jeff screamed.

I wanted to scream so very much, but I didn't.

The wound in Marq's hand dripped, and again, the blood was absorbed within the sand. I watched the hole in his palm close as inky blackness swam from the shadows tucked around his jacket and filled the space. He used one finger to scrape off the excess in two quick motions and flung it to the ground like unwanted mortar. It vanished just like the blood.

Marq smiled again, his needle-like teeth gleaming in the night, and he turned to walk away. Jeff started to cry; I think he even pissed himself.

"He's not my lover." I looked at Jeff but spoke loudly, wanting Marq to hear. I turned from the crier and closed the distance with a trot. "You're leaving already?

Marq stopped and turned. "You followed me? You're unafraid?" He whispered, raised an eyebrow, and leaned in close. He sounded surprised more than anything.

"Why? Because of the hand thing?" I shifted my stance, hands on hips. "Not anymore. Yeah, it was scary as hell. But the moment it closed, I knew it didn't matter to you. It was just a scare tactic."

His stance went less ridged. I hoped that meant amusement, not anger or suspicion.

"What are you?" I asked.

"And give you another thing to forget about?" He smirked. "Not likely. You've seen enough. It was my mistake to let you watch." He took a few steps to be at my side. He was taller than me and looked down to meet my eyes. Shadows crept along his face and chiseled his moonlight-colored cheeks and nose.

"I've killed enough tonight," he said, regret tingeing his voice. "I don't want to kill again."

"At least I'd go out with more knowledge than I should." I tried to sound playful and coy to what was obviously a threat. I was afraid, sure, but I was in too far to back down. I may not make the best decisions, but I'm used to bouncing back after making wrong choices.

My world can't be going back to Jeff, and others like him.

"I live dangerously." Damn, that sounded lame. I followed it up with a hip twist and a cute smile. I was in rare form tonight. This man was clearly dangerous and yet oddly seductive.

Marq shrugged and grinned. It was slight and sharp, but I sensed no malice. Still, his features were a carving of moonlight ivory.

"By all means, live dangerously. But remember, you'd do well to forget." And with that, he turned into the breeze and walked away.

"Wait." I wasn't done, even if he was. I felt bold. "I have questions. Are you a vampire?" Excitement fueled my tongue.

His stony visage broke, and he smiled. It wasn't the one meant to frighten, but something playful. His eyes gleamed in the moonlight, and he laughed from his gut.

"My, aren't we persistent? No, my dear. I'm not a vampire, but I've been called far worse." His tongue moved about quickly over his pointed teeth. "Although I am a creature of the night..." He paused and stared at me with a sudden, introspective look. "You know my name," he said. "What's yours?"

"Honey," I lied. That was the name I gave to all the boys.

He half closed his eyes in a skeptical way and looked at me—through me, perhaps. "And I bet you're just as sweet, but that isn't the truth."

I never used my real name. If anyone came looking for Honey, I'd be in the clear.

"Fine." I felt ashamed at being caught in the lie. "It's Bethany." No one had questioned my fake name before. How did Marq know I was lying?

"Bethany." He let the name roll off his tongue as if saying it for the first time. "It's lovely. Named after the local beach town?"

"Yes... No... It's just...everyone asks that. Or, well, they used to, anyway."

"It has a classic feel. And, it's quite fitting.'" He turned again and walked away—a slow stroll that would take him right out of my life.

"What do you mean?" I followed. "You can't just say something like that and walk away."

"Bethany in Aramaic means house of figs." He nodded. "How fitting you chose 'Honey' as your moniker—something as sweet as the delicate fruit."

I nodded, listening to his melodic voice.

"And, let's not forget the biblical reference. Bethany is the site of Lazarus's resurrection." He smirked and raised an eyebrow. "But perhaps your name is merely coincidental to these things."

When I paused, he continued walking.

"Will I ever see you again?" I don't know why I kept after him. Curiosity, perhaps. If Marq was going to kill me, he'd have done it by now.

Without stopping, he replied, "I'll be here again in one week. Same time. Same spot. It'll be your choice, Honey. Just remember, in the end, it's best you both forget."

With that, he continued up the beach, and I returned to the quieted but utterly piss-soaked Jeff. Damnit, I'd driven us here, and neither of us had a change of clothes. Thankfully, I kept a blanket in the trunk for emergencies. Jeff's urine better not bleed through the Christmas-tree-colored fleece.

I helped the kid to his feet and walked him to the car. He sniffled once or twice but was otherwise silent. I'm sure he was embarrassed; I just didn't care.

I had other things spinning around my mind.

I arranged the blanket like Jeff was a dirty swimmer soaked in seawater and drove him home. The car ride was just as silent until I pulled over in front of his rented house.

"Are you going to see him again?" he asked, one foot already resting on the curb.

"Yes." I didn't even think about it.

"You're crazy." He slammed the door.

I shrugged and drove off. Bye, Jeff, have a nice life.

But as I passed the closed stores and dark houses, I wondered, was

I crazy? Marq was something out of this world, something completely different and strange. And yet, I was excited about seeing him again.

One week. I could wait a week.

I went home and slept the rest of that night and most of the next morning, too. Thankfully, my shift at the bar started at five, so no big deal. I had the time to run a few errands.

At the ATM, the guy in a pink golf shirt ahead of me had antlers. No joke—like the kind my uncle had hanging on his wall in upstate Pennsylvania. He turned to me, smiled, and nodded like nothing was out of the ordinary. He tipped his sunglasses, and I caught his eyes on my chest. He nodded ever so slightly and winked in that way I've come to recognize. That was normal, at least. Maybe, just maybe, the antlers were real. People did crazy stuff beyond tattoos.

On my shift that night, a few of the customers were...different. One guy had leaves for hair. I shit you not. I passed him a beer, and a little red leaf fell off his head. I waited for the two guys next to him to say something, acknowledge the leaf, anything. But nope. I ignored it until I scooped it into the trash.

I also served vodka shots to a pair of bearded biker-types in leather. Their eyes were jet black, and when they spoke, it was like an inky mist escaped their mouths. They joked about the long ride ahead, tipped well, and went on their way. Again, I just kept my mouth shut.

I called off the next few days. Someone had given me the flu, and no one wanted me sneezing into the drinks.

The reality was this was a bit much, even for me.

I couldn't get away from them all. They were anyone at any time. The guy who bagged your groceries. The mailman. The cop who just gave you a ticket.

Marq, what did you do to me?

Over the next few days, I ventured out. Did normal things but watched carefully. I really paid attention to who was around. The beach during the summer was a crowded place, and people from all over came here. I just never knew from how far.

After those initial few days, I hoped, prayed even, that Marq could explain.

When the week had passed, I made sure I was at the beach early. I wanted to sit and observe. Mainly, I needed to gather strength—and this time, oddly enough, without the aid of whiskey or rum.

I sat in my car on the street at the end of the boardwalk—the same spot where I'd parked with Jeff one week ago.

Marq had said it was my choice. Truth was, I had no choice. Things were different now.

I zipped up my favorite black hoodie and settled in to watch the sunset. At least the car seat was comfortable. The breeze started, and with the windows down, the air was already starting to cool. It would be a few hours before Marq would show. Theoretically, no one would disturb me.

There was a rumble in the lot trash can behind me, and in the side-view mirror, I saw a vagrant rummaging through it. I recognized him—Charly. The rat's-nest of brown hair and the ratty, orange backpack were a dead giveaway. Only this time, instead of the pack, there was a twisted shell protruding from his back, and his normally gloved hands were instead the bulbous dactyls of crab claws. He picked through the garbage and held the wrappers and fountain soda cups to his mouth, where a smaller set of claws picked at the scraps and slid morsels onto his tongue.

I'd never seen that before, even though I'd given Charly food many times. I admit, he wasn't all there mentally, but he was harmless. I simply had no idea he was also a crab.

He scoured for a few minutes, then scuttled off. He didn't notice me watching, or he didn't care. I wasn't bothering him. Why should he bother me?

Charly left the parking lot and moved towards the beach, eventually disappearing behind the sand dunes.

Strange, the things you never noticed. I waited and pondered. I've always been drawn to shadows and stars. Was Marq something of shadow and moonlight?

I was anxious for the hour to arrive. I was done with the boys of summer. That life was over. Marq opened my eyes to something more. There was no returning now.

A NIGHT AT THE FOUR WINDS
by Brian D. Gibson

"It was just after midnight when the vampire walked into my club.

Alright, maybe that was a little dramatic. After all, I'm a vampire, too, so it's not like it's all that unusual to see one in the Four Winds Bar, just not one as low-rent as Angelica.

Now don't get the idea that the place is incredibly up-scale. As a crossroads for the supernatural beasties of Philadelphia (at least, those able to pass as human), the club gets all kinds. From street-level werewolf thugs to obscenely rich wizards, from criminals looking to avail themselves of special skills they might not fully understand to society kids flirting with dangers they *definitely* don't understand, the Four Winds is a real melting pot.

But even in the kind of menagerie that frequents my establishment, Angelica was an anomaly. Rumor had it she slept her days hidden somewhere in the maze of tunnels that serviced the abandoned underground concourse south of the Convention Center. She preyed on the homeless population that sheltered there. She certainly dressed to fit in with that crowd. Her jeans were filthy and threadbare and hanging off her, at least a size or more too large. The sole of her right shoe was separating from the fabric, and the stains on her footwear were more than a little suspect. The hoodie that cast her eyes in impenetrable shadow was equally disreputable, the pale skin of her left elbow visible through a rent in the stained fabric. Altogether, she didn't look like someone who'd be eagerly welcomed into any nightclub, regardless of where they sat in the respectability spectrum.

I watched her cross the dimly lit VIP floor to the bar, where she leaned across and snapped her fingers impatiently to get the bartender's attention. Carrie finished up with the young wizard at the end of the bar – a regular who only goes by Valentine – and walked over to the vampire. Ordinarily, she'd lean in towards a customer to be sure she heard them over the music thumping from the lower level, but in Angelica's case, she stood with her back against the old fashioned map of the city that papered the wall behind the bar (we don't go in for mirrors at the Four Winds, for obvious reasons). I don't know if it's because Angelica was more unsettling than the run-of-the-mill vampire or fear that a touch from her would visibly soil the pristine white of the nurse's uniform that Carrie wore when tending bar. Angelica leaned towards her.

Any hopes I had that this would have nothing to do with me were dashed when, a moment later, Carrie pointed a finger in my direction.

I must have groaned because the club kid pressed up against me in my darkened corner booth (damned if I can remember his name, or damned, regardless, depending on your perspective), cut off whatever mindless patter he'd been trying to impress me with to say "Hey, babe, what's wrong?"

I turned my gaze down to him and smiled, exerting a little of the mental pressure that had captured his attention earlier in the evening. To him, for as long as I wished it, I would be his dearest fascination, and he would be quite amenable to trying to please me. Later, he would be donating a bit of his own life to prolong mine.

"I need a few minutes. Why don't you tell Miss Carrie Nurse I told her to give you something on the house? I'll catch up with you when I'm done." I held his eyes captured with my own as he gave a dreamy smile and nodded. "I promise to make it worth the wait."

He squeezed my leg and slipped out of the booth, his smile faltering when he suddenly noticed Angelica nearly on top of us. She stopped at the edge of my table, her hands thrust into the front pocket of her hoodie and frowned at my companion as he tried to squeeze past without accidentally brushing against her.

I couldn't blame him; even I found her a little unnerving.

She watched him silently until he was well out of earshot before swiveling her head back to me. With the club's dim lighting deepening the shadows beneath her hood, her eyes were all but invisible. I looked where I figured them to be and assumed we were making eye contact.

"I need to find a wizard."

"Just straight to it, huh?" I smiled broadly at her, leaning back and spreading my arms across the back of the booth. "No 'Hi, Randall, how ya been?'"

"Hi, Randall. How about you kiss my ass?"

"Well, aren't you the picture of refinement?" I replied. She screwed up her lips in a frown, but before she could retort, I leaned forward and dropped my voice to a near growl. "You shouldn't come asking for favors if you can't even pretend to be polite about it. Pluto won't like it at all if I have to ban you from the Four Winds for your mouth." Pluto is the vampire who turned Angelica, her Sire, an old and powerful creature living beneath the city for longer than I'd been undead. He rarely comes above ground these nights, and most vamps in Philly know he uses Angelica as his eyes on the surface.

I could feel, more than see, her eyes roll, but Angelica managed to squeeze her next words out - between gritted teeth and bared fangs - in a slightly more conciliatory tone. She may not be the brightest of the undead, but she's not entirely unteachable.

"Look, I need to find a wizard. I'll owe you a favor."

A few minutes later, Angelica was safely ensconced in my booth with Valentine, the curtain pulled closed and a white noise generator helping to ensure their privacy. I wasn't even recording them or anything.

Instead, I was standing at the railing of the VIP section, looking out over the club's main floor. I had asked my companion (Dennis? Kevin? Something like that? Hey, don't try to tell me you remember every meal you've ever had) to join me in my office with a fresh round of drinks. In the meantime, I wanted to take a quick look at how my little domain was faring that evening.

On the dance floor below, bodies writhed and jumped in time with the sounds emanating from the speakers. These were provided by my childe, Lehland, who insisted they qualified as music. He was busily keying up and mixing selections at the DJ booth that occupied the small stage at the room's far end. The bar, to my right, was a larger version of the one upstairs. Behind it, Suzy Dear and Velveteen plied their trade, doling out a steady stream of the alcohol that fueled the activities on the dance floor (and helped to obfuscate the activities in the shadows). Suzy, like Carrie, had her youth and vitality extended by regular infusions of my blood, which had the additional benefit of ensuring their deepest devotion. Velveteen, being of fae extraction, was sustained by the emotional energies of the revelers.

Above the dancers, the ceiling was a reproduction of the night sky, pinpoints of light on a black background imitating the spill of the Milky Way with the constellation Sirius picked out extra bright. A bank of windows, small and tinted dark to make it nearly impossible to make out the interior from outside, looked out onto Christopher Columbus Avenue and the Philadelphia riverfront through wrought iron bars.

The VIP section overlooking it all is restricted solely to the supernatural denizens of the city and their guests. It has its own private entrance at the back of the building, but a set of spiral stairs grant access to the public floor. Both the rear entrance and the stairs are guarded at all times.

That night, guard duty was being handled by Chip. That's the only name he's ever given me; it's not his real one, and I have no idea why he chose it. Maybe he wanted something to take the edge off the intimidating aura that followed him everywhere. At six foot seven, Chip was a large man covered with slabs of muscle and ropes of scar tissue that he dressed to display. But the aura was more than just his appearance. There was a wildness about him, an intensity of gaze, and a predatory way of moving through the world that screamed danger to anyone with the wit to notice.

As I looked down from the railing, I noticed a knot of four men who lacked that wit making their way toward him through the crowd.

With the club being so dark and what lighting there was constantly shifting, it's unlikely that a mortal man might have seen the swastika tattooed on the leader's neck from where I was standing. But I did.

I long ago lost the habit of sighing, even when exasperated (at least, when I'm not playacting at being alive), but rolling my eyes has stuck with me. I started to descend the stairs.

By the time I reached the bottom, the men were confronting Chip, where he stood fully athwart the stairs with his arms crossed in front of his chest.

"Sign says VIPs only," Chip was saying, his voice a deep rumble that could nearly be felt in the chest and heard in the ears.

"Well, hell, we're VIPs!" the leader of the men replied, looking up at the bouncer with a smirk. His eyes flickered toward me as I approached Chip from behind, but my arrival only seemed to broaden his grin. "Ain't a mongrel among us!" That set the chuckleheads in his wake to laughing. Really, except for minor differences in height and build, it'd be hard to tell them apart. White skin, blonde hair buzzed close on the sides and longer on top, plenty of tattoos on what little skin was visible, black jackets with jeans and work boots – might as well have been a uniform.

I could sense Chip stiffen slightly at the taunt. He's a pretty thorough mix of ethnicities, and these idiots were trying to use that to get under his skin. But he held his position and didn't rise to the bait since most of what he's paid for is to keep the peace. He keeps questions to a minimum, and, of course, he has his secrets to keep.

"Got me there," he rumbled. "Lookin' at nothin' but purebred poodle." Alright, maybe he rose to the bait just a little.

The laughter stopped.

These guys were looking for trouble, and the feigned humor had been nothing but a façade, to begin with. That and a bit of swagger to help work themselves up to said trouble.

"Listen up, half-breed," the leader stepped toward Chip and thrust a finger into his chest. It was almost funny how far he had to crane his head back to maintain eye contact with the bouncer, and I couldn't tell how much I should admire his courage or disdain his stupidity. But the three near clones backing him up may have accounted for both. "You let your betters by, or you can end your shift in a body cast."

Chip didn't move a muscle. "You pups are pretty damn funny, but I don't think I can laugh *that* hard."

I decided to intervene.

"Gentlemen!" I edged forward off the stairs to stand beside Chip, pouring a bit of the same supernatural energy into my words that I'd used to captivate my date. "I'm Roland Forester, the owner of the Four Winds. I do hope my employee here hasn't put you off our fine establishment. Why don't you join me upstairs for some drinks on the house to make up for any inconvenience."

It was hard to maintain an ingratiating smile in the face of the stupid looks they turned my way. But dead muscle kept the rictus grin on my face as their dull-eyed expressions returned to the swaggering grins they'd been affecting when they muscled up to Chip in the first place. The idiots thought they were getting their way as Chip and I stepped aside to clear their path up the stairs. In response to the bouncer's questioning frown, I tilted my head in the direction of the stairs to indicate he should follow us.

Of course, I intended to get them quietly out of public view without creating a scene. The following day would find them a few memories and a few pints, short. They would also be miles away and strongly inclined never to return. Why does nothing ever turn out as it should?

You see, the mistake I made was letting them go up first.

They must've reached the top just as Angelica and Valentine came out of their booth. From up ahead, I heard one of them exclaim, "You call these VIPs? A bag lady and her soyboy?!"

They surged ahead, and by the time I'd cleared the stairs, they surrounded the vampire and the wizard, shoving them back and forth between them. Angelica kept her head down, keeping her eyes hidden away in the deep shadow of her hood. The thug brigade must've taken that for meekness because they kept getting more aggressive. Valentine did his best to force his way between her and the leader. He seemed to be trying to cool the situation off.

"Hey, baby, why don't ya let some real men buy you a drink?" the leader leered over Valentine's shoulder as the wizard interposed himself.

"Why don't you boys cool it, and we'll be on our way."

"Oh ho! Got ourselves a white knight here, boys!" Valentine had, at least, succeeded in drawing their attention, and one of them shoved him from behind so that he stumbled into the leader's chest. That unworthy seized Valentine's shirt in both fists. "Don't get aggressive with me, cuck. I'll pound you bloody."

"Lay off," Angelica all but snarled. "I'm still using that guy." This drew a burst of guffaws from the ruffians, and their captain shoved Valentine backward so that he fell back into the booth. That was when I decided that I no longer cared about the gentle approach.

Angelica turned her hooded head toward me, the corners of her mouth turned down in a scowl. "Really, Roland? You're gonna let this shit go on in your club?" I shrugged my shoulders and spread my hands to my sides while offering my best ingratiating smile.

"Do with them as you like. Just try not to break the furniture."

The men laughed, evidently thinking this was quite the joke. I was conscious of Valentine trying to extricate himself from the booth and getting shoved back by one of the thugs. Of more interest was the fact that the leader of the group chose this moment to snatch Angelica's hood back and reveal her face for the first time since she'd come in. "Let's see that..."

I'm not sure how he planned to finish that sentence since the face that was revealed stopped the words in his throat. I think I've already noted the paleness of her skin, and I was in no way surprised that the dirty-blonde hair was dirty. Filthy, even. But her eyes were what really grabbed attention. They were red-rimmed, burning in the depths of hollow sockets and surrounded by a dark webwork of prominent veins that spread in fine threads over her cheeks and tangled more densely the closer they got to her eyes. Without her eyes hidden, she looked an awful lot like the dead thing she truly was.

Her lips pulled back in a fierce grin, revealing a surprisingly healthy-looking set of teeth. Her upper incisors slid down as we watched, elongating into prominent and very sharp fangs.

Angelica was barely pushing five-foot-four and slightly built, whereas the leader of her harassers must've been at least a six-foot slab of beef, but at that moment, he was the one who flinched back.

One of the guys had been balling up a fist to go into the booth after Valentine and hadn't noticed the sudden end to the laughter. He was entirely caught by surprise when Angelica seized said fist in one hand and squeezed. I heard bones snap, and the man let out a scream of pain.

And then she leaped straight for the leader's throat, leaving the man clutching his mangled hand behind her.

You know those movies where the sexy vampire bites seductively into their beautiful victim's neck, drawing a gasp of pleasure as they collapse into near-coital bliss? This was not that.

Angelica launched herself in the air, grasping the man's head between her hands and clamping her legs tightly around his waist. In the blink of an eye, she'd wrenched his head to one side and buried her fangs in his neck. Blood spurted from the corners of her mouth, and he screamed.

I'll credit him with having a manly, deep-throated scream. From our brief acquaintance, I'm sure he'd have been proud to know that.

For a moment, his companions gaped at the violent scene in shock. But when the wordless scream was replaced with bellows of "Get her off! Get her off! Get this bitch off of me!" they were finally broken out of their paralysis.

One fellow, who'd been keeping Valentine penned in the booth, turned his back on the wizard and pulled a switchblade out of the pocket of his jacket. I would have to have a conversation with Chip about that – his bouncers should never have let that into the club. The other guy grabbed Angelica by the shoulders and tried to yank her off of his friend but succeeded only in pulling the struggling pair into an awkward, lurching dance around the VIP room floor.

The smell of blood in the air reminded me that I'd been about to eat before all this started up. Hunger welled up, a near physical impulse to throw myself into the mix, sink my fangs into whatever blood vessel presented itself, and feast.

I was already stepping toward the fray when a blast of light shocked me back to myself. A glowing ball of force had flown out of Valentine's booth, knocking the knife-wielding thug sprawling onto his face and sending the knife skittering across the floor to fetch up against Chip's booted foot. Its owner scrambled after the weapon, but his reach to snatch it up was interrupted when Chip stepped on the knife. The ruffian turned his head up, and his threatening scowl turned into a gape-mouthed stare. His face blanched white with terror.

"Why," you might ask when the group hadn't seemed all that scared of Chip earlier? Well, things had changed. Specifically, Chip had changed.

He was now about half a foot taller and even more heavily muscled than before. The hair on his arms and head had grown longer and coarser, though still interrupted by crisscrossing scars, and had spread over his cheeks. His features were sharper, faintly hinting at the merest suggestion of a muzzle. Beneath eyes that had taken on a faintly yellow tinge, his lips were pulled back in a feral smile, revealing that his upper and lower canines had grown longer and now came to distinct points. He growled as he stooped to reach toward the man on the floor at his feet, and suddenly a less appetizing odor was tainting the air.

Meanwhile, Angelica's dance partner had dropped to his knees. He had stopped yelling, now entirely focused on trying to push her off. But his struggles were in vain, blood loss weakening him even as it fed his attacker and made her stronger. She gulped his life from the wound in his neck in deep draughts, ignoring his companion's attempts to yank her away.

Valentine emerged from the booth, a steel rod engraved with strange runes whose shapes seemed to slip from my memory even as I saw them grasped in his right hand. He looked with alarm between the struggling mass on the floor and where Chip was hauling the man who'd soiled himself to his feet. His eyes focused back on Angelica and her partners, and I saw a look of determination set in as he started to step towards them. I've spoken with him enough to know that he was probably about to do something naïve and stupid (he'd probably call it "noble," or maybe just "right") to try and save someone's life.

In the blink of a mortal's eye, I put myself between him and the brawl, my hand placed firmly on his chest. "Don't"

He startled back at what must have seemed to him like me materializing in front of him, but he regained himself quickly. "She's going to kill him!"

"Didn't you notice? They're goddamned Nazis. Or at least wannabes, so why should you care?" I heard a meaty thud behind me, and Valentine's eyes flickered past me in the direction of Chip and his victim. The violence that way mustn't have been too awful since it didn't change his focus. He tried to push through me towards Angelica; when he found he couldn't budge me, he raised the metal rod as if to strike me instead.

"Do that, and every wizard in the city will be barred from the premises. You want that on your head?" At first, I wasn't certain he wouldn't go ahead and strike me, and I briefly considered seizing his will with my own. But, even though he was pretty inexperienced, wizards tend to be tougher to pull that on than run-of-the-mill mortals. What's worse, they can be ridiculously adept at sensing the attempts. Part of the agreement at the Four Winds is that we don't use our powers on each other, and I was not going to be the first to break my own rules.

Fortunately, sense broke through, and he lowered the rod. He looked past me to where gulping sounds and sobs came from the direction of the scuffle and then back. "Please, Roland." His voice was almost plaintive.

I rolled my eyes and feigned a sigh for his benefit. It wouldn't hurt to keep in the wizard's good graces when all it cost me was going back to the original plan.

"Alright, I'll see what I can do."

It was a few hours later when I finally reentered my office. My erstwhile companion from the beginning of the evening had been sent home untasted (a pity; he'd imbibed just enough substances in the course of my seduction that I'd been looking forward to the pleasant buzz that drinking his blood would have brought). He'd been carefully managed to avoid letting him witness any unpleasantness. I was sure he'd be back on another night so that it would be a pleasure delayed rather than aborted.

The leader of the little pack of white power assholes was lying on the couch, focusing on me with bleary eyes set in a deathly pale face.

His tattoos stood out starkly against the whiteness of his skin. There was no sign of the wound he'd suffered when Angelica bit into his neck. His hands and wrists were cuffed, and a rag from behind the bar shoved into his mouth prevented anything more than weak and muffled grunts from passing his lips.

His companions had been rendered unconscious, their memories altered to ensure that they wouldn't trace their troubles back to the Four Winds or recall any of what they had seen here. The terror I'd left intact as an incentive not to return. Sparing them had mollified Valentine enough to prevent a real incident. Their leader, however...

I crossed the office floor and lowered myself to the edge of the couch next to him. He rolled his eyes toward me, trembling with reaction and fear.

"You," I purred, leaning down and cupping a hand behind his head, "have been an inconvenience. You interrupted my meal and the cleanup." I shook my head and gripped his more tightly as I leaned down until I was just about whispering in his ear. "I wasn't planning to kill him. But sometimes accidents happen. So, who knows? Maybe you saved a life more worthwhile than your own tonight."

And then I bit, and he whimpered softly at the pleasure and the pain of it. The blood flow from his neck was sluggish – Angie had taken quite a bit already - but the taste was full and rich, and there would be enough to sustain me into another night.

WILD SYNERGY

by Nicholas Leamy

As the alarm echoed through his skull, Henry slowly opened his eyes. As he reached to deal with it, the voices started their daily back and forth.

Time to start another magical day!

For fucks sake. Turn that shit off! It's downright cruel to expect anyone to wake up this early for any reason.

Now, while I might enjoy a small snooze, this is a work day. We can't be late again.

We hate that job. What do we care if we get fired?

"For the millionth time, this debate is pointless! Once you two start bickering like this, it's done. I'm up. Period. Now, give me some peace and quiet while I get ready."

Thus began Henry's morning, just as it had every day since the collision. The moment just after waking was the one part of his day he always looked forward to—sweet, blessed silence. As long as he kept to his normal routines, the voices stayed quiet. Breakfast could be cereal or pancakes. Never eggs, ever since the great hot sauce debate of last year. News on the television in the morning was okay, but it had to be music during the car ride. As for clothes... clothes could be tricky.

A tie! Why the hell do we need a tie today?

Don't you remember? Today is the day we are meeting up with Henry's mother for lunch.

Oh shit, no! No, no, no! We need less of her in our lives, not more of it. I refuse to let you do this!

"We have been over this countless times. This is better for all of us. Family is an important part of everyone's life, even for me, and my mother should have a place in mine. Besides, I promised you beer afterward. You like beer, remember?""

I do like beer, but that can't be your answer to everything! Especially when your mother is guaranteed to sour every drop. Sounds more like a whiskey night to me.

Do we have to remind you, Shay, that anytime you have whiskey, you become a terrible hassle?

Keep your damned mouth out of this, Dorielle!

"Both of you cut it out! I'm seeing my mother this afternoon, and nothing either of you can say will change that. That being said… I apologize for this."

Henry reached into his dresser and pulled out his tie pin and began fastening it in place.

What the fuck are you thinking!?

That is quite distasteful, Henry! Please!

"It was given to me by my Mom, and she'll expect me to be wearing it. It'll be under my vest until we see her, and no one else will even know it's there."

We'll know, you prick.

With that last derision, Shay and Dorielle settled down. Henry finished getting ready for work. He had learned a long time ago that his commute could be mitigated by taking the longer but more consistent routes. As long as he was on time, Dorielle would be pleased. As long as they didn't hit traffic or construction, Shay would not try to argue the merits of keeping a weapon in the car.

Arriving at work, Henry avoided the large crowds and larger people. He gave Maurice the Minotaur a wide birth as he headed towards the front entrance. Dorielle would be nervous, and Shay had a tendency to over-confidently push for "measuring contests." While he could not avoid triggers 100% of the time, Henry was doing his best to find a way to live with his condition. Not everyone was so lucky.

"Good morning, Grace."

Grace looked up at Henry with the biggest smile he'd ever seen on a living face. Her eyes literally glittered with their own inner light. Wrapped around her ears were a pair of bags that bloomed as she replied, "Such a joy to see you today, Henry! I hope it is a bright and cheerful workday for you!!!"

Most people did not actively engage with Grace since her ears erupted with glitter every time she had a chance to gush about the glories of life, beauty, and love. Henry couldn't imagine letting someone live a life that lonely just to minimize their own discomfort. He was also very sympathetic to her situation. He couldn't imagine living his life with two Dorielles in his head. Life was saccharine enough with the one.

Entering his workspace, Henry could see the diversity program was working as intended. His company had taken in several elves, a fair number of dwarves, a handful of minotaurs, and there was one rock creature in the break room that Henry was unfamiliar with, but it made the best coffee he had ever had in his life.

No one knew the precise cause of what was colloquially referred to as "The Great Collision." Through some poor illustrations, descriptions from authorities, word of mouth, and pure guesswork, the common understanding was that a world or dimension of fantastical races collided with ours, and a number of them were violently displaced. A less understanding subset of humanity assumed that since only members of the other universe were displaced and not vice versa, they had somehow rammed into us on purpose and should be held accountable. Henry personally found social media to be a hellscape of the uninformed. He high-fived a seven-foot-tall elf named Rolim as he approached his desk.

Sitting down, Henry logged in and began working. After almost a year as an accountant with the firm, he was already bored with the job, though he felt he did an exceptional job at it, except for an unfortunate incident or two that shadowed his record. To make up for those outbursts, he worked twice as hard to show he was worth it, not that they could have fired him for them anyway.

Opening his email, Henry saw a large Excel file attachment and a message from his manager, "Henry. I need you to rerun the Jacoby numbers again with these inclusions. They forgot to attach them with their last batch of submissions. I need it on my desk no later than first thing tomorrow morning."

I know what this means.

Henry put his hands over his ears, lowered his head, and began his slow breathing exercises. He could sense an incident brewing, and while he wasn't sure if his breathing helped, he felt obligated to try anything and everything.

In the calmest and most soothing voice he could muster, Henry began whispering to himself, "Shay, you are jumping to conclusions. We don't know how bad this is going..."

I think we can all agree on the following. We have to see the racist twisted sack of flesh you call a mother for lunch, come back to work, and then be stuck here ALL DAMNED NIGHT! No whiskey! Not even beer. Your shittwat of a manager has FUCKED ME!

Can you please keep it down with the profanity? Every time you open your mouth, my ears sting and ache.

"Dorielle, please stay out of this; I can handle it."

Always sticking that holier than thou schnoz into my business. This is going to be your fault. Every time I miss out on a chance to drink, it's because you've convinced this pushover to work late again.

How dare you! All I have ever done is make suggestions for the betterment of our situation. Just because you can't see past the top of your beer glass doesn't mean you get to insult me.

Henry could see what was coming and realized he couldn't stop it. If it had been only one or the other obstacle, he could have de-escalated the situation, but working late and seeing his mother was too much. He stood to leave, silently praying that he still had time.

In a deeply sarcastic tone, Shay replied, **Oh boo hoo hoo. Woe is me. I'm the only one who cares about us. Damn it! We deserve to have a good time too, you know, you miserable excuse for a Tinkerbell!**

"... Say it again. I dare you. Call me that one more time."

With his blood pressure building, his heart pounding, and the doorknob to the hallway only ten feet away, Henry again prayed that maybe just this once, Shay could...

Tinkerbell!!! You pouting, everything is roses, pain in my ass. Your warrior wings are wasted on you.

THAT DOES IT!

With the doorknob only a foot away, the pain that ripped through Henry's head stopped him dead in his tracks. Two tiny little hands slowly pushed their way out of his right ear and started pulling the ear canal open. Henry fell to his knees and channeled his pain into a silent cry, with his eyes slammed shut and his hands violently shaking beside his head.

Ignorant of his pain, Dorielle pulled herself out of his head, her armor roughly scratching Henry on his way out. Exiting, her wings fully expanded, and she flew up to look at Henry, shouting, *"Come out here and say that to my face if you have the balls!"*

Hovering just under six inches tall, Dorielle was resplendent in her full plate armor, with long blonde hair flowing in the non-existent breeze. She drew her longsword and took a battle stance. From three desks over, George looked up and saw what was beginning. He cried, "Shit! Not again!" and then ran to the manager's office.

Two more long-nailed hands protruded from Henry's left ear, exiting in much the same way, except instead of armor, it was the metal studs on his leather jacket that played havoc with his delicate skin. Shay quickly climbed up on top of Henry's head, standing there at equal height to Dorielle in full biker leathers, black sunglasses, a black mohawk, and a goatee. He pulled his hammer from his belt and said, **"What I said was, it's a shame to see one who was appointed to her queen's royal guard reduced to some office jockeying TINKERBELL with no understanding of how to truly live!"**

Screaming a battle cry, Dorielle flew in with her sword raised high, ready to cleave Shay in twain. Unfortunately, Shay's taunts had riled her up enough that she was not prepared to dodge his hammer swing. Swinging from below, he caught Dorielle in her gut, flinging her across the room.

She first hit a laptop, sending it crashing to the floor, and then slid into the filing cabinets. Everyone in the office began to scatter to avoid the tussle.

With fantastical speed, Shay lept from desk to desk, spraying office supplies in his wake. He leaped up onto the filing cabinets and squished down between them and the wall. Wedged against the wall, his back started to push the cabinet out and down onto Dorielle. His pain subsided, Henry turned and looked on in defeated agony at the chaos he couldn't avoid.

Dorielle quickly rolled to avoid the crashing cabinet and snuck along its side toward the wall. Shay leaped up onto the fallen cabinet with a triumphant shout of glee, screaming, "**FINALLY!!! I'm finally free of you, you weak...**" But he never finished the sentence. Dorielle came up from behind and slammed the butt of her sword into the back of his head. Shay tumbled under the desks, tripping a coworker named Rachel and sending her sprawling to the floor. Dorielle stood proudly, looking down at Shay. Shay shook his head, turned around, and stood up to look at Dorielle. Both screamed at each other, picked up the closest desk to them by the leg, and began running at each other when the door to the Manager's office burst open. "WHAT THE HELL IS GOING ON OUT HERE?!?!"

Both combatants stopped in their tracks, looking at the manager with the kind of face only a small child caught with their hand in the cookie jar can give. They both dropped their desks, ran to Henry, and leaped back into his head. Henry fell backward and lay there. "I can't believe you did this again!"

Henry's talk with his manager was short and to the point. He knew he was in trouble the moment he heard them using the calm, quiet, and understanding voice. His time had come. He collected his things in a box and walked to the HR office.

Entering the room, his eyes were immediately transfixed by Argora. She had a way of entrancing anyone who looked her way. She was turned away from him, searching a filing cabinet. His eyes admired her wavy brown hair and traced the line of her neck to her blue dress, following the curve of the dress down around her ample behind to the slit where her thigh poked out. Down her legs, where her brown fur perfectly accented her reversed knee and hoof.

After the great collision, many fantastical creatures were left alone in a foreign world with no way to cope or survive. The government decided that they should be treated as refugees and integrated into society as smoothly as possible. As such, each fantasy creature was put through a series of tests to see what jobs they were best suited for, and then a government agency took those results and worked hard to make sure everyone was appointed to a position that gave them the best chance of success in this new world.

No one was more shocked than Argora when her results came back as HR representative. To her credit, she was the best rep Henry had ever worked with. Her skills were second to none. She always managed to resolve things quickly and in a way that somehow made both the company and the workers happy. It was impressive, even if you could always see her holding back a few of her more ingrained instincts.

She turned around, walking to her desk while holding up a file. "Found you. Come on in, Henry. Have a seat."

Henry came in and turned around, bending over to grab the chair to pull it a bit closer to the desk. He knew he had messed up a half second before he heard the sound of wood being gouged. He quickly spun around and sat. "I'm so sorry. I didn't mean to do that."

Argora sat there, her head lowered and her eyes staring fire into Henry. Her nails were resting at the end of four long, deep grooves in the wood of her desk. Good at her job or not, it was well known to be bad manners to bend over, i.e., enter a presenting position, in front of any satyr unless you meant it as an invitation. Argora closed her eyes, took a deep breath, shook her head, and began anew.

"Anyway, as I was saying. I have your file right here. I understand that this is your third outburst this year."

Did you see the way she was looking at you? If I could get my hands on...

Quiet! We're already in enough trouble as it is without you...

"They're yammering at each other right now, aren't they? I can see it in your eyes."

Dorielle and Shay went quiet. Henry looked up meekly at Argora and said, "I've been doing my best. I've been sticking to my routines. I've been doing the suggested breathing exercises. I'm so sorry for what happened today."

Pointing at the file on her desk, Argora said, "I see we've had to replace five laptops, three desks, and... a blouse?"

Henry looked down, embarrassed, and said, "Yeah. Shay got an idea in his head that if he planted a flag in Dorielle, he could claim her as his own, and she would have to keep quiet from then on. He ripped off Jamie's blouse and made a makeshift flag out of it. The company compensated her for the loss."

Hehehe! I really liked that idea. I still think it would have worked.

Shay, we just need to get through this meeting. Please be quiet.

Closing the file, Argora said, "These are some serious issues with you at the center. Between the physical cost to the company and the distress caused to your coworkers. I'm afraid we can't let things continue the way they have been."

Standing up, Henry said, "I understand. It has been a pleasure working for you. I will see myself out."

Pointing to the chair with her long, manicured nail, Argora said, "Sit!"

Henry sat and waited for Argora to finish. She stood up and began pacing around the office. There was a worn track circling the office. It was clear she would rather be running free through a forest than trapped in this office, and she kept moving to keep her spirits up.

"As you are well aware, faeries are considered an ADA-protected condition. The company has gone out of its way to accommodate workers such as yourself so you can enjoy the benefits of working here. That being said, your case has proven itself to require special attention. I think I have just the solution for you. We're moving you up to the third floor.

Wait! Shay starts a fight, and you're being rewarded for it!

It's nice to be recognized for once!

"I'm being promoted?"

Argora smirked at Henry's confused look and said, "No. This is not a promotion. This is a lateral move. You're heading for the accounting office run under Xavier Rotmutzen. He's a new recruit from Germany, and he has already worked wonders with some of our other refugees who have been having trouble adapting. I have already spoken with him, and he's eager to work with you."

Henry leaped up with a smile on his face and said, "I greatly appreciate this seco… this additional chance. I promise I won't let you down."

"You better not. If you can't make it work with Rotmutzen, I'm not sure what else I'll be able to do for you."

The elevator door opened onto a standard office hallway. Henry walked down to door 379. Entering the room was like walking into a different era. While there was some construction tape in place showing that the office was still a work in progress, the floor was well on its way to being entirely redone. Dark wood paneling was more than halfway installed around the room. The desks had been replaced with wooden versions that matched the paneling. While all desks still had laptops in place, many accountants seemed to be hard at work with piles of paper and pencils. One of them was even using an abacus. All of them were fantastical creatures from various races, and all worked in total silence, focused on the job at hand.

Would you look at that, Henry! Everyone seems so content and focused. This may be just what we've needed.

Shay replied sarcastically, **Yeah. But be careful of that one. He seems to be the real life of the party.**

Henry felt his gaze drawn to a goblin sitting at a nearby desk. He appeared to have come to a full stop and was just drooling on his desktop. "I'm not familiar with goblins personally. Maybe this is some standard afternoon nap he takes?" He didn't need either of them to reply to feel their doubts.

Henry made his way to the manager's office. It was still being renovated as well. The windows had been framed with dark wood trim. The whole design scheme reminded him of some old-timey black-and-white movie that he couldn't put his finger on. Inside, he could see an older man sitting at the desk. He wore thin, horn-rimmed spectacles and was dressed like George Banks from Mary Poppins, down to the bowler hat on the nearby coat rack. He looked up and waved Henry in.

Walking through the door, Henry said, "Hello, Mr. Rotmutzen. My name's Henry Bottom. It's a pleasure to meet you."

"Please, call me Xavier. Come on in. Have a seat."

Henry looked around as he sat, marveling at the office. To him, it felt like spending time here could eventually lead one to believe the last century had been nothing but a daydream. Xavier saw him looking around and said, "I know. It's a bit eccentric of a look and not especially cheap. I had to put up quite a fuss to get all this in place. But, when I get the results I do, the company works hard to accommodate my quirkier desires. I always thought there was something magical about this era, and I try to recreate it wherever I go."

Henry smiled, "While unexpected, I like it. Feels warmer. I bet that works to your advantage when dealing with your specialized staff."

Yeah! I bet that works well with your zombies out there.

Xavier's eye darted to Henry's left ear for just a moment. Henry thought, "Wait, did he hear that?"

Before he could address the question out loud, Xavier said, "But enough about me, let's talk about you. I'm sure most of your previous bosses have worked hard to discuss your situation without ever actually saying its name for fear of reprisals from HR." Xavier stood with his hands on his desk and said, "You're suffering from a case of faeries."

Suffering? How rude!

You're about to be suffering from a case of my fist up your arse if you don't watch it!

Xavier smiled and walked to the other side of the table. "Uh oh! They didn't like that, did they? I can see it in your eyes. You are not the first person I've worked with who had a particularly ornery bunch of passengers riding shotgun." Xavier sat on the desk just in front of Henry. "What if I told you I knew exactly what you needed? That I could make your days going forward easier than you could ever have imagined for yourself?"

Henry, he's scaring me.

You're a coward and a fool, Dorielle. That being said, this prick is too close. Tell him to back up.

Xavier leaned forward and looked into Henry's eyes. "Henry, I've made the lives of many others so much simpler. I like to think my mission in life is to bring a little more peace to this world. I've learned a lot in my time that modern medicine couldn't even begin to comprehend. What if I told you I could cure you of these interlopers?"

I'm not the clap! You pile of rancid dog diarrhea!

Henry scrunched up his eyes and said, "Please be careful. You're making them mad."

Xavier replied, "Henry, look at me." Henry looked up and locked eyes with Xavier. Xavier replied, "Will you trust me? Just for this moment?"

Desperate for a solution, for a change, Henry guiltily whispered, "I'll trust you." He could silently feel the disappointment and disgust deep inside his head.

Xavier smiled, reached out, and cupped Henry's head in his hands. Looking into his eyes, he said, "So, who's in there?" Taking a deep sniff, Xavier said, "I detect the trace odor of a failed Sidhe knight. I assume your queen died on your watch? You do know it's your disgrace that allowed you to be dislocated from your homeworld, right?"

Henry could hear the furious gasps of air coming from Dorielle. He could feel her heat as she was winding up like a tornado.

Xavier's eyes slipped to Henry's left and said, "And what about you, you pathetic excuse for a Nocker? Stuck up in this man's head, not fixing or building anything. Your existence is nothing but a waste!"

I'm going to rip out his eyeballs and skull fuck this liverspotted piece of rat dung!!!

Xavier leaned back and smiled. "That's alright. Why don't you both come out, and we'll have a little chat."

Before Henry could protest, Shay and Dorielle started to work their way out of his head. They stood on his shoulders, staring daggers at Xavier while Henry's head throbbed.

Xavier looked back and forth at each of them before confidently saying, "Living embodiments of extremes. It's no surprise the only way you found to survive in this reality was to become psychic parasites of the moral choices of humanity. But, being living extremes, you are much too easy to manipulate."

Through clenched teeth, Dorielle asked, *"How did you know about the fate of my queen?"*

Shay used his hammer to punctuate his sentences, saying, **"How'd you know I was a Docker? And Dorielle a Sidhe? What the hell are you?"**

Xavier met Henry's pained eyes and said, "I can smell it on him. You permeate throughout his essence with your infection. You both deserve to be excised." Xavier's eyes were wide, and he licked his lower lip.

"Enough talk. I'm taking you out!" Shay put the hammer away and leaped forward. His fist slammed into Xavier's face, knocking him onto the desk. Shay proceeded to punch him into the desk six more times before stopping breathlessly and turning to Dorielle. "He had it coming!" Dorielle just met his gaze and gave a slight nod of her head. Henry looked at his new boss in terror.

Jaw agape, Henry said, "You killed him. My one last chance, and you murdered him."

Dorielle sighed and said, *"Shay chose punches over his hammer. He held back. As angry as he was, he had no intention of killing this man. I'm sure in a few hours he'll be..."*

Xavier shivered. His body started to flop in place. Shay quickly jumped off of him and back onto Henry's shoulder. The three of them watched in terror as Xavier convulsed in what looked like a small seizure. His body then flipped over onto his chest, still on the desk.

The back of Xavier's neck started pulsing. Something under his suit began to swell up and out. The seam down the middle of the suit and shirt ripped open as a jagged spine escaped. A second head pulled itself out of Xavier's neck. The new face was wrinkled, the hair white and matted with blood. Its eyes were black except for blood-red pupils. The new head kept moving up and out until a whole body had emerged with it. Standing about a foot and a half tall, the creature reached deep into Xavier's body and pulled out a blood-soaked red cap, which it then put on its head. It smiled, revealing impossibly large, white, strong, protruding, and sharp teeth.

"FUCK ME!" "*FUCK ME!*" "𝔉𝔲𝔠𝔨 𝔪𝔢!"

The three of them screamed in unison, and then Shay and Dorielle made for Henry's ears. The Xavier creature, who had clearly been puppeteering the body on the desk, shrieked so loud that the windows in the office shook. Henry could feel his ear canals close tight at the sound. While the two faeries desperately tried to re-enter his head, they could find no purchase.

The pair looked up at Xavier in terror. He cackled and said, "IT'S TRUE. WHAT THEY SAY. YOU CAN'T GO HOME AGAIN."

Leaping forward, Xavier landed on Henry's chest, bowling him over. Henry fell backward in his chair, with the faeries landing sprawled out in either direction. Dorielle stood and brandished her sword. "*Your foulness can not defeat me! I've battled worse than you across multiple realms, and I shall not fall here!*"

Xavier responded with a malevolent smile and rushed forward. Dorielle sidestepped him and rammed her longsword deep into his side. The blade exited his opposite side. She twisted the blade and then pulled it down his side. She leaned in and whispered, "*Return to the filth from whence you spawned you evil beast!*"

Henry and Shay got up and stared in amazement. Henry yelped in victory, and Shay said, "**I knew you had it in you, ya daft fucker! Skin him and make a coat out of him.**"

Hearing Shay's words, Dorielle smiled with pride, but her smile faded as she noticed no blood coming from the wound she had inflicted. Xavier slowly turned his head to just an inch away from Dorielle's, stared into her eyes, and said "YOU FORGET. CHILD OF LIGHT. THIS REALM HAS DIFFERENT RULES. YOU FOUGHT WELL. BUT THIS ENDS NOW."

Xavier's startlingly large hand shot out, grabbing Dorielle around the waist. Pulling her away from her sword, he grasped her in both hands. His mouth unhinged like a snake as he shoved her, head first, inside. She had only a moment to cry out in alarm when his bite snapped her cleanly in half like a dry branch. Henry and Shay cried out, tears brimming in their eyes as Xavier quickly finished her off with a second swallow.

Turning on the remaining pair, Xavier said, "WE ARE ALMOST DONE, HENRY. SOON, YOU WILL BE FREE OF YOUR DEMONS. YOU WILL JOIN ME, AND WE WILL FLOURISH IN THIS REALM TOGETHER, OR YOU CAN JOIN YOUR FRIENDS HERE. THE CHOICE IS YOURS."

Looking up at Henry, Shay sighed deeply and said, "Honestly, dying this way will be better than having to put up with your mother at lunch. God, that woman can make a man's scrotum retreat into his chest cavity. Do me at least this much, and get out of here while you can. Don't join this poor excuse for latrine water. It'll break my heart."

With that, Shay pulled out his hammer and rushed forward. Henry seemed to go glassy-eyed for a second and muttered pensively, "... My mother."

Shay came in hard and fast, swinging his hammer in forceful and hopefully deadly arcs. Each hit to Xavier seemed to leave a crippling wound, but each was healed by the time the next blow landed. Xavier laughed as he was pushed back. Shay grabbed his hammer with both hands and raised it high above him, only for Xavier's hands to shoot out and grab him.

Henry again said, "My Mother!!!" loudly this time, and reached into his vest. He grabbed the tie pin and ripped it off. The pin looked like a small spear. Henry held it tightly in his grasp and rushed forward.

Xavier smiled into Shay's eyes and said, "YOU KNEW THIS WAS THE ONLY WAY THIS COULD END WHEN YOU FIRST SAW ME. TELL YOUR MAKER I SAID HI." Xavier opened his mouth wide again and started to fill it with Shay.

Henry screamed as he ran toward them. Cocky and sure of himself, Xavier ignored him. Henry brought his hand crashing down onto Xavier's head, the cold iron of the tie pin piercing his skull. The effect was instantaneous.

Xavier's eyes became round with terror. His unhinged mouth issued a deep scream of pain, agony, and fear. His grip on Shay failed, and Shay fell to the floor. He scooched backward till Henry grabbed him and ran to the wall. They sat huddled together, staring as smoke began to issue from Xavier's head.

Xavier's hands tried to rise up to grab the spear, but he didn't have the strength. His body writhed in agony. His legs appeared to be deflating as blood and ichor dripped from his mouth. The whole scene lasted maybe thirty seconds, but it felt like hours to Henry. In the end, all that was left of Xavier was a pool of various goos with a cold iron tie pin sitting, filthy and unharmed, right in the middle.

They had run back to Argora and filled her in on everything. Like the badass that she was, she took it in calmly and began damage control immediately. She called the police, answered most of the officers' questions for Henry, and informed them that if they had any more questions, she'd be happy to have the company lawyers work with them. Not excited about having to deal with a fantastic creature case in the first place, they informed Henry to not leave the state and that the district attorney would be setting up a meeting with his lawyers in the near future, and then they booked it out of there.

Argora gave Henry the rest of the day off. He now stood in front of his office building, with Shay comfortably back in his ear, unsure of what to do. He glanced at his watch and saw it was almost noon. He closed his eyes, knowing a comment was coming.

"Alright, hear me out. Your mother is a bitch, and I hate her. Her hideous tie-pin did save my life, though. Maybe I can consider trying to give the old bat a bit more leeway in the future. That being said, we did just live through some serious shit! I say we write off the rest of the day. We go drinking right now! We drink until the sun rises and reprimands us for our bad decisions. Hell, you and I both heard that Argora likes to hang out at the Prancing Pony. Maybe we go drinking there and see what fate has in store for us tonight? Maybe we'll get lucky! What do you say?"

Henry waited in vain for the conflicting response. His heart was heavy at the silence that followed, and he found that he had no ability to argue. "Fuck it. If you can keep your shit together, I'll buy you a beer you can drink yourself on the counter. Deal?"

"DEAL!"

WALLY'S DISCOUNT WORLD
by Zach Davis

Eddie wasn't sure, but if this job was not scraping the bottom of the barrel, then it was scraping the thin layer that sat on top of the bottom of the barrel. She'd been hired after filling out an application on Friday, getting a call on Saturday, and being told to show up at 9 AM Monday.

Wally's Discount World looked like hell from the outside. Only three of the lights in the overly large parking lot worked. It was in a part of town where you didn't want to walk amongst the shadows and whatever might lurk in them.

As Eddie parked under one of the functioning lights, she was struck by how it felt like a portal had been opened into the past. The seemingly abandoned fuel pumps on the edge of the parking lot showed that gas was $1 per gallon. When she entered the store, Eddie had the distinct impression of stepping into a time capsule.

Being *in* Wally's and being outside of it were entirely separate experiences. Eddie felt a queer sensation of having committed herself to something by crossing through the doors. She looked around as she moved through the store, taking in the sights of Wally's Discount World.

To the right of the front doors, a pair of pay phones stood at the ready, apparently unaware they were obsolete, waiting in vain for someone with a quarter and a desperate need to make a public phone call.

The prices for everything were so low Eddie assumed they had to be a joke. *How in the hell can a dozen eggs only be $1.09?* She thought. Canned goods could be had for a trio of dimes, which seemed antithetical to reason. Eddie assumed the can itself cost more to produce than it sold for.

Also, it sounded like *NOW: That's What I Call Music Vol. 1* was playing at random over the loudspeaker.

It's like 1998 never ended here, Eddie thought.

Anachronistic and weirdly specific pop culture references were peppered throughout the store. In Produce, a display of iceberg lettuce was accompanied by a cardboard cutout of Wally standing on the prow of a ship, arms outstretched, holding a head of lettuce in each hand. Across the front was "Our savings are TITANIC!"

The lettuce itself sat in a bin Eddie assumed was refrigerated somehow since there was a long cable in the back that ran along the floor where it met an extension cord, which ran further back and into an outlet. There was another, thicker cable that ran up the back of the cardboard Wally, for some reason. The setup was a sure tripping hazard, and an enterprising shopper with a litigious nature could easily end up owning Wally's.

It was the *Titanic* reference, though, that bothered Eddie more than anything. She thought about walking out of the store as soon as she saw it, on general principle.

Our savings make you feel like you're king of the world, she thought, *would be so much better.*

As Eddie made her way toward the office in the back, the sense that maybe Wally's was less of a deliberate throwback and more of a place that only sold old, outdated junk overwhelmed her. She passed the meat bunker and shuddered at the thought of re-stamped sell-by dates so numerous you could never tell the meat's true age.

Bleary-eyed drunks, either at the end of a late night or getting an early start on one, stood in front of the beer cooler. There were no name brands, but the labels were deliberately designed to invoke feelings of familiarity, if not to outright trick customers into buying cheap-ass knock-offs. One of the drunks struggled with a case of "Lerna Light." It had a split along the bottom and every time the drunk shoved one of the cans back in to keep it from falling out, two more popped out in its place.

An old woman looked out at the world from behind a one-eyed squint so tight Eddie would be surprised if light could pass through it. Her cart appeared to be the only thing keeping her upright. She leaned onto it as she wended her way down the aisle at a glacial pace, stopping occasionally to pick out a can with shaking hands, frown at it with her single heavy-lidded eye, then put it back on the shelf in a location other than where she picked it up originally.

This place sucked, and judging by the customers, it appeared to be sucking the life out of them. Eddie stopped and looked back toward the front entrance. She knew what was out there, and there wasn't a whole hell of a lot. And here, at least, there was the promise of a paycheck.

Fuck it, Eddie thought and walked through the double doors into the back area of Wally's.

An employee wearing a faded red and blue vest shuffled down the hall, and Eddie had to sidestep to keep from running into them.

"Excuse you," Eddie said, as snotty she could manage. It was weird to be deliberately getting into a confrontation as "MMMBop" exploded from the loudspeakers, but Eddie had no control over the soundtrack.

The vest-wearer stopped and turned its head, looking at Eddie out of the side of its eye.

"You talking to me?" it said. It was a woman's voice, and there was something familiar about it. Her tone, maybe. There was a harshness to her voice, and it sounded strained and tired. Eddie had been there before, coming off a seemingly endless shift and just wanting to get the hell out without interacting with anyone. She could sympathize. Still, nothing said she *had* to sympathize.

"No," Eddie said, "I was talking to the *other* person who almost ran into me. You must've missed her."

The vest-wearer turned her head to face Eddie. Her eyes caught the crappy fluorescent light and almost seemed to glow. There was no distinction between pupil and iris, just thoroughly unimpressed blackness.

"I remember when I was you," she said. "You oughta remember this when *you* become *me.*"

With that weird-ass pronouncement, the vest-wearer walked out the double doors. Feeling good about sticking up for herself, Eddie headed toward the tiny office at the end of the hall.

The office was taken up largely by filing cabinets that stretched from floor to ceiling. Everything else appeared to be an afterthought, including the short, balding man who sat on a crappy swivel chair in front of an ancient computer. He looked as generic as everything else in the office, like you could pick him up in the Bland Older Gentleman section.

He looked at Eddie with a smile stretched across his face, the same painted-on expression he wore in those innumerable cardboard cutouts all around the store.

"Hi, there," Eddie said after what felt like an eternity of silence.

"Hello," the man said through his smile. "Welcome to Wally's. You're..." he said as he shuffled some papers on his desk.

"I'm Eddie Róas. Edwina, actually, but I go by Eddie."

"Right. You would, wouldn't you? Anyhow, do you have any questions now that you've had the grand tour?"

"I'm sorry?"

"Billie's tour of the place? She showed you everything and told you what you'd be doing?"

"No, that didn't happen. I don't even know who Billie is."

The man's smile didn't fade, but his face registered confusion. It was as if the smile were permanently affixed to his face, and he'd learned to emote around it.

"Billie left before you came in. I had some misgivings when she gave her report. It didn't much sound like her. She told me she'd shown you everything you need to know."

"I hope not," Eddie said. "The only thing she showed me was disrespect."

"Well, that does sound more like Billie. My apologies for the false start. I assume you're ready to work?"

It was a ridiculous question. She was there, wasn't she?

"Yeah, I'm ready," she said.

Her first day at Wally's went pretty much the way Eddie imagined it would.

She met the other members of the floor crew, including Caity, a middle-aged divorcee who operated at the lowest energy output Eddie had ever seen, and Larry, a rat-faced scarecrow of a man who had as many teeth as he did toes, and one of his toes was missing. It was the middle toe, Eddie discovered. Larry didn't understand or had no tolerance for the concept of professionalism in the workplace, and he whipped his boot off at every opportunity to showcase his unusual injury.

"Most times when something falls on you," he said as he pulled an ancient and crusted sock off his foot, "it'll smash a whole bunch of toes. Doctor said it was the only time he'd ever seen something that big hit just one."

Eddie stocked a few end caps, to the side of which was another cardboard Wally, this one wearing tights and a frilled collar. The caption was "Even Shakespeare's in Love With Our Savings!" The back of this one had a large battery pack affixed to it. Eddie looked but couldn't discern what the battery pack was supposed to power. It was loaded with batteries dubiously named "Permacell."

Tags indicated where merchandise should go, but the Wally's floor crew took those as more suggestions than rigid guidelines. After finishing her first cart, Eddie saw Caity still working on placing her first jar. Caity held it in her hand, her arm slightly bent, not putting it on the shelf. She looked as if she was posing for a sculpture.

"Did you make this display?" Eddie asked. "Zoot Suit Riot" was playing at an aggressive volume, and Eddie had to raise her voice to be heard over it.

Slowly, and still without placing the jar of pickles on the shelf, Caity looked toward Eddie.

"No," Caity said. "Wally does all of them. He's super creative. The ideas just come to him."

Talking to Caity felt like trying to hold a conversation with a semi-animate statue. It felt wrong somehow, and the odd sensation that Caity was an inhabitant of the uncanny valley freaked Eddie out. She concentrated on work and on trying not to let Caity slip within eyeshot. She was always there, though, lingering in the periphery, which made it so much worse. Finally, Eddie had to find work on the other side of the store just to get clear of Caity.

The rest of the day was almost nothing special. Eddie helped customers find things they were looking for, and then she was forced to clean up an old lady's pee.

Apparently, an old woman came in every other day or so and walked down an aisle, staring at merchandise, until she let her bladder loose. She'd then drop whatever she was holding, abandon her cart, and calmly leave the store.

There was splash back onto some canned goods on the lower shelves, and there was some debate among the floor crew as to whether the cans should be thrown out. Eddie spoke up in favor of getting rid of them, and the rest of the floor crew decided that was a good idea and that Eddie should be the one to dispose of them after logging them as damaged merchandise.

Taking the cans to Reclamation, Eddie wrote down bar codes on a form labeled "Record of Loss." On the same form, there were boxes for Item Returned and Item Damaged. Eddie put a check next to the latter. Under Damage Description, Eddie was at a loss as to how descriptive to be, especially given her rather strong feelings at having to carry the cans wrapped in thin paper towels to the back of the store. "Cans covered in pee" seemed to sum up the situation perfectly, but Eddie was unsure if that level of directness would be appreciated.

A large stack of "Record of Loss" sheets sat in a haphazard pile. It looked like no one bothered to file these things, let alone read them. Still, it was worth the effort to check how they were typically filled out.

Eddie pulled a few pages off the top pile, careful to settle the remainder so they didn't go ass over teakettle all over the floor.

On the first sheet, under item description, was "Oscillating xarlot." The next page was for "Canned Baldander Meat." According to the record, two dozen cans of Baldander meat had been reclaimed due to a defect in the recipe. There was significantly less goat in the batch than there should have been.

The page after that was for something called "The Unstaring Eye of Aeryx," which had been returned—not for the first time—because of the curse upon it that affected the craven-hearted.

The rest of the pages went on in similar fashion, with weird items occasionally peppered with things like cream of mushroom soup or scented toilet paper. The more Eddie looked at the handwriting, the more she was certain the person who filled out the forms was the same one who made the *Titanic* display out front.

Wally does all of them, Eddie thought. *He's super creative.*

For the rest of her shift, Eddie felt ill at ease. It wasn't just that Wally was a weirdo who came up with fake products. The "Record of Loss" forms weren't presented as fantastic or strange. They were like anything else on the shelves. As she wandered the store, stocking merchandise and arranging displays, she kept an eye out for odd items. She saw smoked oysters in a can but no Baldander meat. There were cheap reading glasses but no Unstaring Eye of Aeryx. There may have been things that oscillated, but Eddie had no idea as to a fit comparison for a xarlot.

With five minutes left to go, Eddie headed toward the back. *Be like Caity,* she told herself. *It'll take five minutes just to get back there, then you can get the hell out of here.*

All told, Eddie didn't think there was much chance of her staying with this job for long. There had to be better ones, with better people, doing better things.

And bosses who weren't insane.

"Sex and Candy" was interrupted by an electric squeal, and a familiar voice came over the loudspeaker.

"Yeah," Larry said, somehow dividing the word into two distinct syllables, "can I get Eddie to the cardboard baler for assistance? Eddie to the baler for assistance."

Eddie picked up the pace. She pushed through the double doors and turned left toward the time clock.

"Hey, Eddie!" she heard from the long corridor behind her. "Baler's this way."

Goddamnit, shit, fuck, Eddie repeated to herself on a loop as she walked to the great blue cardboard baler. It was stuffed to capacity. A wooden pallet sat in front.

"Ya ever done one of these before?" Larry asked.

"No," Eddie said as Lenny Kravitz belted out that he wanted to get away. Sometimes, it seemed, the universe had a perverse sense of humor.

"Alright, well, first thing we do is squish it." Larry turned the key on an electric switch, and the hydraulic press went down, pushing the cardboard flat.

"Imagine putting somebody in there," Larry said, a faraway look in his eye. Eddie could see that wherever Larry's mind had wandered, he was kept company by horrible visions. "That'd be a *huge* mess," he said.

Larry pushed a lever before Eddie could respond, and the press stopped. Larry opened the door of the baler, grabbed a long metal pole, and began shoving it into the cardboard.

"See? Ya gotta clear a path all the way back so the wires can go through." He thrust the pole repeatedly, grunting the whole time. "Ya really gotta shove it in hard sometimes," he said.

The pole slamming into the cardboard made an ungodly sound.

"Alright, squeeze on behind there," Larry said.

"What, behind the baler?"

"Yeah. I'm gonna run the wires through the top, then you loop 'em through the bottom. They tie in front so's the bale stays together."

"Why don't you get in back, and I'll run the wires through?"

"I don't go back there. That's where I lost my toe. You'll be fine, though."

Eddie was cautious. She kept her eyes on Larry as she moved behind the baler. There was more room than she thought there would be. Also, there were several more poles like Larry had used stored back there. She'd grab one if needed.

"Ok, watch your eyes, here's the first wire."

A length of steel baling wire rocketed through to Eddie's left, smacking the wall.

"Now run that through the bottom."

Eddie took hold of the wire and ducked down to guide it into the narrow channel at the bottom of the baler. Another wire shot through above her head, pulling her hair.

"Jesus, Larry! You nearly hit me in the head with that fucking wire."

"Sorry, I'm trying to get you as far as I can. I gotta clock out. You got this from here?"

"What? No, I don't know what the hell I'm doing with this thing," Eddie yelled as she wriggled her way out from behind the baler, trying to avoid getting caught. When she finally got out, Larry was gone.

"Creepy son of a bitch!"

Eddie had no idea what to do. She stared at the baler for a while, trying to see if there was something she could learn about the baling process through observation. She noticed one side of the wire had a loop, so she guided the straight end through that, then twisted the wire until it was taut. The cardboard wasn't going to move unless she could figure out how to raise the hydraulic press. She didn't want to just start flipping switches and turning keys, feeling that there was a better than even chance of fucking something up if she did.

A few Google searches on her phone filled in the gaps, for the most part. However, she was unable to find anything at all about this specific model on the Internet; it was, apparently, a model of baler unknown beyond Wally's, which wasn't much of a surprise. Still, the basic mechanics seemed to be similar, aside from this baler having a few extra settings that Eddie didn't see on any other pictures of these machines. There was a lever where the blue paint was worn away that Eddie rightly identified as the release. Next to it was a bright red switch currently in the Off position. On a strip of masking tape, someone had written "Only flip for Quærñèz!!!"

Eddie was reasonably sure the mysterious Switch of Quærñèz did not need to be flipped, so she raised the lever to get the compacted cardboard out of the baler and onto the pallet.

By the time Eddie found what appeared to be Wally's only pallet jack to drag the bale out back, it was well past 7 PM, and "Flagpole Sitta" was blaring from the loudspeakers. Eddie pumped the jack and pulled the bale close to the overhead door. A drawing of a stick figure receiving a serious spinal fracture warned her to exercise caution when the door was raised. Eddie lifted the door and thrust up, sending the door sliding on its track. She pulled the bale and released the jack, and then the overhead door slid down.

"Fuck!" Eddie yelled as she tried the door, knowing it would be locked. Feeling like it was now a certainty that she would never work another day at this place, Eddie ran around to the front of the store, singularly focused on getting back in, clocking out, and getting the hell out of there.

She hurried through the automatic doors and into Wally's, which had become something other on a fundamental level.

Being in Wally's at the beginning of the day and now were separate experiences. Eddie felt a radical sensation of change by crossing through the doors. She looked around as she moved through the store, taking in the sights of Wally's Discount World.

The roof stretched hundreds of feet in the air. Vast and immane things walked with thundering footsteps, their great heads nearly touching the roof. Racks upon racks of merchandise stood in rows, infinite varieties of items ready for an uncountable number of consumers. The floor was reinforced with strong metals and stone. It felt unyielding and adamantine through her sneakers. The air buzzed and fluttered with the sound of wings. Glittering portals wavered and winked into existence, letting beings pass through before closing and disappearing from reality.

Eddie looked back at the parking lot. A long line of vehicles stood in front of the gas pumps. The vehicles ranged from what looked like big-ass Buicks and hovering discs to what were clearly living creatures being ridden for conveyance. After they filled up with gas, or finished absorbing iridescent crystals, or finished eating blood-red fruit that screamed with the voices of men long dead when bitten, the vehicles moved through rifts in reality. Bright pulses of light winked from deep within as they went.

Eddie turned around, and Wally's was alive with oddities. A creature shambled toward her, pointing at her red and blue vest. Long ropes of flesh, like settled candle wax, sat massed on the creature's face. There was an eye where a person might typically find one and another where a person might find an Adam's apple.

"Shüb nar gauthurk?" the creature said.

"Flarey's Meatpies and jams are on aisle 112," Eddie said, surprising herself with this knowledge of the language, the store, and its bizarre offerings.

"Ckhorp szyim blaüt."

"You're welcome. Thank you for shopping at Wally's."

Eddie never saw such variation. There were creatures covered in hair and some completely bald. The spectrum of colors extended beyond her perception. There were beings made of light and those made of shadow. There were things that appeared to be dead, which were somehow ambulatory and seeking retail comfort.

And over all the multivariate noises, warbles, beeps, cries, and screeches, there was the sound of "Barbie Girl" over the loudspeaker.

Eddie felt like she should be overwhelmed, but strangely, she wasn't. She supposed she should be horrified at the eldritch, chthonian, and impossibly angled shoppers, but they weren't there to terrorize. They were just looking for things on their shopping lists.

Some of the strange new customers were reflections of ones Eddie saw earlier in the day, in behavior, if not looks. A cadre of literally glassy-eyed men with long, snout-like appendages on their faces stared longingly at what had once been the beer cooler. An ancient woman trailing clouds of dust shuffled slowly down an aisle, frowning at items and occasionally plucking a bottle of *Claret uv Catoblepas* off the shelf. Eventually, she stopped in place and released a stream of brownish liquid, placed the bottle on a shelf where it didn't belong, and then meandered off.

"Jesus," Eddie said, "this place is a magnet for assholes."

A hand fell on Eddie's shoulder. She turned and saw Wally's ever-present smile smeared across his face.

"Have you clocked out? I didn't go over this, but we don't really do overtime."

"Wally, what the hell *is* going on?"

"Foundation Day Eve shopping. It's a holiday in every realm, and there's always huge crowds. Listen, come to the back real quick, clock out, and I'll answer your questions."

Eddie walked to the back with Wally. As they headed to the office, Wally stopped.

"Clock out, please. I'm serious about the overtime thing."

Eddie clocked out and followed Wally to his still shitty-looking office. Wally sat down and looked expectantly at Eddie.

"Are you not gonna talk?" Eddie said.

"It seems you should, first. After all, this is normal for me."

It was hard to think as the Backstreet Boys belted out "As Long as You Love Me." Finally, Eddie settled on a question that felt right.

"What the hell is this place?"

"It's one of several places where the barriers between existences are thin and dimensions intermingle. Ours is the only one with an all-purpose store."

"How did you find it?"

"I'm not originally from this world, but everyone's heard of it, and eventually, almost everyone passes through it. This is, for one reason or another, a popular destination. Visits were routine and have been for millennia. Visitors were highly complementary, but the big complaint was that there was no place to get supplies. Enter me. There are entranceways to innumerable existences that intersect right here, and because of that, this reality is mutable, able to expand and contract as needed, if you know what you're doing. It occurred to me that an enterprising being could import goods from other realities at very cheap prices and store them here, having them available for who and whatever might want them."

"What about the people who work here?"

"Travelers, too, by and large. Caity, for instance, comes from a place of living statuary. Beings like her are carved into existence. It takes them decades to shed some of their more obviously statuesque tendencies."

"What world is Larry from? That has to be the creepiest fucker I've ever met."

"Oh, he's from here. This world spits out Larrys from time to time."

The Backstreet Boys ended, and Tonic came on, kicking into "If You Could Only See."

"Ok, what's the deal with the music? And the weird displays? Why is stepping in this place like stepping into 1998?"

"1998 is the foundation point for all existences. In that year, the Queen of Nothingness and All led her army of Unmakers against life itself. Disgusted with the havoc life had wreaked across all worlds, the Queen bid her Unmakers to poise their shadow blades at the throats of every reality. For nine days, the Queen held court at the Precipice of Life and Death, having called emissaries from every realm to make the case as to why existence should continue. No gifts would appease the Queen. No great achievements could sway her judgment. She was about to give the order to slice, when a lone traveler prostrated herself before the throne. In her outstretched hands, she held a copy of *NOW: That's What I Call Music Volume 1*. The gift pacified the Queen, and this day and year was proclaimed sacred across all realities. Technically speaking, right now, we're *in* 1998. It's the nexus of existence. And, the prices are cheap, which helps business. The displays are my creation. You've noticed, perhaps, the battery packs?"

"I did," Eddie said. "I was wondering what the hell they were for."

"They send a beacon call to many of the known worlds, letting them know we're here for whatever a wandering interdimensional being might need."

"You advertise across realities?"

"A man's gotta eat, so the saying goes, even though I only have to eat every 38 years."

"So, why did you hire me?"

"I've hired aspects of you from numerous realms. You're attracted to this place in every reality in which you exist. Usually, you come here as something like a last resort, and it is here that you reach your fullest potential."

"What do you mean, aspects of me?"

"You've met some of them. They are versions of you from neighboring dimensions. Incidentally, it was Billie who gifted *NOW: That's What I Call Music Volume 1* to the Queen of Nothingness and All. She's responsible for the continued existence of life, and she picked up that CD here. She also singlehandedly repelled an invasion by the Reflected World by destroying the mirrors they planned to use for incursion. She logged each shattered mirror with a 'Record of Loss' form. While working here, they performed great works that echo through the halls of infinity."

"So, what? Are you saying this is my destiny or something?"

"As far as I've seen, there is no such thing as destiny. I think this is simply the place you feel you should be. There's important work to be done, or at least *different* work, and you're awfully good at it. So, do you think this is something you can see yourself doing?"

Eddie thought about it. She *was* good at this job, and it *was* different work, at least.

"I'll stay, but only on one condition," Eddie said.

Eddie learned how to draw a customer's eye, how to display clearance items so they looked both attractive and low-cost. She'd learned how to quiet a grundek that someone let off its flaming leash. Bleary-eyed drunks stared at the beer. Old ladies stared at merchandise on store shelves, walking slowly down the aisles. There were also new customers, ones attracted to the recent changes. They loved the new displays.

Eddie's improvements increased the broadcast scope of the displays, drawing in customers and carving out market share in territories Wally's never had before. The Burning Plains was well represented, and the Cavalcade of Nightmares now exclusively ordered all their shadow manipulators from Wally's.

Eddie, wearing her red and blue vest, stood in front of a Wally wearing an army helmet, surrounded by a barrage of falling prices, with the caption "Savings Private Ryan."

Eddie shook her head at the sad display and lamented the lack of cleverness. This was one of the last displays needing to be replaced, and she was glad of it. Eddie thought of the new displays she'd created. There was one for powdered donuts with a cardboard Wally, whose hair sat up in a wave. The caption was "There's Something About Wally's Savings." Another for oatmeal had Wally covered in rose petals that read "Our Prices Are an American Beauty."

They were pretty good, and Eddie was proud to have made them. This next one, though, was going to be the best of them all.

It would really tie the place together.

LOVE POTION #10
by Mark Bruce

"You know, a few hundred years ago, they would have burned me."

Martin's client said this with perfect equanimity. She was tall, lean, dark-haired. Her ruby-red lips came straight from a Grimm's Fairy Tale. She dressed in a long, flowing purple dress. Her dark eyes watched Martin with amusement.

"Burned you?" Martin said. "Like Joan of Arc?"

She shook her head.

"Like in England during the witch hunts."

"Oh."

Another one, Martin thought.

Recently the Public Defender's Office had given him clients who didn't want to be part of the real world. First, it was the young redheaded girl who insisted she was a faerie from the woodlands. Then, it was the dissipated old man who called himself Bacchus, god of wine. Now, this one. Who believed she was a—

"Witch, I'm a witch," the woman said.

And a damned fine-looking one at that, Martin thought.

"Thank you," she said, smiling at him.

"Did I say that out loud?" Martin asked.

"You might as well have. Not all of us look like Margaret Hamilton from *The Wizard of Oz*. In fact, we witches see that movie as a bigoted portrayal of our ancient and honorable coven."

"I see," Martin said.

"You don't believe me," she said. There was no disappointment in her voice.

"Not really," Martin admitted.

"It doesn't matter," she said. "I'm not going to use my witchy ways to seduce you."

Too bad, Martin thought, looking at the client's lovely face. He, himself, was pudgy and short, his brown hair streaked with gray.

"Thank you again," she said, dimpling another smile at him.

"Uh, ok," Martin said. He'd better watch what he thought as well as what he said when talking to this woman.

"A good idea," the woman said. "Keep it professional."

"Of course," Martin said. They sat in the Public Defender conference room, a glorified name for a simple room with no pictures on the white walls and a long Formica table with eight cloth-covered chairs surrounding it. Martin asked his investigator to be with him during the conversation. The investigator had refused. The client spooked him, he said.

He pulled up the case of *People v Stevens* on his iPad. The police report was almost comic:

CW ("Complaining Witness") Charles Breton reports that suspect lured him into her place of business on 7th Avenue in Victorville, "The Coven Shop." In the shop, CW insists that suspect attempted to sell him illegal substance known as "Ecstasy," which is Methylenedioxymethamphetamine, or MDMA. She indicated that it would make him virile and attractive. She called it "Love Potion No. 10." She told CW that "Love Potion No. 9 wasn't strong enough for him."

CW reports that when he declined to purchase the MDMA, suspect became belligerent and began to chant what she called a "hex." CW states that she then pulled a knife from her robes and attacked him with it. CW reports that she stated that she could not let him live because he knew her secrets, and witches cannot allow those who know their secrets to live.

CW reports that he was able to disarm her and flee from the shop. He called 911 on his cell phone. Police arrived within three minutes.

Suspect was arrested in her shop. No knife was on the countertop when officers arrived, and suspect did not attempt to assault the officers.

When asked if she had attempted to stab CW, suspect admitted it. She stated she was a witch and that CW had come to the store to try to destroy her with magic. She was only defending herself, she stated.

Suspect was booked on suspicion of selling MDMA and attempted murder. Bail was set at $500,000.

Martin stole a glance at his client. Five hundred thousand dollars bail was a hefty amount to have posted. Even at ten percent, it was fifty thousand. That would be a lot of sales of Love Potion No. 10.

"My sisters posted the bail money," she said.

"I see," Martin said. "Miss Stevens..."

"Call me Izora," she said, laying an elegant white hand on Martin's sleeve. Her hand spread tendrils of warmth through his body. It distracted him for a moment.

"Miss Stevens," he said, "I'm having a problem believing that you admitted trying to kill this guy. There don't appear to be any recordings." The report stated: *Audio and video recordings of the arrest and statement appear to have been erased. The department is looking into this problem.*

"No. Such devices are rendered mute in a witch's presence."

"I didn't know that."

"It's a modern phenomenon," she said.

"So they have no proof that you admitted trying to kill this guy, other than their word. Which is still evidence, Miss Stevens..."

"Izora."

"Izora," he said, "but it's still somewhat disturbing that such a thing would happen to perfectly good equipment. I think we might have a suppression motion in regards to the suspected coverup of the recordings."

"Don't bother," she said.

"Say again?"

"I did try to kill the little mouse. I should have just turned him into a mouse and been done with it, but I was so angry I couldn't remember the spell."

"Okay," Martin said. "Any reason why?"

"He thought he was going to destroy me," she said simply.

"With magic?"

She nodded.

Oh boy, Martin thought.

"So you see, it's self-defense. That will get me off, won't it?" she said, giving him a dazzling smile.

"Sure," he said. *Depending on the magic,* he thought to himself.

Her red lips pouted.

"You don't believe in magic," she said.

"Um, no."

"Despite the fact that you have in your hands a magical device created by your mortal culture," she said, pointing to his iPad.

"There are technical reasons this device works," he said.

"None of which you, yourself, understand," she said.

"Um, no."

"So, for all you know, it could be magic which is cloaked in technical jargon."

"You got me there." Martin smiled at her. She was crazy, but she was smart.

"Thank you again," she said. "I appreciate that you recognize my intelligence."

Okay, Martin thought.

"Do you know what happened to the knife?" Martin asked.

"There was no knife. A witch is not allowed to use iron or steel. It makes us sick to carry such things."

"No...but you confessed."

"I said I tried to kill him," she said. "I didn't say I used a knife."

Something the cops will be able to cover because there's no recording, Martin thought.

"So, how did you try to kill him?" Martin asked. He should have expected the answer.

"With magic, of course. After all, I *am* a witch. It's sort of the thing that we do."

"Of course," Martin said.

Her prior lawyer, a private solo hired by the "sisters," had waived preliminary hearing in fear that she might be charged with more crimes after the hearing. Martin couldn't figure out what worse crimes than dealing illegal drugs and attempted murder could be extracted from the facts. But this was how a lot of solo lawyers worked felonies: They waived prelim so they wouldn't have to prepare, then parachuted out of the case at the trial level.

Not that it mattered. In California, the police are allowed to testify at prelim as to statements made to them by witnesses. This saved wear and tear on the witnesses. No one cared about the wear and tear on justice, Martin thought.

He sat in the office, looking over the police report again and again. Izora Stevens had insisted on a jury trial, insisted that when the jury heard her part of the case, she would be acquitted and carried from the room on their shoulders. Martin suspected that Izora Stevens intended to place a spell on the jurors to make them acquit her. He smiled to himself. If she could do that, perhaps the Public Defender should hire her as a juror consultant.

He thought about Izora. She had a warm and sensual way about her. When she talked to Martin, it was as if she was pulling him toward her bed, which was ridiculous. The woman was attractive, in her early 30s. Martin was a chubby man with a sad face, about to jump off the cliff into his 60s. There was no way they would ever end up in bed together. Still, it was an appetizing thought. Martin was still a man. And he reacted predictably to Izora's come-hither ways.

He shook his head. He'd been through this before a dozen times. A beautiful client would often act seductively so that her Public Defender would spend more time on her case. Usually, it was because the client had no defense and was hoping for some magic.

Magic. There was that word again.

Martin shook his head and reread the police report. As he read, he tried to play the events depicted in the police report as if they were a movie. He saw Izora standing behind the counter of her shop, the "mouse" asking her for a love potion. Then he suddenly has a change of heart (why?) and told her no. She pulls the knife from her robes and attacks him...

With the counter between them. That makes no sense.

The "mouse" disarms her. How? And why didn't he just run out of the shop when she pulled the knife? There was a counter between them. She would have had to have leaped across the counter...

There were parts missing in the story. He went into the case files, looking for the investigation. Martin had asked to have the "mouse" interviewed. The report was short. The alleged victim had refused an interview.

Which made Martin wonder. Often, victims would reluctantly tell their stories to the investigators. Usually, their stories jibed with the police reports, and the client, upon being shown the interview, would plead guilty.

"I'm not pleading guilty," she said. Her voice had suddenly sounded in his head.

"You confessed," he said aloud.

"I said it was self-defense," her voice said again.

Martin shook his head at his own foolishness. Magic, indeed.

Martin found The Coven Shop on 7th Street, across from the Kentucky Fried Chicken. He took a deep breath as he pushed the door open. He almost hadn't come at all. But he had to look over the scene of the crime—the alleged crime, he told himself. His cross-examination was always better when he knew the layout.

"Martin!" Izora said, delighted. "I didn't expect you, or I would've put on tea."

"Love Potion No. 10?" he asked with a smile.

"That would not be necessary if we were so inclined," she said. "You are already infatuated with me."

Martin didn't deny it. He had a quick and tawdry vision in his head of Izora pulling him behind the dark blue velvet curtains behind the counter and stripping naked.

"Well," he said, "I'm here actually to get the layout. I have some questions."

"Certainly," she said.

Today, she wore a long, dark red robe. Out of one of the side pockets, he saw the wooden handle of a weapon. Some people never learn.

He looked over the shop. It was about twenty by forty, with a small row of shelves with various strange packages. In vain, he looked for eye of newt and wing of bat, but he did find organic flour and herbs.

"Where's the magic stuff?" he asked.

"I keep it in the back," she said. "In case someone tries to shoplift something they don't know how to handle."

"Smart," he said.

"The Coven has rules. They were somewhat wary of me opening this shop to begin with. Now I know why."

Izora stood behind a glass counter, about waist high. In the glass were magic wands and little pots with labels.

"I see you haven't run out of Love Potion No. 10," Martin said, reading one of the pots.

"It's one of my best sellers," Izora said, reaching down and placing the pot on the counter.

"Is it Ecstasy?" he asked. She laughed.

"No chemicals," she said. "Completely organic."

Another reason to have a prelim, Martin thought to himself. The cops would have been forced to admit that the potion in the pot was not MDMA.

"What's in it?" Martin asked.

"I can't tell you. Only that it contains completely legal herbs and spices."

"A bit like the Kentucky Fried Chicken across the street. Secret recipe with herbs and spices."

She smiled indulgently.

"I suppose so. Except this pot will make anyone fall in love with you."

"So, you're telling me that if I gave this to Scarlett Johansson while we were out on a date—say, I secretly put it into her cocktail—she would fall madly in love with me?"

"The trick," Izora said, fixing him with a saucy gaze, "is getting her to go out on a date with you in the first place."

He smiled.

"And if you gave this to me right now, I'd fall in love with you?"

She laughed a sexual, dark laughter that went straight to his little man.

"Dear Martin, you are already in love with me. But yes, if I desired to have you as my love slave, I could give this to you. It would work for a little while."

"It wears off."

"As love always does," she said, smiling.

He gave her a sheepish smile.

"You know that, because you're a client, I'm not allowed to make sexual comments to you, or I'll lose my bar card," he said.

"I understand, darling," she said. "I will refrain from being too forward in the future. Until the case is over."

Ah, Martin thought. There it was again. *She's laying the incentive for me to work magic in the courtroom and get her acquitted. The implication is that she'll take me into her bed and work magic on me.* It somehow made him sad.

"I suppose," he said, changing the subject, "that you get some kooks coming in here."

"The Catholic gift shop is just down the street," she said.

"This guy, Charles Breton, had he ever come in before?"

"No. But I knew who he was as soon as he walked in."

"Crazy Catholic?" Martin, himself, was Catholic, so he knew the type: Wild-eyed, chubby, usually with a Messianic complex to rid the world of the Devil's children.

"No. A wizard."

"A...what?"

"Wizards and witches are fierce competitors in this world," she said calmly as if it were the most reasonable thing to say. "Sometimes we come together to make magical offspring—they are always girls—but for the most part we are deadly enemies."

"Harry Potter notwithstanding," Martin said.

Izora laughed.

"Those books are quite comic and entertaining. But they have as much to do with real witchcraft as your superhero comics have to do with real heroes."

Martin strolled over to a bookshelf. As expected, spell books and something called "The Witches' Bible."

"How did you know he was a wizard?" Martin asked.

"We can always tell one another. Though he tried to convince me he was just a mortal who needed help with love."

"A mortal?" Martin asked. "I thought we were called Muggles."

"Again, Harry Potter. No, non-witch folk are called Mortals because their lifespans are so pitifully short."

"Lifespans..." Martin said.

"Yes. I, for instance, am three hundred seventeen years old. I barely missed the Salem trials. In fact, my mother barely escaped from being hanged."

"I thought you said they burned witches."

"Only in England. Here in America, it was thought hanging was sufficient."

"And was it?"

"For the poor mortal girls who were mistaken as witches, yes," she said. Her expression had darkened. Martin decided to change the subject.

"So, you're three hundred years old. Here I was, thinking you were far too young for me."

She smiled complacently.

"Perhaps someday you'll find out," she said. "But then, we agreed we were not going to talk about such things until the case was over."

"Fair enough," Martin said. "I wonder why Charles Breton didn't tell the cops he was a wizard."

"They would not have believed him," she said. "Wizards are a dishonest lot."

"I see," Martin said. "So he'll lie about that on the witness stand."

"Probably not."

"No?"

"When any witch or wizard takes an oath to tell the truth, they are bound by it and will suffer a dire consequence by breaking it."

"Really? What kind of consequence?"

"It's pretty horrible to watch. They sort of implode. Their bodies cave in, and they disappear in a rather disgusting mass of flesh and fire."

"That would be something to see," Martin said. "Talk about a Perry Mason moment."

"A what?"

"Lawyer magic," Martin said. "When you get a witness to admit he's lying and that he, himself, is the killer."

She folded her arms and looked to the skies.

"So you would unmask him in front of the jury. If only, dear Martin, you could work that kind of magic for me."

"If you could magically turn me into Perry Mason, perhaps I might," Martin said.

"And why did you go into the shop?" Cindy Young asked. Her dark eyes regarded the witness with professionalism. Martin, goat that he was, could not help but notice Cindy's shapely form encased in a gray business suit. The two of them had been lovers once or twice, though Cindy never wanted to commit to a relationship. Her lovely face still made Martin's heart palpitate. He believed Asian women were the most beautiful in the world, and Cindy was exquisite evidence of that belief.

Izora Stevens leaned over.

"I could let you have some Love Potion for her, gratis," she said, nudging him in the ribs.

"As you said, it wears off," Martin said. "Which is the problem Cindy and I keep having."

"I sympathize," his client said. They'd missed the answer to Cindy's question.

"Did you intend to attack her?" Cindy asked.

"Not really," he said. "It was self-defense." He was a pale man with a pronounced Adam's apple. He wore horn-rimmed glasses. His short, chubby body reminded Martin of a mouse. He wore a slightly wrinkled gray suit.

"You had completely innocent intentions, then?" Cindy said.

"Objection, leading. Calls for a legal conclusion." Martin said.

"Sustained," Judge Jackson said. She was an older black woman who had once been a Public Defender.

"You did not intend to kill her, then?" Cindy said.

The witness squirmed a bit. Interesting, Martin thought.

"I intended to see what love potions she was selling," he finally said. It wasn't exactly an answer to her question.

"Did she show you potions?"

"Yes. She called it *Love Potion No. 10.*"

"What was in it?" Cindy asked.

"Objection. Calls for an expert conclusion, and this witness has not been called as an expert," Martin said from the defense table.

"Sustained," Judge Jackson said, shooting an irritated look to Cindy Young. "I assume you will have an expert testify as to the contents of the potion, Ms. Young."

Cindy Young looked down at her file and acted as if she didn't hear the judge. Martin knew her well enough to suspect trickery.

"Ms. Young?" the judge said, her irritation rising.

"Your honor, may we approach the bench?" Cindy said. Judge Jackson sighed.

"Come on," she said. Martin roused himself to his feet and walked to the bench, allowing Cindy to walk in front of him.

"What's the story?" Judge Jackson said.

"We're going to dismiss the second count," Cindy Young said. Judge Jackson sat back in her chair, her face a mask of amazement.

"Why?" she asked.

"We can't get results on the potion," Cindy said in her best beaurocratese.

"You can't...how long have you known this?" the judge said.

"We hoped to have results by the time we presented our case," Cindy said. "But there have been problems."

"And in the meantime, you've allowed the jury to hear that the defendant was charged with possession of MDMA," the judge said, her voice dark.

"We thought—"

"You will dismiss now," the judge said peremptorily. "In front of the jury."

"But..."

"Or you will present evidence on the charge. If not, Mr. Berry will likely move for a mistrial, and I will likely grant it. And you know what happens if a mistrial is declared after a jury has been impaneled, Ms. Young."

Cindy lowered her head. Martin almost felt sorry for her. Almost.

"I'll phone the expert at the break," Cindy said. "If there are no results, I will dismiss the charge."

"In front of the jury," Judge Jackson said.

"As your Honor wishes," Cindy said with a smidge of resentment in her voice.

They went back to their tables. Charles Breton looked curiously at them from the stand.

"Did she show you the potion?" Cindy said.

"Yes. It smelled awful."

"It smelled like turpentine and looked like India Ink?" Cindy said, smiling.

"Something like that," Charles Breton said. He clearly did not recognize the reference to the old Fifties song.

"What did you do?" Cindy asked.

"I refused it. It was disgusting."

"It won't work if it's not disgusting," Izora whispered in his ear. His body tingled with the feel of her hot breath.

"What happened next?" Cindy asked.

"She took out a weapon and pointed it at me," Charles said.

"What did you do?"

"I defended myself."

"What happened next?"

"I ran out of the store."

"Because my magic was stronger than his," Izora whispered to him. It was hard to concentrate on what she was saying when his body kept responding to the sensation of warmth and sensuality her breath gave him.

"No more questions," Cindy said, sitting.

Which was interesting. There were a hundred holes in the story. Charles Breton got up as if to leave.

"No, Mr. Breton, you need to stay there," Judge Jackson said. "Mr. Berry has questions for you."

"Questions?" he asked sickly. "I thought I just had to answer the prosecutor's questions."

"I'm not sure who you've been talking to," Judge Jackson said with forbearance, "but in a court of law, both sides ask questions of a witness."

"Can't we do it differently just this once?" he asked. Judge Jackson's face turned menacing.

"This is a trial for attempted murder," she said sternly. "We take this seriously, and we don't bend the rules for anyone."

Meekly—like a mouse, Martin thought—he sat back down in the witness box.

Martin stood and regarded the man for a minute. Where to start? He decided to go for the prosaic.

"Why did you enter Ms. Stevens' shop in the first place?" Martin asked.

The mouse squirmed.

"Curiosity," he finally said. Martin almost said *Curiosity is for cats, not mice.*

"Curiosity about what?"

"I wanted to see what she was selling. I'd never seen a witch running a business."

"You've seen witches before?" Martin asked.

"Objection, relevance," Cindy Young cried out. It was a bit too vociferous an objection. There was something she was afraid of. Did she know he was a wizard? Martin smiled at the thought.

"Sustained," Judge Jackson said.

Martin pursed his lips.

"Did you go in specifically for a love potion?"

The song sounded in his head. He almost asked *Are you a flop with chicks?*

"No," the mouse said. "But she was very pushy in showing it to me."

Because mice like him always have problems getting women, Izora's voice sounded in his head. He turned to look at her. She merely smiled.

"It was in a little pot, right?" Martin asked.

"Yes."

"She brought it from under a glass counter, right?"

"Yes."

"In fact, that glass counter was between you and Ms. Stevens during this entire transaction."

"Yes."

"She never leaped over the counter at you?"

"Uh, no." He started to look a little worried. He knew he'd just made a mistake, but he didn't know what it was.

"You say Ms. Stevens pulled out a weapon," Martin said. "But you didn't specify the weapon. Was it a knife?"

"Uh...yes." The Mouse seemed to quiver at that answer as if his stomach hurt him.

"Can you describe the knife?" Martin asked. This was dangerous. No knife had been found, and by asking Breton to describe it, he would place a knife in the jury's mind. But Martin was running on instinct.

"Uh, it was a knife like any other knife," Breton said, clutching his stomach again.

"Mr. Breton, are you quite all right?" the Judge asked.

"Yes, your Honor. Just a little gas."

The jury tittered at that.

"Proceed, Mr. Berry," the Judge said.

"There are all kinds of knives, as we all learned by watching *Crocodile*

Dundee," Martin said. "Was it a big knife or a small knife?"

"Yes," the mouse said. His face twitched.

"Which was it? Big or small?"

"Small," Breton said. He seemed relieved not to have to use the word *knife.*

"Describe the blade."

"It happened so fast I didn't see the blade," the mouse said. Again, he seemed relieved.

"You said you defended yourself," Martin said.

"Yes."

"How?" Martin followed up.

"How?"

"That is my question. How did you defend yourself?"

"I, uh, that is..." Breton clutched the witness stand. "The way I told the police." His face twitched again.

"You weren't under oath when you talked to the police, were you?" Martin asked.

"No."

"You are now. Please answer the question. How did you defend yourself?"

"I grabbed..." his face twitched again. "That is, she pointed the knife..." His body convulsed, and he let out a groan. The bailiff stood and ran toward the witness stand, intending to perform CPR on the man.

But Breton beat him to it. He reached into his suit coat pocket and whipped out a thin black rod with a knife handle. He pointed it at Martin and cried out something in Latin. Martin found himself struck dumb.

The bailiff flinched, seeing the rod, and reached for his gun.

Breton then spun the rod toward the Bailiff and yelled another Latin phrase. The Bailiff froze in his tracks. But the mouse had forgotten his true adversary.

Izora leapt to her feet. In her hands was a thin white rod with a wooden handle. She pointed it at Breton. *"Mus Procedent!"* she cried.

Breton collapsed beneath the witness stand. As he did, he emitted a little squeak.

Both Martin and the Bailiff reanimated at the same time. The Bailiff charged the witness stand. Martin sat down next to his client, looking at her with new wonder and fear.

"Don't worry," she whispered. "I won't do anything to you."

The Bailiff picked up the chair in the witness box and looked under it. He searched the area around the witness box and even apologized as he searched the judge's bench. He had called for backup. Other sheriff's deputies poured in through the courtroom doors.

"Did you see him run out?" the Bailiff asked his brother officers. They all shrugged.

"I'm sorry, your Honor," he said to the judge. "He seems to have disappeared."

Martin noticed a small gray mouse skittering away from the witness box. He looked back to Izora sitting calmly, a slight smile playing on her face.

Since the complaining witness did not stick around to complete cross-examination, Cindy Young was forced to move to dismiss the case. As she did so, she gave a sidelong venomous glance to Izora.

They walked out of the courtroom, Izora's arm snaked around Martin's.

"I don't know why I didn't remember that spell before," she said. "It's actually rather simple."

"Latin," Martin said.

"*Mus Procedent,*" she murmured. "Mouse, come forth."

"Simple if you know your Latin," Martin said. He felt dizzy. He had already convinced himself that he hadn't seen what he thought he saw. Somehow, Breton had escaped from the courtroom to avoid being charged with lying to the police. The gray mouse probably lived in a niche in the courtroom, living off the remnants of the clerk's lunches.

The case was over. Izora was no longer a client. Implied promises of sensual delight played in his head. He tried to tamp them down.

"Don't worry," Izora said. "I am no threat to you."

"Meaning?" Martin asked, nearly breathless.

"Meaning there are rules for witches, just as there are rules for lawyers."

"You can't sleep with a client?"

She laughed.

"Oh, no. That kind of rule would ruin everything. Often, the client needs to be slept with in order to diagnose his or her problem. No, there is a greater rule I am forbidden to break. A rule which saves you from the dilemma of going to bed with me."

"And that is," Martin asked, his throat thick with excitement and disappointment.

"We are not allowed to interfere with true love."

"True what?"

Izora gestured to Cindy Young, who was stalking from the courtroom, her boxy-wheeled briefcase trailing behind her.

"True love," she said. She winked at Martin. "What you do is your decision. But I always have Love Potion No. 10 to nudge things along for you, if you wish."

CUE THE RAIN

by Riv Rains

Everything it falls upon becomes equal.

Beneath the rain, right now, I look no different to the rest of you. A blank face in a crowd. Just a pane for drops to slide upon. The painted face of nothing.

Yeah. That suits. I'm nothing.

I untangle my legs from the peak of a jungle-gym tower and drop to the wood chips. The powerland is optional, of course, but it keeps the mystery alive for anyone watching.

In this business, a little mystery goes a long way.

Rain means work. Work means coffee. One of those conjunctions is excellent; the other less so. I'll let you work out which is which while I get coffee. Lots and lots of coffee.

The bell rings over my head as I enter. They always amuse me; I'm used to absolute silence when I move. I could muzzle it, but why waste the juice? I'm about to beckon the attention of you humans anyway.

"What can I get youu...uh, h...hello!"

I smile for her. She can't help it. I'm everything. Everything and nothing. I feel her heartbeat quicken; her warm brown eyes slide over my face. She can't meet my gaze, and I know why.

"Double espresso, no-nothing."

"Sure. Umm ah... what name, honey?" Her eyes can't seem to settle.

I smile, throwing her an anchor. She locks to it, breathes out long and loud.

"C U E. Just mark it down for Cue." I shouldn't, but I wink, heavy lashes stroking her pulse. The click of my tongue was an extravagance, but right now? I need the buzz.

I'm off to work, after all.

Sally made my coffee herself. Not only did I watch her hip and shoulder the younger lad out the way to do it, but she burned herself twice because she watched me. My cup is laced with two extra shots and sugared with beads of her shaky self-worth.

It's almost as sweet as she is.

Had I been in the market, Sally would be delicious.

Obligation ratchets my ribs together, urging me to unknown places. Fuck, I hate that feeling; me, the soft, pliable metal, your struggles, my twisting vice.

But we'll get to that.

First, let's take a walk.

Sally tried to touch my finger as she passed me the cup. I let her, if only to taste the sweetness of her soul for a moment. I disturbed nothing within her. She's lost so much in this life, yet she's mending. She's the best of you, but I'm not here for her. Instead, I amble out into the glistening, simpering street, take a swig of coffee and savor that soft pink glow on my left index finger.

Too sweet. This world keeps spitting her out like rotten teeth.

You might think I'm going to a car, but you'd be wrong. I don't drive. I can, I could, I have a plastic card with a full name on it and everything, but I don't. Driving is lonely—just me in a tin can.

In my line of work, better to be on the tube. Faces, voices, hearts. Blood beating. *Thump, thump, thump.* Much, much better.

Bet you're wondering what I am.

Me too.

They call me Cupid, Kintsugi, Ixtab, or Algos. Bringer of love, mender of parts, the journey, the trial, the test. I am the equalizer—the one who takes and gives in the same breath.

What does that mean? Today? Let's find out.

The platform is crowded. Beautiful people who don't believe they are. As usual, you burrow underground at the first sign of sleet. Some would say like sheep. I don't agree. I like sheep. They don't hide their fears like humans. You all think you should learn to be bold and brave—unique, challenging—but you shouldn't. You don't need to lick up the leftovers from any flicker of fame like a starving dog, hoping to ingest something magical.

On a good day, all you need is each other. Pure, simple—hearts as fireflies, chasing through the night.

Magic.

On a bad day, you'll need me.

The rattling drag of air precedes the train. I can't help but breathe deep against it. Sure, it's polluted as hell, but it's still energy—my fuel of sorts—like a stiff drink. Can I live off it? Nope, and I don't have a USB port, though I'd surely enjoy your search for one.

No, I live off *you*.

On the street, in the park, on the train. I feel you. All of you. The parts you want me to see evaporating under the weight of those you don't.

The latter are my meal ticket.

Don't get me wrong; I've not materialized to leer at the insidious lust hiding within Sharon here—even if she does have delicious cleavage. No, she'd be fun, but I'm after Gerald, there.

Yep, *him*.

Reading the self-help book. Golf socks a foot clear from beige business cuffs. That's my meat. Sharon would only be an appetizer.

Gerald doesn't move much when I drop down opposite him on the tube. He's engrossed. He's desperate to be going somewhere—up—in life and love, hopes he'll solve it all before his stop, wearing those socks, and reading that book.

It's almost hard to break it to him. Almost.

'You got a light?' I use my thickest drawl, knowing the combination will drive him to distraction—to irritation. I need him lit. I need him to *feel*.

Gerald doesn't lower his read. His elbows ride that briefcase like a pro, the idiot's path to inner peace bobbing up and down in his tidy office hands. The white scar from his wedding band sways like a siren call from the depths of his desperation.

Luckily, I can swim.

I hook one long finger over the spine of his book, pull down, and peer over. Gerald gets his first look at me. Both his brows raise—my left one answers.

There it is. Instant dislike. Poor Gerald. He can't land me; knows I'm too much. He clears his throat and tries to raise his book.

I hold it down.

Gerald clears his throat. "No smoking on a train."

Finally, some spunk from Gerald. Wasn't sure he'd let me see it.

"You never asked what I'd light." I lean in like a conspirator. "Truth is, I just wanted your attention, and see? Now, I've got it." I wink.

Sometimes honesty works the fastest.

My mark looks at his fellow passengers—every one of them is focussed elsewhere—books, screens, their own quest for Camelot—like he longs to be. All are oblivious to the life-altering events going on beside them.

I follow his gaze. "Beautiful things, humans." I sit back. "They won't notice us unless I want them to. And today? I'm only here for *you*."

To illustrate, I lean over to Furle next to me, obnoxiously sniff her auburn hair, untuck the fall of it from behind her ear.

Gerald's jaw drops as he watches her absently tuck it away again.

It's just the spark I need for my smile.

As I said, sometimes the show is everything.

"How did you...?" The tremor of his tone is cute, like the soft place between awe and fear.

My smile widens. "Gerald, we've got work to do, my friend."

There it is—power of a name.

He's mine now. Though he doesn't know it. He looks at Furle once more, then at me. I mean, *really* looks. It was inevitable, so I let him wash over me. I take my ease, hook my arm over the corner of the bench and lean back. Manspreading, they call it. What's it called if you're nonbinary? Non-spreading? I really should look that up. God knows someone will have worked it out. Humanity is brilliant at the small problems—catastrophic at the large.

Gerald here—taking me in—is on the cusp of his largest.

What's he seeing? Everything. My angled jaw, lazy dimples, shoulder-length sandy hair, and utterly impeccable dark eyebrows. He's seeing the bar through the left brow—pulled tight while it's cocked—amused at being appraised by him. He's interested in my neon pink t-shirt and black leather jacket, confused by the snug silver chain around my neck, yet reassured by sensible black jeans and boots.

Who wouldn't be? Footwear is everything.

So. Gerald's doing some appraising, and me? I'm checking him out—not physically, obviously—don't be dumb. Sharon was more my type, although that guy over there with his 'don't tell mum I smoked weed' smile would be in the running. But no. I'm reading Gerald's heart.

Every facet of it. Every burn, every brand. Those bright spots where he keeps his memories. That name—half-written—before the teacher snatched the note in 6th grade. The gentle curve that cradles his children. The perfectly round puncture in his left ventricle that fits his mother's death.

Finally, I find the source of the wound—the one *she* made.

The bleed; the one I'm here for. The one that's spilling all down his shirt in red—running rivulets off his briefcase—dripping to the floor beneath our feet. The one that drove him to the brink.

"Gerald, we have work to do."

Gerald stares at me. Fish mouth—open and shut.

"And I'm afraid you're absolutely gonna get wet."

"In your books, they call it closure."

We've been chatting for a while now. Off one train, onto another, off again. He's given me the whole sorry story, opened up like a stroked clam. As for me? I've given him the space to tell it. You haven't missed much. I've only just begun poking holes in his colander of self-pity.

We're strolling down a rain-soaked street. Well, I might've been strolling; Gerald was scampering—or hopping—or whatever the thing is when you can't keep up because I'm 6'6" and you can't run because you're in a suit and tie. Jog-hop-skip. Whatever. He was doing that, dodging puddles, leaving a trail of haphazard red skid marks in the water behind him.

He also listened like a champ.

I talked like a god. "Without it, can you move on? Is that it for Gerald? You think your song ended? You think you're all sewn up? Everyone else is squared away, life packed up and labeled?"

He bobbed up and down and tried to think of something impossibly pointless to say.

Now, I know it sounds like I don't like Gerald, but don't get my vibe wrong. I truly do. It's just that it's hard to like Gerald right now. You must understand; Gerald doesn't even like Gerald right now, and that, my pretties, is part of the problem.

"I...don't know. I have a cat?"

Ladies and gentlemen of the jury; The Problem.

I don't care about Gerald's cat. The problem is, you humans get lost. No, not like when your GPS sticks two wheels in a lake then says, 'in two hundred meters, turn right.' Not like that.

Let's delve a little deeper here, shall we? Beyond the fleece?

Internally, emotionally, mentally.

In any of those ways, most of you couldn't find your way out of a wet paper bag. You get lost when you try to follow each other—nose to tail—like those woolly clouds-on-legs I mentioned earlier.

I don't do the making. That's above my pay grade, but as far as I can tell, someone nodded off in creation class. You're a mess! You have so much free thinking, so much choice, and so much chaos. The more you learn, the worse it gets. You're a veritable flock of fuckery!

All I'll say is, where the hell is your shepherd?!

Somehow, it's my job to curtail your messes. Do I like it? About as much as the rain. However, I do like *you*. So, in order to help Gerald, I look up. Into streaks of sunlight that are fighting free of the grey. Into rainbows and clouds yawning in retreat.

Game time is ticking. Gerald is skipping, and I may have gotten slightly side-tracked.

Blame the coffee.

Back to Gerald.

He's about to get my short shift.

My boots splash to a stop on the sidewalk. I pull him by the sleeve to face me. "No, Gerald. Not your cat." I give him a little shake. "Tell me, do you believe there's one person for everyone? Do you believe that your wife—who left you for that car detailer in Florida—found hers? Do you believe that the .45 caliber you purchased today—while still dusting the crumbs from your tie after your tuna roll—was a good deal? Do you think because you're all about solid investments and it was a good package price—even though you only need it for one shot—that the touch of revolver nostalgia was worth it? Do you hear it now, taunting you, rattling around, cuddling up to that photo of your kids in that fake leather briefcase—which, by the way—she bought on sale on the way back from screwing *him?* Will it solve it all, Gerald? Do you believe that?"

I stare at him. His fish mouth. His eyes as moons, his heart chewing up the tails of his mind. I hunt those eyes, my hands on his shoulders, leaning from the waist so I'm on the level, rain and sun ticking down on my back, watching, watching, the spinning penny.

"I..."

Nothing. Gerald. The blank man. So browbeaten he can't find a second syllable. Why do you do this to each other? Where's the gain?

Not good enough.

Clear! My energy hits him like a power surge, pounding down through the rain, feeding off everything it touches, spidering through my veins, crackling across his teeth, eclipsing his dusk—the collective consciousness of you all—white lightning in the storm.

My mental powerland.

Gerald blinks.

Something blossoms on his shirt front. Beauty coughed up from the red.

Passion. Purpose. Hope.

Any moment now.

Then he's with me. Pulse on the run, ignited parts of him burning towards the soggy sack of truth in the center of his heart. *Thump, thump,*

thump. That spark of epiphany I deliver, his lit fuse.

He's cackling, crying, choking.

I feed him some air. A subtle push that rocks him back in his golf socks.

"Gerald. Do you believe it?"

"I... well, no!"

We stand. Him, a quiver of epiphany. Me, the fading catalyst.

The final heavy drops make halos out of discarded bloody puddles.

If I had bills, this is what would pay them.

Existing quietly, in our tiny, large moment.

Slow as the brightening sun, Gerald grins with me. A shower of teeth still sparking with purpose. Beneath his skin, my special brew of jungle juice glues a patch for his bleed. The stain on his shirt dissolves, running scared from his oncoming enlightenment.

Melancholy escapes with the rain.

I slap his left cheek, the splash and sting binding this moment as his.

This belongs to him now.

We start strolling. Both of us walking the street in the lifting, steaming dregs. Like old friends. Like it was paved for us. No more bouncing from his bag. The intent within silent in the shafts of sun.

I hear sighs of relief from his children's children.

I join them, warmed by the world—by you.

I can't save you all, but today, I've saved Gerald.

The clouds thin, and I'm on my way out. I shift with their shadows. I appear with the rain, evaporate without it.

The bell over the door amuses me.

I'm the drips upon the door handle, the mist sweeping behind his step. Gerald enters, unsure why he's on this street and soaking wet on a cloudless day.

"What can I get youu...wow! What happened to you?" A sweet voice, apron wrung in both hands.

"I... I'm not sure, life, I think?" His smile is crooked and kind, the light of you all warming his left cheek. "And anything hot if you please. I'm goddamned soaked!"

They share a smile. It always starts with a smile.

"You poor thing! Pick a table, drip all you like. Coffee and a towel coming right up! We'll get you wrung out in no time. How's banana bread still warm from the oven? On the house?"

Gerald throws down his briefcase, ignoring its thud. "That'd be wonderful, thank you. I'm so grateful I wandered in here."

"We aim to please! New, bedraggled customers always welcome. Now, what name am I gonna scribble on this, honey?"

"Gerald. And maybe—do you mind if I ask yours?"

There's that smile again, tipped from the heart.

"Well, ain't you a sweet one?" She fusses with the sugar and menu on the table—scorch marks bright on two fingers—and gives his soul a glance through her lashes.

I feed her some air.

"Why Gerald, I'm happy to meet you. Soaked or not, you can call me Sally."

PULSES

by Jacob Jones-Goldstein

I started having the dreams a few days after Lorna disappeared. Weird, surreal, unknowable dreams of America's Wild West, buccaneers on the high seas, and Bob Dylan. They were feverish flights of subconsciousness with no narrative or structure. The only anchor I could hold onto was the image of Dylan in the center of the illusionary maelstrom.

Each morning, I would wake twisted in my sheets, drenched in sweat. I lived in a one-room apartment above a bar in Exeter. The same bar where I met Lorna. The flat wasn't bad, but it wasn't the kind of place where you would bring your parents either.

Lorna had worked downstairs in the pub called McWane's for a few weeks before we hooked up. Seeing as I lived upstairs, I was in there most nights. I liked to sit in one of the quiet corners and read while I nursed a beer. It wasn't a noisy place. Students from the University mostly went to other pubs in town and left this one to the townies. It was a spot for people who didn't want to be bothered as we drowned whatever we had that needed drowning.

Typically, I left the people who worked there alone. I didn't chat up the bartenders or any of the servers. A friendly hello, maybe a bit of small talk about the weather or football, but that was it. We were all familiar strangers and tried to keep it that way.

Lorna was different. Right from her first day, she went out of her way to get to know people. I think some of the other barflies found it off-putting, but I enjoyed it. We got to talking about music and books and whatever else.

I'm a generally solitary person. My family is long gone. I have a few friends who check in once every couple of weeks, but most are busy with their own lives. Chatting with Lorna in the bar was a bright spot in an otherwise dreary existence.

One night, I worked up the nerve to ask her if she wanted to come back to my place. She said no but that I could come back to hers. I had imagined she lived in a place like mine since she never talked about family or friends either, but I was wrong.

She lived in a beautiful house overlooking the river. It was impeccably decorated with antique furniture and fresh flowers. I could barely make myself move past the threshold, feeling like I was intruding in a life that I didn't belong in. She laughed at my nerves and led me by the hand to the living room. I sat on the couch, feeling out of place, when I noticed the picture of Lorna and a handsome man on the mantle above her fireplace.

I walked over and picked up the picture. I was looking at it when she returned with two glasses of wine.

"That's Paul," she said. She walked over and took the photo from me, looked at it for a moment, then put it back on the mantle. She then tapped the vase next to the picture, and I realized it had an inscription with a pair of dates on it. I started to say something, and she just waved her hand and smiled at me. It was a sad smile, but one that told me she'd heard everything I was going to say before.

I went over and sat down on the couch with the glass of wine. She put a record on and then sat down beside me.

"Do you like Bob Dylan?" she asked as the sounds of 'Tangled Up in Blue' began to fill the room.

She woke up screaming that night. The bed was soaked in her sweat, and she was shaking. I calmed her down enough that her screams turned into deep sobs, filled with so much sadness my heart nearly broke.

Once she had gathered herself enough to talk, she told me about her marriage, her family, her home, everything. Even with her husband dead, she felt trapped. It was a life that felt planned out. She said she felt like she was playing a role rather than actually living. Her voice in the bar had always been filled with cheerfulness. When we talked downstairs, it was filled with a melancholic sadness. Now, all of that was replaced with a desperation so complete it was almost frightening.

I just listened, but deep inside, in a way I couldn't articulate, I understood everything she said. The part of her that was speaking was the same part of me that I ignored except for very late at night when everything was quiet. Before too long she had exhausted whatever her nightmares had awoken and fell back to sleep. I watched her sleep until dawn and then slipped out quietly.

We talked in the bar the next evening, and she thanked me for the lovely evening. We still chatted, but nothing progressed out of it.

A week later, she didn't show up for work.

After a few more days of her absence, I asked the owner of the bar, Jerry, if she had quit. He shrugged and said he hadn't heard from her. He was going to give her another day or two, but after that, he would have to hire someone to replace her.

That night was when the dreams started. I didn't wake up screaming, but right on the edge of it. I couldn't shake the dream and got no more sleep that night. It had been a bizarre nightmare where I walked out of the apartment and got into a car driven by Bob Dylan. Together, we drove through a nightmarishly weird landscape that I could barely describe.

I wasn't a Dylan guy, not really. Lorna had been a big fan. During our night together, she talked about her love of his music and, among other things, the freedom it represented. We had listened to a few of his albums while we chatted. I had laughed when she said she wished either Dylan had been English or that she had been American.

The next morning, I went over to her place to check on her. The house was dark, and her car wasn't there. I knocked at the front door and waited a few moments just in case, but it was clear she wasn't home. Her door had a mail slot in it, and after looking around to make sure no one on the street was watching me, I opened it and peeked inside. There was a pile of mail on the floor. It was early, so I was pretty sure the mail hadn't arrived that day. If it had, her postal carrier was a lot better than mine. I guessed she had probably taken a holiday.

When I got home after work that night, I saw a help wanted sign in the bar window. It made me more sad than I would have thought and I just went straight up to my apartment. That night, I had another dream. It started the same as the other, with me getting in the car with Dylan, but the landscape changed. It was still nightmarish but different than it had been before. I couldn't begin to describe it if I were willing to remember it enough to try. Each night, the dream would repeat itself, with Dylan and I traveling through ever-worsening worlds.

I began to worry I was losing my mind. I'd had the occasional nightmare, but never anything like this before. Each night, I would wake up soaked and almost breathless.

After a week, I went by Lorna's house again. It was still dark, and the car was still gone. I looked in the slot and saw the mail pile was still there but much larger now. During the night I had spent there, she had mentioned her mother-in-law lived two doors up, so I decided to see if she knew where Lorna was.

I felt awkward as I knocked on the door. I barely knew Lorna. All we had shared was a few pleasant conversations and one intense night. It wasn't a lot, and I felt a bit stalkerish. To tell the truth, I don't know if I would have pursued it if it wasn't for the dreams. I had barely slept, and on some level, it felt like she was connected to that, both because of when they started and Bob Dylan's repeated appearances.

The woman who answered the door looked me up and down with no small amount of disdain. It occured to me that I looked a mess. I was wearing old jeans with beat-up trainers and a worn-out hoodie. I told her that I was a friend of Lorna's and asked if she had seen her. She eyed me for a moment and then said she hadn't. I wanted to ask more, but it became clear very quickly that she wouldn't tell me anything even if she knew. I thanked her for her time and asked her to have Lorna give me a call when she saw her. She snorted and closed the door.

I didn't know what else I could do and thought that would be the end of the line. After work, I went back to the bar and took up my usual corner. The help wanted sign was gone, and a new server was working. I talked briefly with Jerry to let him know about her mother-in-law's place, in case Lorna had left any personal belongings at the job. She hadn't. She had disappeared without a trace.

The dreams didn't go away. They got so bad I really thought I would crack. I called and made an appointment with a doctor. I didn't have any idea if she could help me, but I had to do something. I also bought a Bob Dylan album, Blood on the Tracks. It was the one that Lorna had played that night. I thought maybe I could somehow exorcise him by listening to it again. It didn't work, of course. The doctor gave me some pills that helped me fall asleep but did nothing about the dreams, and when I woke up, I'd be utterly disoriented after taking them. I started missing work and trying to sleep during the day, but that didn't help either.

After several weeks of this, I was drinking in the bar when the mail arrived, and Jerry called me over. He handed me a postcard. It was sent to the bar but addressed to me. There was nothing else written on it besides the address. The front was a picture of a hotel on a hill by the sea, and it read 'Tintagel Castle Hotel.'

"That's out in Cornwall, innit?" Jerry asked.

I nodded.

"Neat looking hotel. Friends staying there?"

"Not that I'm aware."

I walked back to my corner, staring at the card. I couldn't think of anyone I knew who would have sent it. Certainly not from a place that was maybe an hour away. After contemplating it for a while, I tucked it into the back of the book I was reading and forgot about it.

I dreamt of the hotel on the postcard that night. It was surrounded by fire and smoke. Light poured out of the windows and blinded me as I stood in front of it. I could feel the heat on my face and smell the smoke, but I was not burning. Gradually, the blinding light from the hotel coalesced into a beam that shone across the water onto a real castle. The other castle, the real one, was built on a rock and looked ancient. Slowly, the light receded back into the hotel.

When I looked around again, the fire was gone. Everything started to look normal as the front door to the hotel opened. Lorna emerged. I tried to call out to her, but this being a dream, I had no voice. She walked over to me in that slow, liquid way that things move in dreams. After what felt like an eternity, she reached me. There was no doubt it was her, but her eyes were closed, and she had not said a word.

She stood in front of me, and I in front of her for millennia, until her eyes began to slowly open and light poured out. The world lit up in an impossibly bright flash.

I sat bolt upright in my head. The apartment was cold, but my body felt like pure fire. I was panting like I'd run for miles. I sat there, trying to catch my breath and bring my mind back to reality.

It took time, but eventually, I was able to calm down enough to get up and get a glass of water. My throat was parched to the point where I wondered if I had been screaming in my sleep. My hands shook hard enough that I had to use both of them to hold the glass.

It was dark out but it would be dawn soon. I put the glass down and wondered if I should go back to bed. That was when I heard the car horn. Two sharp bursts from right downstairs. It was too early for any traffic and way too late for anyone to be waiting for a cab at the bar.

I walked over to the window that overlooked that street and looked down. I wasn't surprised by what I saw, not really, but my mind still rebelled against it.

Down on the street, standing by the open driver's side door of an old Vauxhall Viva from the 70s, was Bob Dylan. It was Dylan as he looked in 1975, with the huge head of black curly hair and the scruffy midwestern beard, not the old man he was today. He was looking up at my window and waved when he saw me, beckoning me to come down.

I stared for a long time at him, and he looked up at me. Finally, he reached back into the car and honked the horn again, and then he shouted, "Come on, we don't have all day" at me. It was that same voice, familiar from the songs.

I made a decision. Whatever this was, I would follow it. If I was losing my mind, so be it. If it made the dreams stop, even better.

I grabbed my bag and tossed some clothes in it, along with my passport and the book with the postcard. I slung the bag over my shoulder, took a look around, and then headed out for God knows where.

When I opened the door to the street, I saw that it was no trick of light. Standing by the car was Bob Dylan as he was. He looked annoyed at me but pointed to the passenger door. "Come on. I'm on the clock here."

Without any more hesitation, I got in. He started the car, put it in gear, and off we went down the street. The radio was playing 'Space Oddity' by David Bowie.

I asked where we were going.

"Tintagel," he replied with the kind of sarcastic annoyance that he always displayed in interviews.

"Why?"

"Because that's the place to go."

I had more questions, but I guessed they would be as cryptically answered. Slowly, the world woke up around us as we got on the A30 and headed west.

After driving for about 45 minutes, I decided to ask, "Are you really Bob Dylan?"

Without looking up, he responded, "I am what you needed me to be."

"I don't know what that means."

He grinned and half sang, "Who among us isn't a little mad?" and then winked at me.

I didn't find that very encouraging.

I could tell from the signs that we were nearing the town of Tintagel when he spoke again in that affected nasally voice, "Change of plans. We're running a bit late, so we're going right to the rock next door."

"What are you talking about?"

He didn't respond. Instead, he sped the car up as we careened down the windy Cornwall roads. In the distance, I could see a storm rolling in. As we got closer, the dawn light we had been chasing was snuffed out like a candle after church.

He slowed down some as we entered the empty early morning streets of the town. With the menacing sky, pregnant with rain and lightning, there was no one out on the streets. Finally, he made a right, and I could see the hotel from the postcard in the distance, overlooking the ocean.

Instead of driving there, he made a sharp turn and drove down into the gulf between the jetty the hotel was on and the one next to it with signs for 'Tintagel Castle.' He drove about halfway down the hill leading to the ocean before stopping at a gate.

"This is your stop."

"Not the hotel?"

"Nope. You're heading up there."

He pointed to what looked like a giant grass-covered rock sitting in the ocean. I could see old ruins on it from here and a winding staircase to the top.

"What's up there?"

"Maybe the future. Maybe the past. Maybe a way out. Maybe a way in."

He shrugged jovially.

As I got out of the car and shut the door, the rain started pouring down. I heard a chuckle from inside. He pulled away, and I began walking down the hill towards the staircase leading up to the top of the rock. Not for the first time, I wondered if I was dreaming all this.

The deluge of rain and wind picked up as I walked down the hill. I could see the ocean at the bottom roiling. I vaguely remembered something about sea caves here that Merlin supposedly lived in. That added to the surreality of all this. I considered that my driver may actually have been the ancient wizard taking on a different form. It seemed just as plausible as anything else that had happened.

The storm did not let up when I reached the bottom of the staircase. It was a half-wooden, half-stone, switchback set of steps that looked like it was designed to terrify visitors. Waves were crashing against the rocks at the bottom, and the wind was whipping my coat like a flag on a pole.

I stood at the bottom, looking up. This was pure madness. I could still turn back. Surely, I was having some sort of nervous breakdown. I would break my neck climbing this giant stone in the middle of a hurricane.

The reality was there was nothing to go back to.

I lived in a small apartment and spent my evenings and some days in a bar filled with people who wouldn't notice if I never showed up again. The landlord would wait a week, dump my stuff in the bin out back, and then rent the room. I had no family. No real friends. My job would take a week to even realize I wasn't there. I was a shadow, living day to day, just waiting for the sun to come out and erase me from the world.

I began to climb.

The wind howled. The rain pounded. And I climbed.

At the top was an archway. I walked under it. Soaked to the bone, I pressed on through ruins that wrapped around the side of the rock, heading to the top. It was as dark as midnight until I crested the plateau. There was an enormous crash of thunder, and a brilliant flash of lightning illuminated the whole world.

On the far side of the rock, overlooking the ocean, was a figure silhouetted in the burst of light. I pushed through the wind, fighting to keep my balance towards it.

As I got close, there was another flash, and suddenly, a second figure was standing there. As I looked, the second figure raised a hand in greeting, and I heard, somehow clear as a bell over the howling wind, "Frank!"

It was Lorna's voice.

I walked the final yards until I could see her clearly. Next to her, the other figure was a larger-than-life statue of a cloaked figure leaning on a sword. She was as drenched as I was. I stopped a few feet from her, and we stared at each other. She smiled.

"I waited for you."

"I looked for you."

"What's happening?" I pleaded.

"We were ghosts, living ghost lives. We weren't meant to be ghosts, Frank," she then raised her arms to the storm and screamed, "WE ARE ALIVE!"

The statue raised its sword, and a bolt of lightning struck it. Tendrils of lightning flared down its sides and into the earth below. Jagged lines of electricity coursed across the plateau, through the rock and grass like rivers of light. The bolts coursed down the sides of the rock, through the ruins, and out into the ocean.

I felt my body dissolve into pure energy. My consciousness was sucked into a vortex, and suddenly I was flying along the lines of lightning. I saw Tintagel rush past at a speed too fast to truly comprehend, but somehow I did. I saw fields, and farms, and roads, and rivers, and cities as my mind roared across all of England. I saw people and animals. I felt their joy, and love, and sadness, and pain, and desperation. I saw all of it, and I understood this green and pleasant land for the first time.

We are not shadows. We are not ghosts. We are not meant to live our lives in the dark.

We are the beating heart of the land.

We are alive.

Jerry had been having nightmares for a week or two when he got the postcard. It was of an old hotel up in Wales. He had stayed there once on a family trip to Snowdonia. There was an old tower up the hill behind it that he had explored on a clear and cold Autumn afternoon. It made him smile to see the picture.

The card was blank, but the handwriting on the address looked familiar to him. He wasn't entirely sure why. He shrugged and tucked it into the book he was reading and went back to work, whistling an old Bob Dylan song that had been stuck in his head for days.

He hoped he would have a better sleep that night.

ACKNOWLEDGEMENTS

We would first like to again thank Jennifer Marang for the incredible job she did on the cover art and the layout of the book. Her art captured the spirit of the stories contained within in a way that feels truly magical.

This book was long delayed from its original inception in 2021. We faced challenges too numerous to list between then and now and we wanted to extend our thanks and gratitude to the patient and talented writers who stuck with us during the process. We hope you love the book as much as we do.

We would also like to thank all the folks who backed and helped promote this project on Kickstarter. Crowdfunding is a challenging and stressful process, but seeing the project funded in roughly eight hours after launch was both a relief and an affirmation of the work we are doing. The kind of support we received is rare and precious, and we thank everyone for it.

Additional thanks go to Captain Blue Hen Comics, they are a rock of support in the local creative community and have always gone above and beyond in promoting and supporting Oddity Prodigy Productions. Not everyone is lucky enough to have an LCS like them, and we are always thankful.

Jacob would like to thank Frank Turner, whose song 'I Am Disappeared' from the album 'England Keep My Bones' inspired his story 'Pulses.'

The editors would like to thank the rest of Oddity Prodigy Productions. Working with you is like working with family, which means it is no work at all.

And a final shout out to our families, who were very accepting and supportive of our long nights working on this. You make everything worthwhile.

MEET THE AUTHORS

COLIN ANDERSON drifts through life under the oppression of the City of Newark and writes short stories every now and then. Go to storybarf.com to read some of them.

ALICE AVOY is an emerging writer from Poland who graduated from the Institute of English Studies and worked as a journalist, reviewer, editor, and translator. One of her short stories appeared in 34 Orchard and another in Fanatical Magazine. She's mainly interested in horror, high fantasy, and urban fantasy, but she follows where her muse leads her. She loves to travel, play ttrpgs, and get lost for hours in the land of video games. You can find her on Twitter @AliceAvoy.

MARK BRUCE is a disabled Vietnam-Era Veteran who practices criminal and family law in San Bernardino. He was a Deputy Public Defender for 17 of his 34 years as a lawyer. He won the 2018 Black Orchid Novella Award and has been published in Alfred Hitchcock Mystery Magazine, Writer's Digest, Rattle, and other publications. His comic essays on the life of a lawyer have been used by the California State Bar as training material. He lives in Barstow, California with Mariah (a stuffed mermaid) and his writing support dragon Ferdinand.

J. PATRICK CONLON — see page 283.

ZACH DAVIS is a peddler of weird tales whose work has cluttered the darkened corners of otherwise respectable print and online journals for over a decade. Some of the places nice enough to take a chance on his stuff include *Carve, The First Line, Berkeley Fiction Review, Drunk Monkeys, Gravel,* and the *Anthology of Appalachian Writers* (numerous volumes).

BRIAN D. GIBSON is a lifelong fan of science fiction, horror, and fantasy (urban or otherwise), who has allowed a career in mechanical engineering to distract him from putting thoughts to paper for far too long. A father of three and husband of one, all beloved, he makes his living in the wilds of suburban Lancaster County, Pennsylvania. There, he occasionally dabbles in a writing process that could best be described as ponderous chaos.

JOHNNY GUZMAN was born on July 1st in Los Angeles, California. Raised in Delaware, has lived in Texas, Illinois, and Maryland. He enjoys the works of Edgar Allan Poe and Victor Hugo. He is a huge DC Comics fan and enjoys anything that involves the Batman family. He is a self-described Pro Wrestling "mark". Born to a wonderful mother, and a proud Mexican-American citizen.

JACOB JONES-GOLDSTEIN — see page 283.

NICHOLAS LEAMY — see page 284.

JAY T. LEVY, devoted writer of genre fiction and role-playing games, spends much of his free time reading stacks of comic books, and taking walks with his lovely shield-maiden wife and dogs. His other works can be found at in such anthologies as *Dark Halloween, Scarry Snippets: Valentine's Day, Scarry Snippets: Halloween, Scarry Snippets: Christmas, Scarry Snippets: Virtual, Fatal Fairies, A Guide to Useless Sidekicks,* and *Guilty Pleasures and Other Dark Delights.* To contact, visit his blog: https://jaylevyswritingadventures.blogspot.com.

MORD MCGHEE is the author of *Ironblood* (Golden Storyline Books, 2023 London UK) & *The Stroke of Oars* (Nat1 Publishing, LLC 2023 USA). He writes from Lowcountry South Carolina in the USA. Mordmcghee.com for more information.

TORI MILLER (they/she) is an IT/Physical Security Professional and creative from Indiana. They originally wrote guest anthology stories for a podcast called: *The Grey Rooms* for two episodes and *Baseline Feed* for one episode. They now perform in drag under the stage name of Lucy Furr and hopes to travel while participating in the performing arts. As a creative, they value storytelling that is authentic and intellectual. When they are not writing or putting on wigs, they enjoy spending time with their partner on lazy weekend afternoons.

BRENDA MORRIS is a Rhode Island native whose passion in life is writing epic young adult fantasy stories. After living in New York while attending Sarah Lawrence College, she currently resides in Southern California. When she isn't working, puppy-sitting for friends, or cheering on her favorite football team, you can find her creating new worlds, creatures, and characters from the comfort of her favorite desk chair.

RIV RAINS is a collection of rusting gears lubricated exclusively by chocolate. Bookgeek, author, and conjurer of creative daemons, she'd have a lot more time if she wasn't also captain and chief to two kids, four boats, and one husband. Born amid the sticks of rural Australia, she finds words in the magick of sunsets and river swells, chassis and unsuspecting rib cages. Riv welcomes you to seek out the spawn of her tumultuous mind at rivrains.com or @rivrains, and hopes to reach for you through the gaps of many more heartfelt pages.

JORIE ANN RAO has an MFA in Writing Arts and Composition Theory. She is currently teaching freshman composition at a small community college in New Jersey.

KATHRYN REILLY By day, Kathryn helps students investigate words' power; by night, she resurrects goddesses and ghosts, spinning new speculative tales. Sometimes, she even writes the truth. Enjoy poetry in *Shadow Atlas, A Flight of Dragons, Last Girls Club, Paris Morning* and fiction in *Seaside Gothic, Diet Milk, Blink Ink,* and *Fish Gather to Listen.* Her rescue mutts hear all the stories first. When she's not working or writing, you can find her rewilding suburban spaces. Follow at @Katecanwrite or visit katecanwrite.com.

DAVID T. SHOEMAKER describes himself as a "Poet, artist, philomath, endomorph, undocumented art historian, and occasional paraprosdokianist." None of these pay well, so he currently works as a Harbor Patrol Officer to pay the bills. His poetry has been featured in two group anthologies and in *Dreamstreets* magazine. David's first CD, *Bardsongs,* was released in 2017. He published his first book of poetry, *A Living Art and other poems* in 2018. In 2019, David premiered a walking tour based on the life and works of Charles Demuth. He also scripted a documentary film about Demuth which was produced that year by Natural Light Films. He has since published *Smoke and Souvenirs: the Essence of Charles Demuth,* a work of creative nonfiction that combines poems and essays to paint a word portrait of the famous artist. David lives with his wife Sue and a rescued feral kitten named Shadow.

M.C. ST. JOHN is a writer living in Chicago. He is the author of the short story collection *Other Music.* His stories have appeared, as if by luck or magic, in *Cosmorama, Nightscript, Flame Tree Publishing, Thirteen Podcast,* and *Wyldblood Press.* He is also a member of the Great Lakes Association of Horror Writers, serving as co-editor for the horror anthology *Recurring Nightmares.* See what he's writing next at www.mcstjohn.com.

ROSE STRICKMAN is a fantasy, horror and science fiction author living in Seattle, Washington. Her work has appeared in anthologies such as *Sword and Sorceress 32, Seers and Sibyls* and *The Bicyclist's Guide to the Galaxy,* as well as several e-zines such as *Luna Station Quarterly* and *Eternal Haunted Summer.* She has also published several novellas on Amazon. Check out her Amazon author's page at https://www.amazon.com/author/rosestrickman.

DJ TYRER is the person behind *Atlantean Publishing* and has been widely published in anthologies and magazines around the world, such as *Chilling Horror Short Stories* (Flame Tree), *The Horror Zine's Book of Ghost Stories* (Hellbound Books), *Occult Detectives* (Emby Press), and *Sherlock Holmes and the Occult Detectives, Volume Four* (Belanger Books), and issues of *Sirens Call, Hypnos, Occult Detective Magazine, parABnormal,* and *Weirdbook,* and in addition, has a novella available in paperback and on the Kindle, *The Yellow House* (Dunhams Manor). DJ Tyrer's website is at https://djtyrer.blogspot.co.uk. DJ Tyrer's Facebook page is at https://www.facebook.com/DJTyrerwriter. The Atlantean Publishing website is at https://atlanteanpublishing.wordpress.com.

THE ODDITY PRODIGY TEAM

MARCELLA HARTE CONLON has been fascinated with art and illustration since childhood. The same passion and attention to detail that won her school a sizable arts scholarship followed her to the University of the Arts, where she earned her bachelor of fine arts in illustration. She is currently working on a children's literature project. Her publishing credits include the anthology *The Stories in Between* by Fantasist Press, a collection of science fiction and fantasy stories published in 2009; cover art for the *All-Out Monster Revolt Online Magazine* in 2015; and most notably *The Mermaid in Rehoboth Bay*, a national award winning children's book published in 2016.

J. PATRICK CONLON is a genre fiction author currently living in Bear, DE. As a fellow Oddity in Oddity Prodigy Productions, his writing focuses on fantasy and speculative history themes. He has appeared in anthologies and magazines, most notably as Associate Editor for *Beach Pulp,* a collection of pulp fiction put out by Cat and Mouse Press. When he isn't writing, he is tirelessly marketing for his wife, an award winning illustrator and fellow cofounder Marcella Harte.

JACOB JONES-GOLDSTEIN, founding member of Oddity Prodigy Productions, is an internationally published author, journalist, and editor. His short stories have appeared in anthologies and magazines such as *Plague of Shadows* from Smart Rhino Press, *Beach Pulp* from Cat & Mouse Press, and *Lovecraftiana* from Rogue Planet Press. He writes about music for his personal site, ShoutingStreet.com, and has covered the

Philadelphia 76ers for several online publications. Beyond writing, he hosts popular podcast *The Scary Stuff Podcast,* plays Magic the Gathering, Disc Golf, and way too many board games. He loves comic books, movies, exploring, cats, family, friends, Joel Embiid, Tyrese Maxey, and his wife, Jennie [still last, still noted by said wife doing layout for this book ;)].

NICHOLAS LEAMY is a well-known miscreant who has lived in Northern Delaware all his life. Working in a data center, with a B.S. in Computer Science, he is well outside his wheelhouse when it comes to writing fiction. He has decided, however, that the time he's spent running D&D games for his kids, Oliver and Edison, has made him interesting enough to pull it off. He also happens to be a lover of board games, horror movies, and anything bizarre. Nicholas has been published twice before in *Oh Snap it's Oddity Prodigy* and the horror anthology, *Scary Stuff.* Despite his loving wife Hannah's attempts to help him evade capture, he has been apprehended and institutionalized, which allowed him to find the time required to bring you more of his personal madness.

JENNIFER MARANG loves werewolves, writing, and... uh, what else starts with W? Working? God, no. A graphic design/tech person by trade, Jennie did the cover art and interior layout for both *Beneath the Yellow Lights* and *Scary Stuff* anthologies. She's spent most of her life writing and drawing and broke into the industry in grade 6 with the award-winning illustrated story *Indiana Jones and the Last Banana*, released by her own printing press (handwritten on construction paper), distributed at the local library, and published in the newspaper of her tiny outback town in Australia. Look out for her next published work sometime this century; *The Flame's Heart*, a slightly-sweeping fantasy about a complete dick trapped in a sword. Jennifer lives in Delaware, by way of Montana and Australia, with four ridiculous cats, two ghost cats, a variety of wild birds, a chonky sneak-thief raccoon, and a husband she absolutely adores but purposely put last because that's where he put her; looking at you, Jacob.

STEVE MYERS was an award-winning cartoonist and graphic designer who lived in Bear and Newark, Delaware. He spent his days working as a Search Engine Optimization professional, and his evenings drawing comics and cartoons, including *The Adventures of Superchum*. He passed away in December of 2023, and is truly, deeply, missed.

SHASTA SCHATZ is an eager reader, occasional writer, and lifelong fan girl, the latter of which translated into a costuming obsession in her adult life. Her B.A. in English laid the groundwork for Shasta to become an addicted hobbyist with professional leanings. Between HEAs, TPBs, and NDAs, Shasta is a hot mess wife and mother with a penchant for coffee and organized clutter. While she prefers not to be associated with these people, their links can be found on her costuming blog, GreenLinenShirt.com.

CAPTAIN BLUE HEN

After he crashed landed on Earth and saw his favorite stuffies torn from him, The CAPTAIN swore to protect stuffed animals everywhere and create the most amazing comic book and pop culture buying experience this side of the Mississippi. For nearly 40 years, Captain Blue Hen Comics has been your one stop shop for all your pop culture and nerd needs, and we don't plan on stopping anytime soon!

www.captainbluehen.com
302.737.3434

DAYS OF KNIGHTS

The Days of Knights game store has a huge selection of Board & Card games, Magic the Gathering, YuGiOh, Pokemon, RPGs D&D and Pathfinder, Sci-Fi, Miniatures, Warhammer 40K & Bones, Tarot, Chess, Mahjong, and much more! Friendly staff in a business that's been on Main Street in Newark, DE over 40 years!

www.daysofknights.com
302.366.0963

Also available from
ODDITY PRODIGY PRODUCTIONS

SCARY STUFF
Horror Anthology

A tribute to the classic style of horror published in comics from the 60s and 70s, Scary Stuff is at heart a love letter to the kind of scary stories we grew up on.

$18.95 paperback

OH SNAP!
It's Oddity Prodigy

Meet the founders of Oddity Prodigy and get a sampling of everyone's work in this affordable, jam-packed publication!

$2.50 digital
$6.00 paperback

Purchase online at
WWW.ODDITYPRODIGY.COM